D0759049

Adventures in Nowhere

Adventures in Nowhere

John Ames

Pineapple Press

Sarasota, Florida

Inquiries should be addressed to:

Pineapple Press, Inc.

P.O. Box 3889

Sarasota, Florida 34230

www.pineapplepress.com

Library of Congress Cataloging in Publication Data

Ames, John Michael, 1944–

Adventures in nowhere / John Ames. — 1st ed.

p. cm.

ISBN 978-1-56164-484-1 (alk. paper)

1. Florida—History—20th century—Fiction. I. Title.

PS3601.M486A66 2011

813'.6—dc22

2010026688

First Edition

10 9 8 7 6 5 4 3 2 1

Design by Louise OFarrell

Printed in the United States of America

To my sister Shirley

I

It was hyacinth time. The Hillsborough River was so full of them that Danny could hardly spot a patch of open water. Hanna's Whirl was like a green prairie dotted with fabulous purple flowers. People said the hyacinths were a disease to the river, but they were a picturesque disease. However, ten-year-old Danny was not thinking about the beauty of the flowers. His father had been crazy earlier that morning and had nearly killed him.

They had been riding along and, to all appearances, his father had been in a friendly frame of mind. Then something had happened. Danny had missed it, but some other driver may have made a little move with his car that no one else would have thought twice about. Whatever it was, Danny's father suddenly got that twisted look on his face, and he had abruptly swung the car onto the unpaved shoulder of the road. In an instant, the Ryans' old 1937 Dodge was careening along the uneven ground, parallel to the road. Inches from Danny's door on the rider's side was a low cement-block wall and beyond that the pauper's cemetery, where they marked the graves by pounding a coffee can flat on a stake and hammering it into the ground.

Danny was frightened, but he knew that he must remain calm and keep looking down the road as if nothing unusual was going on. Ahead of him he could see the drivers on the roadway swerving as his father appeared un-expectedly on their right, only a foot from their fenders. Harold Ryan was threading a needle, but the clear area in front of the cemetery was running out, and ahead was a big oak tree blocking the way. There was no going to the right because of the wall, no going to the left because of the solid line of traffic, and no going ahead because of the tree. The only sane choice was to stop, but Mr. Ryan was not sane, so he had driven onward with leaden eyes, and Danny had held on to the door handle, silently watching the tree trunk come closer and closer.

Then a driver on the road next to them had jammed on his brakes, maybe out of shock at the sudden appearance of a car where none should be or because he was a quick thinker and saw a way to avert a crash. Anyway, a space opened up, and Danny's dad jerked the car into it with no more emotion than he showed when killing a chicken. His actions might be wild, but his face always had that set, knowing expression, deeply sarcastic, as if he had recognized something meant to be hidden from him, something personal and demeaning.

So they were saved, though Danny did not show his relief any more than he had shown his terror at the prospect of death moments before. He just sat like a statue while the bad expression on his dad's face slowly transformed into the amiable countenance that was the other side of the coin. By the time they had reached the Ryan house, Danny had allowed himself to put his elbow up on the car's window frame. Things had gotten that loose.

Now, sitting by the river, Danny wondered if it wouldn't have been better if they had smashed into the oak tree. Certainly, his mother and his two sisters would be better off. And Danny could not help thinking that he and his father might be better off as well. For his father, there would be no more of those tormented moments when he felt that someone had it in for him. For Danny, there would be an end to his vigilance and dread. But he tried to put such thoughts out of his head. They were probably sinful.

Danny had been struggling with the complexities of sin since his first confession three years earlier. For a while, he had hoped that the Catholic Church might provide some useful advice on coping with his dad. Once his mother had taken him to Sacred Heart Cathedral in downtown Tampa for a quick confession, and Danny had broached the subject by listing among his sins a failure to obey the fifth commandment.

"In what way do you not honor your parents?" the priest had asked.

"It's only my father," Danny had answered.

"How do you not honor him?"

"I don't like him."

"Many children go through periods of not liking their parents, but do you obey him, as is proper for a son?"

"Yes, Father."

"Then you are honoring him. Try to be understanding. A father has many responsibilities that children do not comprehend. He deserves your love."

"But he scares me!"

"In what way?"

Here Danny paused, unsure of how to go on. At the time of this confession, his father's craziness was confined to an occasional attitude of such menace that the whole family trembled, yet he seldom did anything more. Behavior like passing on the shoulder of the road was well in the future.

"Does your father strike you?" the priest eventually asked.

"No, Father."

"What does he do?"

Danny paused again. It was hard to explain why he was so upset about a person whose only sin was seeming as if he were on the verge of doing something awful but never did it.

"He . . ." Danny began, but words failed him.

The priest listened intently.

"He . . ."

Again Danny could not go on. The priest shifted in his chair. Danny's knees were starting to hurt.

"If he does not strike you, does he touch you in other ways?"

"Other ways?"

"Ways that are sinful."

Now Danny was really confused. What on earth was the priest getting at? There was such a multitude of sins and ways of committing them that he couldn't be sure something hadn't cropped up without his knowledge.

"He doesn't touch me that much," Danny said, hopefully.

"Any at all is forbidden," the priest replied, a note of agitation creeping into his voice.

"I hadn't heard of that," Danny said. "It wasn't covered in catechism."

"Catechism is not for such things, not for the young."

"I wish it had been mentioned. You need to know something like that."

"We know it when we come to it," the priest said. "That is why you have told me."

"I'm not sure what I told you," Danny whispered, wiping the perspiration off his lip.

"You have said enough," the priest replied. "You will wait for me and we will speak more in the rectory."

Danny said his act of contrition and fled the confessional, grateful that he was at Sacred Heart, where he was not known. He met his mother at the back of the church and pulled her along toward the exit.

"What about your penance?" she asked.

"I'll say it later," Danny replied.

"Don't be silly. Just kneel down and go through it. We've got time."

"I feel sick."

"Like how?"

"Queasy."

"I wonder what caused that," Marjorie Ryan said softly, putting the back of her hand to his forehead. "Well, you can say your penance in the car on the way home."

It was clear to Danny that he was beyond help by the church. To seek such help was to be drawn into a vortex at the bottom of which waited his father, unchained and enraged. Danny could pray to God, and he could ask his guardian angel for help, but no earthly factotum, neither the nuns who taught him nor the priests who confessed him, could ease his situation. That was a lonely feeling.

Danny shuddered and returned to the present, a summer day with no school in the near future. He dabbled his toe in the Hillsborough and looked to his left at the houses downstream, small in the distance, beginning halfway around Hanna's Whirl. They were tidy and seemed to have been there a long time, but it was strange how they stopped a quarter of a mile past where the creek flowed into the river. Above the creek, woods began and ran nonstop, right up to the dam.

Those downstream houses comprised what Danny thought of as a normal neighborhood, like one you'd see in a movie, where there were sidewalks, and men in nice clothes went away to work every morning, and kids had their own rooms. Danny lived upriver from that neighborhood, in an indescribable place. It wasn't quite the country, though it once must have been. Now it was a patchwork of woods and fields dotted with a few lonely houses. Even the woods were not deep woods, though he sometimes came across the guts of slaughtered animals, probably left there by some person who hadn't realized that things were different than they used to be.

Three years earlier, in 1951, when the family had first arrived in the area, Danny's sister Loretta had said, "My God, we've ended up in the middle of nowhere!" Loretta had little use for their parents, who had taken them from Los Angeles and plopped them down three thousand miles away on the outskirts of Tampa. A Hollywood talent agent had once offered to make Loretta the next Elizabeth Taylor. He had given her his card. Loretta had it in her wallet. She often looked at it, and then glanced out the window ruefully shaking her beautiful head. Danny understood her attitude. Even though he did not consider himself child star material, he would have preferred to at least live someplace recognizable—in the neighborhood down the way or on a real farm—but he was stuck in between, in no place in particular. Nowhere.

Danny had spent many hours on the bank of the nearby Hillsborough River, fishing with a bamboo pole. He seldom caught anything, but he could look over at the overgrown bank opposite him and imagine whatever he wanted. He had gotten good at it, often visualizing something exciting like the castles in knights-in-armor movies that he occasionally saw on Saturdays in nearby Sulphur Springs. The Springs Theater had recently installed a Cinemascope screen, and Danny thought nothing could ever equal being absorbed by that huge world of Technicolor, but today he did not want to imagine anything exciting. His wild ride that morning had been enough excitement.

To cheer himself up, Danny looked across the Hillsborough and imagined a friendly little house with a neatly manicured lawn and a sprinkler running in a circle, going *click, click, click*. He gave the house jalousie windows and painted it aqua, a color Danny liked very much. The house made him feel better, and it seemed so real that he didn't have to concentrate very hard to keep it going. In fact, the more he watched it, the more Danny had the mad thought of trying to get across to the house using the hyacinths. Bigger kids often climbed on them and even rode large clumps downstream to Tampa Bay. Still, it was dangerous to try to make it all the way across the river, especially this early in the season. Though the plants looked solid, there were thin spots where you could fall through. Danny had heard stories of kids being drowned under them, but adults liked to be scary, often for no good reason. He felt he had to make his own judgments about such things.

Laying his pole aside, he clambered to the water's edge, picked up one of the hyacinths and looked it over, as if for the first time. It was a fantastic thing, dark green and healthy, with its roots hanging down, dripping river water on his jeans. He plunged his thumb into one of the many flotation bulbs and felt the familiar punky texture give way. When the plant was old and decayed, those bulbs would pop like little balloons, making a satisfying crack, but that stage was far away. This was the blooming time, when the hyacinth put out a flower so beautiful you couldn't believe it was something bad. Some people called them "water orchids." Even so, everyone said they were choking the river with their beauty.

He looked toward the aqua house and thought he could see a possible path to it, where the hyacinths were more densely packed, a jagged swath of deeper green stretching from his side of the river, right to the opposite bank. It almost seemed as if the path were made for him, created by some hidden entity. But that was crazy thinking. Danny shrugged the notion off. It was just a bunch of hyacinths, and with that thought he started across the river.

The going was tough and scary. Farther out in the channel, his plunging set up vibrations that caused the whole mat of hyacinths to undulate. He was amazed that a kid only ten years old could set up such a commotion in a river forty yards across. Of course, he could never tell anyone about it. Adults wouldn't approve of his being out on the hyacinths, and kids would be sure to make some joke about his weight, which was a bit more than average for his age. His mother assured him that the excess was just "baby fat," destined to melt away of its own accord somewhere down the line. Danny couldn't say he liked the term "baby fat," even though it was coupled with the promise of normalcy. He hated the fact that any special language had to be used in describing him.

The hyacinths were growing more active, but not because of Danny. Underneath the mat, the river's current was gaining speed, causing a gentle rise and fall that soon increased to an alarming bucking motion as the water beneath the hyacinths raced faster. Danny knew what was happening. Upstream, they were opening the dam to flush out the channel. Now, he recalled the occasional warning that had seemed so far-fetched: "Stay out of the river. You never can tell when they'll open the dam."

When the dam opened, the Hillsborough's personality changed from sleepy to murderous. Its flat brown surface erupted in little whitecaps, whipping up islands of foam that caught on the banks. Nobody in his right mind would have gone in the water when the river was in that state or stayed in when he felt it coming, and you could always feel it coming, unless you were an idiot like Danny, not paying attention.

Now it was too late. The hyacinth mat was tearing up around him. He flattened himself out to spread his weight. Soon he would be off like a rocket, headed into the most notorious part of the Hillsborough, Hanna's Whirl. At that point, the river made a big right turn, causing some of its currents to circle back. Danny didn't know who Hanna had been, but he always imagined her as a young woman with long grey hair, being sucked down, with only her frantic arms and her head visible above the whirlpool. Her mouth made an "O!" and her hair stood up straight.

Abruptly, the dense green path Danny had been following broke free and headed downstream, slowly aligning itself with the current. Danny looked back at the bank, but the house was gone. He put his face in the hyacinths and breathed in their watery smell. They would survive. Even if drawn down into Hanna's Whirl, they would eventually bob to the surface, but Danny would stay under, choking, turning grey. That was the price he would pay for trying to get to that house. Perhaps it was for the best.

He looked up as his hyacinth raft began to turn the corner toward Hanna's Whirl. Soon it would be coiling back on him. Round and round it would go, like a piece of spaghetti sucked down the sink drain with the dishwater. As the raft turned, a strange sight came into Danny's view—a red triangle bearing down on him. He blinked the river water out of his eyes and recognized the prow of a canoe. In a moment, its fat side was next to him, blocking everything out with its shining redness.

"Grab on!"

Over the edge of the canoe came a hand and forearm: capable-looking, pinkish brown, covered with fine blond hair. Danny grabbed it, struggled up, and promptly fell into the gap between the hyacinths and the canoe, plunging beneath the brown water, but the hand drew him up. He broke the surface sputtering.

"Let's see how we can work this," someone said. "Can you hold on?"

"Yes, sir," Danny replied.

There was a hearty laugh from above and the owner of the hand peered over the edge of the canoe. He was a teenager with a head of blond curls, smiling and clearly having the time of his life making a rescue in Hanna's Whirl.

"I'm Buddy Connolly, and if you can hold on at the back, I'll get us out of here. If I try to drag you into the canoe, we might go over."

He swung Danny around, back to the narrow stern of the canoe.

"Grab on with both hands. Good! You solid?"

"Yes, sir."

Buddy laughed again.

"Just let yourself trail out. This won't take long, but if you get tired, give a yell."

Buddy's canoe was rounding the bend and beginning to shudder in a crosscurrent. He took up his paddle and dug into the water. Danny felt the canoe jump forward, but hanging on was easy because Buddy didn't fight with the river. He let it take the canoe where it would as long as the direction was generally suitable to his purposes. When it was not, he would dip the paddle in the water and suddenly they would be going correctly again. They made smooth but slow progress toward the shore, and Buddy frequently turned around and asked Danny how he was doing.

Danny was doing fine. He was glad to be on the surface rather than at the bottom of Hanna's Whirl and was beginning to enjoy the sensation of moving with the river, even getting a little cocky and sometimes holding on with only one hand. He used the other to grab at the clumps of hyacinths passing by, testing himself to see how far he could reach. Each stretch was succeeded by a greater one until he went too far and felt his fingers lose contact with the canoe.

He kicked vigorously, trying to catch back up, but as he did so, Buddy changed course and the canoe raced away. One thing was lucky. They were well out of Hanna's Whirl, so the currents here were not as treacherous, but they were swift, and the rafts of hyacinths bore down on him with no Buddy to help him keep pace. In fact, a big one was looming over him now, but it might be a blessing in disguise if he could grab on and ride for a while. Danny reached out and nearly took hold of a water moccasin coiled on the raft. He yanked his hand back, but the current brought the snake forward, toward his face.

There was no time to swim left or right, so Danny took a breath and slipped beneath the surface. As the raft passed over him, it interrupted the brown glow of sunlight from above. He had a funny feeling, as if it didn't matter whether he tried to swim or not. He thought about the coffee-can markers in the pauper's cemetery. Once he had looked at one to see if they had scratched a name on it, but it was too rusty to tell.

Danny recognized that he was thinking strangely, but he found it pleasant, rolling along under the Hillsborough with the hyacinths overhead. Hanna's fate may not have been so bad after all. But then he came to his senses. It was one thing to drown; it was another to accept it without a fight. Danny felt his soul was in peril, and he struck out, looking for a bright patch of water where he could surface, but the hyacinths had closed ranks, and he was stuck like a seal with no blow hole. He twisted desperately around, but it was the same on all sides. There was nothing left to do but take a run at the surface and hope he hit a thin place.

He kicked his way upward and crashed into the mat of hyacinths, hanging there for a moment, suspended by his head. He opened his mouth, and it was flooded with hyacinth-flavored water. Caught between river and air with no time left to try another spot, Danny worked his hand up next to his face and then thrust it above him as hard as he could. He broke through and tore out an opening big enough to accommodate his head. The breath exploding from his lungs sent a spray shooting skyward.

"Is that you?"

Danny could only gargle in reply, but in the next instant, Buddy's arm was around his neck, and he was being towed, face up. The oak limbs overhead meant they must be close to shore. Sure enough, his feet soon touched bottom, and Buddy helped him clamber up on the rocks next to the shuffleboard club at Sulphur Springs.

"You all right?"

"Yeah, but where's the canoe?"

"On its way to Cuba, I guess."

"I'm sorry."

"Forget it! It hardly cost anything. Mostly made of orange crates."

"Well, it's still gone."

"How come you didn't yell when you lost your grip?"

"It was my own fault."

"What's that got to do with it? You nearly drowned."

Danny couldn't say anything. He couldn't put into words his feeling that he had to do everything for himself; that it was embarrassing to be rescued one time, let alone twice; that the world seemed full of betrayals; that asking or accepting favors just increased the possibility of betrayal; that the best course was just to keep quiet.

"I don't know," Danny said.

Still, Buddy didn't seem to have anything wrong in him, no nasty streak or unsettling secret like Danny sensed in many people. He gave the impression of not minding the day's inconvenience, happy and relaxed in spite of having had to pluck a little snot-nose out of the hyacinths and then watch his handmade canoe disappear downriver.

"I'm chilly. How about some fries?" Buddy asked.

Danny was sorely tempted. The french fries sold at a stand near the Springs Pool were famous. The attendant took them hot out of the cooker, placed them in a brown paper bag with some salt, twisted the top and gave them a vigorous shake. When you opened that bag, the contents made you weak in the knees. Danny had heard his sisters discuss why Springs fries were so great. They thought the secret was the grease, which they agreed was either of very high quality or of very low quality. It was a complicated argument, but regardless of who was right, kids would hang around the stand just for the fragrance of those fries. They were especially good when you were water-logged from several hours swimming in the cold spring that fed the swimming pool next door. That was the way Danny felt now, with the breeze cooling him down in his wet clothes. Hot fries would be heavenly.

"No, thanks."

"Why not?"

"I don't have any money."

"Why don't I loan it to you? You can pay me back later."

Normally, Danny wouldn't have indebted himself to a stranger, but nearly drowning must have lowered his resistance, so he agreed. In a moment the two were at the stand, where Danny could look into Sulphur Springs proper, a place he had never figured out. It gave the appearance of having once been a resort or at least some kind of spot where people had wanted to come in times past. The main part was an arcade of stores topped by a hotel. Danny had been up in the hotel a few times, but it had an ominous feel, full of old people, some looking like bums and others just worn out. He had the sense that they'd come to Sulphur Springs long ago and gotten trapped somehow, unable to leave as the place went to seed around them.

The arcade contained numerous stores, among them a drugstore, a hardware store, a general merchandise store, and a pawn shop. The pawn shop was a source of continual fascination due to its extensive window display of switchblade knives and hand guns. Several other kinds of businesses also made their homes in the arcade, including the barber shop where Danny got his hair cut by a man who took a malicious pleasure in rubbing a child's scalp nearly raw during the final application of hair oil.

On the street opposite the arcade was a row of pathetic shops, smelly with deterioration. A man in one of them had tried to sell Danny a plaster dog in a squatting position. Along with it came a bunch of little plugs. You were supposed to stick one in a hole in the dog's rear-end and light it with a match. The man demonstrated the technique with the air of someone sure of a sale. As it burned, the plug produced a winding coil of something like feces but far longer. As it continued to mount up, the disturbing smile on the salesman's face got broader and broader. When the show was finally over, the man turned triumphantly to Danny, who had seldom been so confused. He tried to imagine under what circumstances such a thing was brought out. What kind of people could enjoy it? This was simply more proof that the world was full of dark secrets. He bought a fake ink blot instead.

As he stood in line at the french fry stand, the strangeness of Sulphur Springs hit Danny afresh because of Buddy. Such a normal kid seemed out of place here, yet here he was, talking pleasantly of having gotten the plans for his canoe out of *Boy's Life* magazine. Danny was thinking so hard that he barely listened to what Buddy was saying, so it came as a surprise when he heard him ask, "So you want to?"

"What?"

"You want to help me build another canoe?"

This was too much.

"I'm sorry, I've gotta go home."

"What about the fries?"

"No, I just remembered something I've gotta do. Thanks for pulling me out of the river. Sorry about the canoe."

Danny ran toward the bridge, leaving Buddy holding a brown bag of french fries. It was a long walk back to Nowhere, passing along the roads next to the river, staring curiously at the normal houses, wondering what went on inside them. Probably they were full of children who took *Boy's Life*, like Buddy. Danny knew a few kids, but none of them lived in the regular neighborhood, and even his one real friend could not be invited to Danny's home because it was too embarrassingly strange, strange and dangerous.

By the time he came out of the woods into his backyard, he was dry. His nineteen-year-old sister Ruth was sitting in a chair near the tree line, where she could gaze down at the creek. She was asleep, tired out from the effects of recently having had an atomic cocktail. Danny's father had probably had to carry her down there and would carry her back later. That meant his father was home. His heart sank.

Danny saw that Ruth had her favorite silky scarf, the one with the butterfly on it, wrapped artfully around her neck. She always wore a scarf when she was outside, even in the backyard where nobody could see her. The scarf helped to hide her neck, which was swollen from Hodgkin's disease. Danny tiptoed by without waking her.

2

The day after his near-calamity on the hyacinths, Danny went back to the Hillsborough to retrieve his fishing pole. His friend Alfred Bagley came with him but insisted on going by to see the Ryans' chickens before they started out. Since his father was not home, Danny agreed, though he himself found the chickens depressing. There had once been over a hundred of them. Now there were only twenty, all walking around as if they had a strong inkling of their fate, which was to be slaughtered.

In a way, it was their own fault. They had been given a chance to fashion a different future for themselves. Mr. Ryan had knocked together some neat little coops with ramps leading up to them. And the chickens had climbed the ramps and made nests. Everything seemed to be going well. Harold had shown Danny how to put alluring plastic eggs in the nests so the hens would not feel bereft when the real eggs were collected and sold. This did not do much for Danny's appraisal of chicken acumen.

The hens did lay some eggs, but not nearly as many as hoped, and more and more of them began to look listless. These were killed, processed for cooking, and others substituted, but the trend continued. Eventually, the egg operation was abandoned and the chickens were slaughtered and sold in the neighborhood. This had to be done slowly because Nowhere could absorb only a limited number of freshly killed chickens. Danny had delivered many a package of neatly wrapped chicken parts. It embarrassed him to knock on a door with such an item under his arm, but he was polite and took the money home to his mother.

As usual, Alfred was excited by the chickens, whatever their paltry number. He had a chicken of his own, and this may have been why the Ryan poultry responded so favorably to him, circulating around his legs, clucking and showing off. Toward Danny they were aloof, unless he had a feed pail in his hand, but they loved Alfred and trooped behind him when he went to one of the coops to check for eggs. Alfred was short, and he had to put one knee on the ramp to get high enough to stick his head inside the coop. This was not really necessary, but Alfred was not one to merely peep in when he could actually enter the chickens' domain.

"Just the plastic one," he reported with a note of sorrow in his voice. Then, unaccountably, Alfred turned on his back with his legs dangling out the coop door, one on each side of the ramp. His T-shirt pulled up, exposing his bony ribs and protuberant navel.

"I don't think they ever lay any on the ceiling," Danny observed drily.

"Get out of there."

Danny whirled and looked up at his father. The sun was at the man's back, so Danny could only imagine the dreadful expression on his face, but he knew it must be there. Danny turned back to Alfred and tugged at his friend's jeans, but in true Alfred Bagley fashion, he had managed to get a belt loop hung up on something. He wiggled comically, but comedy was the very thing to drive Danny's father over the edge.

"He's trying," Danny said with all the sincerity he could muster.

It didn't work. Mr. Ryan pushed Danny aside, grabbed Alfred's legs, and gave a yank. Down came the coop, leaving Alfred on his back, head still inside, blinking his eyes amidst a cloud of chicken dust. Danny's father turned and strode away. In a moment, the back door slammed.

"What happened?" Alfred asked in a muffled voice.

"Coop collapsed, you dope. Dad tried to get you out before it went down."

Danny disentangled Alfred, who hopped up with his usual resilience.

"Where's your dad gone to?"

"He had to leave."

This was enough explanation for Alfred. He took a step toward the chickens, all of whom had fled to a far corner of the yard, where they were milling around and cackling fearfully.

"No more chickens," Danny said firmly, grabbing Alfred by the shirt and dragging him toward the gate.

Alfred looked longingly over his shoulder but allowed himself to be led into the woods behind the Ryan house. He showed no ill effects from his chicken coop adventure and apparently forgot about the incident after thirty seconds of walking. Never one to travel silently when he could prattle, Alfred asked one of his signature questions.

"Danny, what'd you do if a big black cigar appeared in your mouth?"

This was typical of Alfred, a boy who seemed completely at home in Nowhere. He was a scrawny, jug-eared child, given to odd pursuits like training his pet chicken to come and eat a cockroach when he slapped the floor. In this he had been extremely successful, and one of Alfred's great diversions was to creep about the house with a fly swatter, looking for cockroaches. The bird was called Nickel because his parents had promised Alfred a nickel for every roach it ate. This was later reduced to a penny, but the name Nickel stuck.

"So, what'd you do?" Alfred urged.

This type of question always stopped Danny cold. He couldn't fathom what he was supposed to do with it.

"I just don't know, Alfred."

"Would you smoke it?"

"Would I have a match?"

"Yeah!" Alfred answered, his voice crackling with excitement.

"Then I guess I might give it a try."

At this answer, Alfred dissolved into uncontrollable giggling. As always, Danny could only watch and wonder. Alfred continued giggling until they were on the verge of the fish hatchery. Danny couldn't understand why it was called the fish hatchery when it was really a place where aquarium plants were grown. Apparently, it had once been a fish hatchery, but its title had not been updated. More confusing still, if a kid had nerve enough to approach the door to the long frame building where the plants were sorted, he could see on the wall yellowing pictures of the hatchery when it had seemingly been a swimming spot, overrun with people in old-fashioned bathing suits. So had it been a fish hatchery before or after it had been a swimming pool? This was what could be expected of Nowhere. One could never get an accurate line on it.

But the real point was that you had to be careful around the fish hatchery. Yelling or loud giggling was ill advised because sometimes bad-tempered men would appear and shoo kids away from the network of concrete pens, each of which was devoted to the growing of a particular plant. These men were one of several obstacles that had to be negotiated in order to get to the river by the shortest route. You could go around by regular roads, but it was out of the way.

On a day when a kid was feeling bold, he might cut right across the pens, zigzagging along the narrow block walls like a tightrope walker. Such a maneuver invited scrutiny and often brought the men out of the big house. They had different techniques for dealing with intruders. One of them would gesture angrily at the kids, as if he truly hated them. The other usually yelled something about getting hurt, which was seen as another adult overstatement. The water was deep, but falling in was rare and all the youngsters in Nowhere could swim.

But after his disaster the day before, Danny was not in a bold mood, and Alfred, whose dad whipped him with a belt, was not much of one to challenge authority. They stuck to the well-hidden trail that skirted the pens. It bordered a different creek than the one that ran behind Danny's house, and at one point it was rather narrow, cutting into the bank six or eight feet above the stream. This was a part of the trail Danny particularly liked, since it reminded him of the mountain paths he sometimes saw in movies, but today it had an unnerving feature.

Sitting on the trail with her legs dangling over the edge above the creek was a young Latin woman. She must have been from the hatchery, because there was no other explanation for her. All such people lived in Ybor City or West Tampa, but every weekday eight or ten dark-skinned Latin ladies got off the bus at Halper's store, where the line stopped, and walked into Nowhere to work at the hatchery. But this girl was hardly the type to be doing such work. Whereas the regular ladies were middle-aged, overweight, and plain, this girl was young, curvaceous, and beautiful with shining dark eyes, jet-black hair, and olive skin. She wore a peasant blouse, which was a fashion Danny liked very much but for some reason made him nervous. The girl turned to Danny and Alfred, smiling as if there was nothing startling about her presence on a path through the woods of Nowhere.

"How are you today?" she asked, her voice full of Spanish inflection.

Alfred was struck dumb and did nothing but peer around Danny's shoulder like a gargoyle. That was just like him! Bend your ear with unanswerable questions when you were alone, but couldn't find a thing to say in an emergency.

"Okay," Danny replied, looking at his toes.

He wished Alfred would stop staring, but he could hardly blame him. This girl belonged on a billboard for Ybor City's fancy Las Novedades Restaurant, not on this crummy trail where nothing happened. She was a finished item, with a definite place in the world—why wasn't she in it?

"Do you wish to go by?" she inquired.

"Okay."

"This must be your favorite word. Can you say another?"

How was he expected to answer a question like that? Any response was bound to sound stupid. Danny tried to take a step backward, but Alfred would not give ground.

"And your friend. Does he not speak?"

"What would you do if a big black cigar appeared in your mouth right now?" Alfred blurted.

Danny was mortified, of course, but he was glad that the girl was getting some of her own medicine. She had asked an impossible question; now she could try her hand at answering one.

"This is something I can tell you of," the girl responded, nodding wisely at Alfred. "My father can still roll cigars in the Spanish style. I know a great deal of cigars. If a cigar appeared in my mouth, and I was a man, I would take it out and test its fragrance. If it smelled of unworthy tobacco, I would curse the devil and cast it away, but if it smelled of fine tobacco, I would thank God and treasure it."

"Then what?" Alfred asked quickly.

"Then I would make ready to enjoy it."

"How would you do that?"

"First one must create a channel through which the smoke may come. An impolite man may bite off the end of the cigar and spit it aside, but a cultured man will have a little machine that neatly does what is needed. Some men will then use the tongue to dampen the cigar."

The girl slowly exposed her tongue and drew an imaginary cigar across it. Something about this motion made Danny breathe more rapidly.

"But, if this does good at all, it does so only for inferior cigars, and as I said, I would have thrown away such a one. A fine cigar is of itself moist enough, though I think some men do the unnecessary in order to have the pleasure of tasting the tobacco before they smoke it."

"How does it taste?"

"Who can tell another of a taste? A poet perhaps, but I am not a poet. You will search out this taste for yourself. You may find it does not suit you."

"I bet it will!" Alfred said.

Danny felt the same. Since seeing this girl lick an imaginary cigar, his interest in tobacco had shot way up.

"What else?" Alfred urged.

"One must be careful when one lights the cigar, not to draw in the gas from the match flame. This is harsh and creates a bad reception for the flavor of the tobacco. Once the cigar is glowing, one must be gentle, be satisfied with a little at a time. Such smoke is to be savored. It must not be gulped. One cannot conquer a cigar. One must dance with it."

This seemed the final word on what to do if a big black cigar appeared in your mouth. Alfred had no more questions, and Danny felt that he had sacrificed his right to further comment by earlier having had nothing more to say than "okay."

The young woman stood gracefully up and walked to a place where the trail was wide enough for the boys to pass comfortably, but they hung back.

"Please, you must not let me keep you from your business," she said quietly.

As they passed, she put her hand for a moment on Danny's shoulder, making the hair on his neck prickle. When they reached the next bend in the trail, Danny and Alfred looked back, and she was still standing there, like a bouquet of fresh flowers on the surface of the moon. Then she was out of sight.

Both boys were quiet the rest of the way to the river, though Danny could hear Alfred making cigar-puffing sounds under his breath. The Hillsborough was just a short distance from the fish hatchery, and they reached Danny's fishing spot in a few minutes, but his equipment was nowhere to be found. That wasn't a great tragedy, because bamboo poles were cheap, but it was unusual for such things to be stolen. Was this a punishment for his having tried to reach the house?

"Where'd it go?" Alfred asked.

"If I knew that, I would have gone there in the first place," Danny answered.

"Did the water wash it away?"

Now, this was a novel theory, perhaps the best one Alfred had ever come up with. The river had risen when the dam was opened, and maybe that accounted for the pole's disappearance.

"Maybe we could find it," Alfred said.

This was just like Alfred, to say something sensible with one breath and something ridiculous with the next, but Danny held his tongue. The odds against finding a pole that had been swept away were astronomical; however, an impossible hunt for a fishing pole was as good a pretext as any to spend time with Alfred, who would no doubt do many entertaining things in the course of the search.

The first time Danny had seen him, just a year before, Alfred had been hunkered in the weeds with a basket of wild blackberries under his arm. In the midst of picking them, he had run across a low-growing plant with leaves like tiny ferns, and when Alfred ran his finger along the spine of a leaf, the fronds tightened. He had greeted Danny brightly and asked him if he wanted to see a plant that moved on its own. At first mention, this seemed interesting, but the reality was so far below what Danny had imagined, that it could have held his attention for only a short time if Alfred had not been so fascinated. As it was, they sat there for an extraordinary length of time, stimulating those weeds, but after only a few minutes, Danny gave up watching the weeds and took up watching Alfred, something he had been doing ever since. Before Alfred, Nowhere had been a much less entertaining place, not to mention much lonelier.

"Where shall we look first?" Danny asked.

"Let's get our bikes," Alfred answered.

The boys ran home with Alfred leading the way, enthused about the great pole hunt. Danny kept pace, hardly thinking about his father. Alfred often had that wonderful effect. The two parted company in the street, and Danny started thinking about his father again. He hoped he could sneak around back and get his bike without being seen, but he didn't make it. His mother came out the back door.

"Danny?"

"Yeah?"

"Did you see Daddy earlier?"

"Yeah."

"Did anything happen?"

"Nothing much. Alfred got stuck in one of the coops, and it fell down."

"Good lord! Did your father do anything?"

"No. Is he still around?"

"He went back to work. Are you sure nothing happened?"

"Everything's fine. Alfred didn't notice anything."

"You're not just trying to make me feel better?"

"No way. Alfred thinks Dad tried to help him. You know how Alfred is. Everything's normal. We're going to look for my fishing pole."

"Did you lose it?"

"We think it floated away."

"Where were you when this happened?"

"I went up to the hatchery for a while. I wasn't catching anything, but I left my pole propped up, just in case."

Mrs. Ryan looked down toward the chicken yard.

"Do you think you'll find it?"

"Not a chance."

"Wait a minute, then."

Mrs. Ryan went back in the house and after a moment came to the window. She unhooked the screen and handed Danny three quarters and his sneakers and socks.

"Get yourself a new fishing pole."

Danny looked doubtful. This was a lot of money.

"I never catch anything, anyway."

"Take it. I'll make lots of tips tonight. We'll be in the chips."

"I don't know."

"Maybe you'd like to come in the house and help me grind this liver."

"I'm gone," Danny said, taking the money.

Danny would rather do anything than grind liver for Ruth. He knew that he should want to help, but everything about the process turned his stomach. He couldn't believe drinking such foulness could possibly do his sister any good, regardless of what the doctor said. Several times a week, Danny's mother clamped a vicious-looking grinder onto the kitchen table and fed it hunks of liver. At first he had been intrigued, thinking perhaps something worthwhile could be done with liver after all, but it remained hateful in his sight. His mother had tried to divert Danny by calling his attention to the workings of the grinder. There was a hole in the top where you stuffed the meat, if you could call liver "meat." At the bottom of that hole was something like a big corkscrew that revolved when his mom turned a crank and drove pieces of flesh through a hellish attachment. What emerged was a shocking mess, which his mother wrapped in cheesecloth and squeezed, producing a brown liquid that was taken to Ruth in a cheerful tumbler. Danny didn't know whether to admire or despise the uncomplaining way Ruth drank that juice. Not that she smiled or anything, but the fact that she swallowed it at all was a triumph. Danny often wondered if he would drink liver squeezings, even to save his life. He might prefer to die.

The boys met back in the street and Alfred waited for Danny to put his sneakers on. Danny considered them a nuisance, but his mother had been worried, and he thought maybe wearing the sneakers would make her feel better. Since riding bikes through the woods was impossible, they took the long way to Hanna's Whirl, where they began their search. Alfred was not satisfied to leave any portion of the riverbank unscrutinized, though when they reached the part of the river where the houses started, this level of attention was increasingly difficult. After they had been yelled at a couple of times for skulking around in someone's backyard, Alfred started marching up the tidy walkways and knocking on doors. A housewife or older man would open the door, and Alfred would make a short statement, whereupon the door would either be closed or he would receive permission to go around to the back where he could scan the riverbank. Sometimes they even escorted him through the house!

"What do you say to them?" Danny asked.

"I tell 'em we're looking for your fishing pole," Alfred answered, as if this concept was the key that would open any door. "Why don't you come, too?"

Danny just shook his head. He was too keenly aware of the potential consequences of a stranger's knocking on the door of his own house. Then again, Alfred showed a tremendous interest in other people's property and their furnishings, while Danny was afraid of what he might find if he were too nosy. These houses looked normal, but looks could be deceiving.

By stages, they worked their way down the Hillsborough until they

reached the bridge to Sulphur Springs. Alfred probably would have followed
Danny's fishing pole to Venezuela if left to his own devices, but here he
had to stop.

"It could be around the next bend," Danny said.

"Naw. Outside my boundaries."

Danny often dealt with Alfred's troublesome boundaries, which stopped
just short of Sulphur Springs. Many a time they had stood together, looking longingly across the bridge toward the pool or arcade, with Alfred
unable to cross over because he hadn't gotten special permission. The best
he could do was call home if he had a dime, and that was usually a dime
wasted. Apparently there was something sacred about starting out from
home with permission, because Alfred's mother seldom granted it on the
fly. And permission always involved some specific errand. It was unthink-
able for Alfred to be given permission to go to the Springs simply to mess
around. In spite of temptation, Alfred rigorously honored his boundaries.
Danny sometimes crossed over one of them just to show how easily it could
be done, and looked back to see Alfred standing there with his bike, shaking his homely head and saying, "Somebody might see me." It would have
been comical if the threat of the belt had not hung so heavily over him.

This was one of the few instances in which Danny felt his situation to be
superior to another person's. His house was so full of uncertainty, sickness,
and fear that there was no time for trivial things like keeping track of an
active child. And even if his parents had set boundaries for him, the family
never socialized or even had conversations with anyone who might observe
him violating them. And supposing he had been observed, his father was
quite the opposite of Alfred's. Rather than being pleasant as long as rules
were obeyed and angry when they were violated, Danny's father was forgiv-
ing of the occasional trespass, but subject to dark anger just when things
were going along fine. It was confounding, but one useful result was that
Danny could do just about what he wanted as long as he did so quietly.

"My mom gave me money for a new pole. We could go over to the hardware store together."

There were few places Alfred liked better than a hardware store, but
again he shook his head.

"I'll stay here and watch for you!" he said enthusiastically.

"Okay," Danny replied.

As he rode along, Danny marveled at how ardently Alfred embraced the idea of hanging around for forty-five minutes just to experience the thrill of seeing Danny coming back from the other side of the river. Meanwhile, Alfred would find some way to amuse himself. He might march up to someone's house and ask if he could come in and look around. If, as any sensible person would, someone said "No," Alfred would not be at all fazed. You had to admire that.

Danny wished he could enjoy Alfred's company as he went through the ritual of choosing a new pole, a neat cork bobber, and yet another hook. Danny thought his failure as a fisherman might be a case of using the wrong-sized hook, so he was going through the whole range. He had started with a tiny hair hook, with which he caught minnows, and was gradually working toward a ridiculously huge one, probably suitable for tarpon. Whatever hook he used, he never pulled in a fish bigger than his hand, though it was always exciting to see the bobber begin to dance, like a message from a secret world. However, Alfred would not have been much help in choosing a pole. He had given up poles, preferring to put on a bathing suit and chase the fish up under the banks, where he trapped them with his bare hands. Using this technique, he caught far more than Danny, but Danny thought the pole was more sporting.

As he rode back toward the bridge, holding his new pole under his arm, he heard a rumble. He pedaled faster, hoping to get back to Alfred before the lightning started.

3

Danny hated riding with a fishing pole. As long as the going was easy, he could carry it over his shoulder and steer one-handed, but that didn't work in tough stretches where leverage on the pedals was needed. In order to get both hands on the handlebars, he had to thrust the pole forward, clamping it beneath his elbow like a lance. By the time he was within sight of the bridge, his fingers were aching and his elbow was numb. Cold raindrops were falling like fifty-cent pieces all around him. He was completing an awkward turn onto the old bridge when lightning struck one of the metal girders. Blinded by the flash, he drove his fishing pole into the bridge railing, catapulting himself so cleanly out of the saddle that his bike continued on across the bridge.

Danny lay in bewilderment, watching the bike's momentum carry it toward Alfred, who was standing on the opposite side, scanning the girders for some sign of the strike. At last, the sound of whirring wheels caught his attention, and he glanced up, gawking at the riderless bike but making no attempt to interfere as it proceeded by him, slowing to a stately pace before collapsing among the roadside weeds. This dashed Alfred's hope that the bicycle had been moving of its own accord, so he turned to see what else might be afoot.

Upon spotting Danny lying in the road, he started forward but stopped abruptly as he remembered his boundaries. Danny gave a pathetic wave and tried to get to his feet but slipped down again, which caused Alfred to break out laughing. The lightning, the bike's ghostly transit, and the sight of Danny flopping in the road, still clasping his shattered fishing pole, constituted the kind of low-comedy situation in which Alfred delighted.

That Danny might be crippled for life didn't occur to him, only how funny it all was.

On his second try, Danny managed to remain upright, and he hobbled across the bridge, dragging the remains of his pole. This increased Alfred's hilarity, until Danny thrust his left fist close to Alfred's face. There was blood trickling from between his fingers. It looked terrible, and even Alfred couldn't get a laugh out of it. Danny glared at him and went to pick up his bike. The rain was coming down harder and lightning flashed more frequently.

"I'm going back to the arcade," Danny said.

"I better not," Alfred replied.

"Look, your folks always tell you to get out of the lightning, right?"

"Yeah."

"Well, isn't this lightning?"

"I'm supposed to ask permission to stay on somebody's porch until it's over."

"You can say you were helping me. I'll show them my hand."

"They'll want to know why I didn't help you someplace inside my boundaries."

Danny knew this was true, so he played his trump card.

"After the rain, we can go over to the swap shop."

There was nothing Alfred liked better than going to the swap shop. He was a natural pack rat and considered it an act of providence that the place was actually called "Al's Swap Shop," though nobody ever called Alfred "Al." Alfred harbored a secret desire to go into the junk business, in spite of his parents' insistence that he become a barber. Alfred was not much for schoolbooks, but it seemed to them he had the patience to cut hair.

Danny thought running a swap shop would be a good career for Alfred, but Mr. and Mrs. Bagley were hard-shell Baptists, and you never could tell what might come through the door of a swap shop. For example, in one of the swap shop's nooks, there was a pile of paper items and among them were some pictures, drawings really, of ladies in skimpy clothes. Danny tried to get a glimpse of these whenever possible. One of them was of a lady wearing nothing but a barrel and a pair of high heels. Underneath her it said: "Barrelly covered." Danny was fascinated by the look on her face. She seemed delighted to be wearing a barrel. Danny instinctively knew that this was the sort of thing that had turned Alfred's parents against the swap shop. Whenever they gave him special permission to go to the pool or somewhere else at the Springs, they usually added, "But you stay out of that swap shop." Without this specific mention, Alfred would certainly go there.

Alfred knew that his parents would not consider Danny's injury to be a sufficient excuse to violate his boundaries, but it might be enough of a factor to eliminate a whipping from the price he would have to pay if he were found out. It was worth the risk. Everywhere a boy looked there was something exciting: Aqua-Lungs, propellers, hula skirts, horse collars—you couldn't name it all. Alfred never dwelled, as Danny so often did, on how out of place many of the items were. He never asked himself how a dogsled had wound up in Sulphur Springs, Florida. Alfred just dreamed of where he might display a dogsled if by some incredible stroke of providence one fell into his hands.

"Okay," he said.

Another crash of thunder sent the boys scurrying for the shelter of the arcade, but riding was impossible because the streets had turned to rivers, so they pushed their bikes, worrying at every moment about being struck by lightning. The rain was icy cold and by the time they reached the arcade, Alfred's lips were turning blue. Once they were well into the central corridor, Danny took off his tennis shoes and wrung out his socks, using one to tie around his hand as a bandage. He didn't look closely at his injury, but he could feel that the skin had been torn back on his palm. Meanwhile, Alfred busied himself by going through the trash can behind the notions store. He found a piece of gum, unwrapped it, and popped it into his mouth.

"That's probably not a good idea," Danny said.

"Why not?" Alfred asked, chewing vigorously and relishing the first rush of gum flavor.

"It's been in the garbage."

"It was all wrapped up."

"Something could have dripped on it."

"Naw. It was clean."

During this debate, Alfred had continued going through the trash and with his usual expertise had come up with something unusual, a cardboard kaleidoscope. Such kaleidoscopes were familiar, but this one had a unique feature, a clear plastic rectangle that slid back and forth on a little track over the lens. The rectangle had four compartments, each containing a teaspoonful of loose objects. One had dried beans, one sequins, and one plastic pearls. Each of these materials created a different sort of pattern. The fourth compartment was broken, its contents lost. Alfred put the kaleidoscope to his eye and turned the lens, sliding the compartments into view one after another.

"I like the beans," he announced.

"You would," Danny replied.

"Let's take it over to the swap shop," Alfred suggested.

"They won't want that. It's trash."

"Things don't have to be perfect to go in the swap shop," Alfred said.

Danny had to admit there was much truth in this, so the boys left the arcade and discovered that there had been one of those amazing Florida turnabouts, and the sun was now shining brightly. Alfred's formerly blue lips were pink again. Steam was rising from the pavement. The boys pushed their bicycles across the street to the swap shop, their noses filling with asphalt vapors.

As they grew closer, the familiar sights came into view. To Danny's mind, Al Gallagher, the proprietor of Al's Swap Shop, was a master of display. Standing between the twin doors leading into the shop, he had propped up one of his most fascinating items, a full diving suit. Danny stopped as usual to look at the suit's oversized feet, heavy but not heavy enough by themselves to keep you underwater. Weight belts were also needed. Danny was familiar with the setup from having read a comic book in which Scrooge McDuck had sent Donald down in a diving suit looking for treasure.

The boys parked their bikes to one side and ventured into the shop. Al Gallagher himself was in the store today. For Danny, he was a figure of mystery, but for Alfred Bagley, he was a god. As usual when Al Gallagher was present, Alfred and Danny went separate ways, Danny to examine the rows of fascinating objects and Alfred to stand admiringly near his hero. As Danny edged toward the nook containing the barrel lady, he could hear Alfred posing one of his favorite questions.

"Mr. Gallagher, what kind of car do you drive?"

This was a question that Mr. Gallagher had heard from Alfred probably ten times, but he never failed to respond and always with the same information.

"I don't drive a car. I drive a truck."

Danny did not have to be over there with them to know that a shiver
went through Alfred when he heard that answer. The idea of driving around
in a truck full of junk was so delicious that Alfred could not let go of it.

"What make?"

"Chevy."

"Chevy," Alfred repeated reverently, falling into a meditative silence.

Meanwhile, Danny had worked his way around the many objects that
cluttered the floor of the swap shop and had arrived in the vicinity of the
paper goods. The lady with the barrel was on top, looking slyly out. Of
course, Danny did not go directly to her. He pretended to examine something nearby. It was like a wire cage with a funnel-shaped opening. It was
interesting, but he kept glancing over at the lady.

"You know what that is?"

He was caught. There was no mistaking the voice of Al Gallagher, who
must have seen Danny looking at the lady and had decided to ask him
one of those questions that had a meaning Danny could not understand.
Anybody could see that she was a lady in a barrel, but she was seemingly
something else, too, something he was incapable of comprehending, so
Danny just stared at the floor and said, "No, sir."

"Crab trap."

How was this to be understood? Danny ventured to glance up at Mr.
Gallagher, who was not seedy-looking like the man who had tried to sell
Danny the pooping dog. Mr. Gallagher looked hardy and self-possessed.
He might have missed a day shaving every now and then, but he was clean,
especially for a man who presided over a store full of dusty objects. He
wore denim pants, a pull-over shirt, and a pair of comfortable sneakers. His
face was plain and unthreatening, his voice unemotional but not unkind.
Danny could not guess his age. He certainly was not old.

"They crawl in through there."

Danny realized with tremendous relief that Mr. Gallagher was referring
to the cage thing and not the lady, but why had Mr. Gallagher picked this
moment to speak to Danny, who had been in and out of the store many
times and received no more notice than if he had been a ghost? Then he
noticed Alfred, standing behind Mr. Gallagher. This looked suspicious.
Had Alfred told Mr. Gallagher something? The only thing for Danny to
do was bluff it through.

"How come they don't crawl back out?" Danny asked, pointing to the little funnel-shaped opening.

"Crabs are not smart enough to figure that out," Mr. Gallagher replied. "What's that in your hand?"

"A sock."

"Is that where you usually keep your sock?"

This sounded as if it might be a joke, but it was hard to tell with Mr. Gallagher. If only the man would give a lame laugh like other adults who were being cute. Danny thought it best to act as if he thought it was a straightforward inquiry.

"No, sir."

"You mind if I take a look?"

This was fraught with possible complications, but the flatness of Mr. Gallagher's voice was somehow reassuring. Danny held out his hand, and Mr. Gallagher knelt down. Alfred looked on with interest.

"Unclench your fist."

Danny flattened out his hand and saw that his white sock was now mostly crimson where he had clutched it. Mr. Gallagher took the sock between his thumb and forefinger and pulled it slowly upward, drawing with it a flap of palm skin that revealed an expanse of raw meat below. Alfred's eyes rolled back into his head, and he fell to the floor with a thump, his broken kaleidoscope clattering out of his hand.

"Oh, fine," Mr. Gallagher muttered, turning away from Danny to stare down at the little bag of bones on the floor.

He gathered Alfred up, tossed him over his shoulder, and headed for the heavy door at the back of the store. While he was inserting the key, he said, "You come along."

"Me?" said Danny.

"Yeah, you."

Danny was torn. He knew he was not to take candy from strangers or get into a car with anyone he didn't know; however, going into a locked room with a famous storekeeper had not been covered in his safety lectures. There was probably something wrong with it, but his pal Alfred was going in under any circumstances, so out of loyalty he followed Mr. Gallagher through the door.

What lay behind that door was a surprisingly large room, quite different from the helter-skelter atmosphere of the swap shop proper. It was not exactly well organized, but it was full of a different kind of objects, just as wonderful as the stuff out front, but less practical: a large model of a suspension bridge made of silver-colored metal, a handsome ventriloquist's dummy in a tuxedo, an elegant chandelier hanging overhead—lots of things to ponder. But in addition to its treasures, the room also contained a bunk, a washbasin, and a refrigerator. Mr. Gallagher put Alfred on the bunk and turned to Danny.

"Come over by the basin. Let's wash your hand."

The idea of running water over his wound did not appeal to Danny, and the word "washing" implied soap, which was a horrible thought. After seeing that flap of skin and what lay under it, he would have preferred to continue clutching his sock for the next few months and hoping for the best. It was not a thing you wanted to let free. But Mr. Gallagher kept beckoning to him, so he went.

"This is just warm water to get the dirt out of it. Don't watch. Look off somewhere."

Danny looked off, but he didn't see much. All of his attention was on his hand. However, Mr. Gallagher turned out to be very competent, letting the warm water flow for a minute or two over Danny's clenched fist. Then he gently forced the hand open and soaked the sock thoroughly before removing it. As the sock departed, Danny's anxiety shot up, but once again he was pleasantly surprised. Nothing rough or excessive happened. Mr. Gallagher just moved Danny's hand to and fro under the water.

"That's looking good. Do you know the difference between iodine and mercurochrome?"

Danny certainly did know the difference. One stung like crazy and one didn't.

"Yes, sir."

"Which do you think I ought to put on?"

Now why did he have to ask it like that? What did Danny know of "ought"? He knew what he desired. If something must be put on, then he deeply desired that it be mercurochrome. What kid would choose iodine? Why should Danny have to answer trick questions with his palm in two parts?

"I don't know," he answered, hoping for the best.

A second later he was skipping around the room shaking his hand and howling in pain. At the sound of this commotion, Alfred sat upright and began to laugh hysterically. Mr. Gallagher looked on impassively as Danny flung drops of iodine onto the room's precious things. In a moment, Danny realized what he was doing and stopped shaking. Though his hand still felt fiery hot, he was suddenly overcome with remorse. The bridge and the other hard things could be wiped off, but the dummy's tuxedo was covered with little dots of iodine. Danny had no idea whether or not they would wash out. He had heard his mother say that some things didn't.

"Come on back over here," said Mr. Gallagher, his tone unchanged. "We'll put a bandage on and then I think you should go right home. How about you, little Al? Do you feel all right?"

Alfred was off the cot and prowling around the room examining everything he could get his hands on.

"I guess you do," Mr. Gallagher said, opening a tin box from which he removed a piece of gauze and some white surgical tape. "Little Al, put that astrolabe down and come over here."

While he sat on the cot, taping gauze on Danny's hand, Mr. Gallagher gave each of the boys a serious look.

"I don't mind you two telling your folks that I put on this bandage, but I would appreciate it if you didn't mention the things in this room. Okay?"

Alfred was atremble. He could hardly believe that he and his idol were to be linked by a secret. Both boys nodded.

"Now, go on."

On his way out of the room, Danny ruefully glanced at the little tuxedo.

"Hey," said Mr. Gallagher, "forget it. I picked iodine."

Danny lowered his head and walked toward the door. He was surprised that Mr. Gallagher had been watching him so closely and seemed to know what was in his mind. Danny made it a habit to be as unobtrusive as possible. He could not afford to be under scrutiny. As much as he disliked the thought, Danny felt he might have to avoid Al's Swap Shop. Mr. Gallagher noticed too much.

On his way through the store, Alfred picked up the broken kaleidoscope and ran back to Al Gallagher.

"What's this?" Al asked.

"You look through it." Alfred said.

"Is that so?"

"Yeah," Alfred said, shaking the kaleidoscope.

"Show me how."

Now, Danny was sure Mr. Gallagher was joking, but he did it with such a straight face! And he didn't seem mean, just . . . well, it was hard to put your finger on what he was.

Of course, Alfred was oblivious to any second level of meaning in Mr. Gallagher's comments. He put the kaleidoscope to his eye and demonstrated how to move the slide.

"Oh, I get it," Mr. Gallagher said, accepting the kaleidoscope from Alfred and putting it to his eye.

"I like the beans," Alfred said.

"I don't wonder," Mr. Gallagher responded.

"Could you sell it?" Alfred asked.

Mr. Gallagher looked over at Danny, who rolled his eyes in embarrassment.

"Well, it's hard to tell what people will buy," Mr. Gallagher said, staring down at Alfred and adding with solemn emphasis, "One man's trash is another man's treasure."

Alfred stared back in stunned silence. He had heard a lot of sayings in his short life, mostly having to do with proper conduct, but he had never heard anything that he understood as well as this. He opened his mouth, but nothing came out.

"I have a few toys over in the corner of the window," Mr. Gallagher said. "I'll put it there, and if anybody buys it, I'll split the proceeds, but you have to let me sell it for what I can get. No griping afterward."

Alfred opened his mouth again, but again nothing emerged. Somehow, through the influence of God or the devil, he was in business with Al of Al's Swap Shop. This was the greatest day of his life. The boys walked out into the steamy afternoon and turned to watch Al Gallagher place the kaleidoscope. Alfred reverently approached the swap shop window and put his nose on it.

Mr. Gallagher stuck the kaleidoscope in a corner and glanced up at Alfred, then he shook his head slightly and moved the toy a few inches into a more prominent spot. Alfred could not tear his eyes off the kaleidoscope until Mr. Gallagher rapped on the window and broke the spell. He pointed forcefully down the sidewalk and mouthed "Go home."

4

Danny and Alfred hurried along Nebraska Avenue, the main drag through Sulphur Springs. It was a busy street, so Alfred was worried about being seen and reported. Danny himself was vaguely uncomfortable about Nebraska Avenue. The state of Nebraska played a murky part in his family history.

Before he was born, his parents and Ruth and Loretta had lived in Nebraska. His father had been born there and had worked for quite some time at a meatpacking plant. "Meatpacking" was the polite term for slaughtering animals. Mr. Ryan had been good at it and sometimes spoke of his skill with a trimming knife. Then the family went to California, supposedly because the winters in Nebraska were too harsh for Ruth.

Danny had been born in California, and he did not understand why the family had not stayed on the West Coast. This mystery was never explained, though Loretta mumbled darkly about something having to do with their father. She would not be specific, and Danny didn't feel it would help him to know.

The boys turned off Nebraska as quickly as possible and circled the Springs Theater, taking the most inconspicuous route to the old bridge, which was seldom used by automobiles. Nearly all motor traffic went over the newer bridge of white cement that took Nebraska Avenue traffic into the heart of the Springs. Once the boys were safely within Alfred's boundaries, they stopped for a few minutes to observe the alligator lying in a storm drainpipe that emptied into the Hillsborough under the bridge.

The creature was almost always there, and Danny had once asked his dad why the gator liked that spot so much. Mr. Ryan had speculated that the water coming out of the drain was probably warmer than the river water, but Danny suspected that the feeling of protection was the real reason he stayed there. It would be reassuring to spend time in a pipe where nothing could sneak up on you.

Once the boys started riding, they made good time back to their street, Florinda, which like most of the byways in Nowhere was unpaved and not very good for bike riding, though there was a rumor around that it would soon be improved. Danny was suspicious of this talk of improvements. He had been told that life in Florida would be an improvement and look what had come of that. After they turned onto Florinda, Danny stopped to walk his bike, and Alfred did the same.

"So, you weren't in Sulphur Springs today," said Danny pointedly.

"Huh?"

"I fell. I went to get help. You stayed inside your boundaries."

"Suppose somebody saw me?"

"I had another kid with me. They thought it was you."

"What kid? What's his name? Where does he live?"

Alfred, suggestible as always, was beginning to get interested in the new kid.

"His name is Buddy. We don't know where he lives. He just came along and helped out. But he's the one that I went to the Springs with. You went a little way out on the bridge when I fell, but then you went right back and waited until I came."

"What did I do while I was waiting?"

"You watched the gator in the pipe."

"Did he do anything?"

"Nope."

At this, Alfred looked disappointed. That gator never seemed to do anything but lie there.

"What else did I do?"

"You sang a song to pass the time."

"No, I didn't."

"Why not?"

"I'm not allowed to sing, except hymns."

"Okay, not a song, a hymn."

Alfred was getting very nervous. Even in this fantasy, he was on danger-ous ground. The Bagleys were incredibly strict: they didn't drink, smoke, dance, or apparently sing. As far as Danny could tell, they were clothed twenty-four hours a day. Once he had been over at the Bagley house early on a Saturday morning and accidentally got a look into the Bagley master bedroom. What he saw was confusing in the extreme. Alfred's parents were sitting up with the covers in their laps, but Mrs. Bagley was in the same sort of house dress she wore during the day, and Mr. Bagley had on a T-shirt, khaki pants, and socks.

"They know I wouldn't sing a hymn if I wasn't in church."

"Okay. You just watched the gator and you got bored. Nothing else happened. That's all you need to say."

Alfred's expression suggested that he might not be able to stick to even this simple story if the heat were turned up ever so slightly.

"You want me to come in and tell it?" Danny asked.

Alfred looked dubious but eventually nodded his head.

"Okay."

Of course, this action involved lying, which the sisters at Danny's Catho-lic school, Our Lady of Perpetual Help, had tried to paint as evil in all forms, but they had not been able to make that precept stick with Danny, who could not see the harm in a lie with no ill effect. If a lie was not mean or nasty or was a matter of survival, he didn't hesitate. However, on the few occasions when he had tried to lie for the wrong reason, he had been a failure. His mother would look at him and say, "Danny, your eyes tell me you're lying."

But Danny was spectacularly good at lying about trivial matters, and he could think of nothing more trivial than Alfred's boundaries, which were arbitrary and enforced with whipping, which made them despicable. There was a great deal in life that Danny was unsure about, but he felt pretty sure that applying a belt to a boy's back was wrong.

The truly confusing thing was that in some ways, Mr. Bagley was a neat father. He was usually in good spirits, and you could depend on him to stay that way as long as you toed the line. He let Alfred have a goat, which with proper goading would pull a little cart, and of course, Alfred had his own personal chicken. Nickel alone was sufficient evidence that Alfred should never be whipped. She was a tribute to the boy's nurturing powers, having started out as a dyed Easter chick, a seasonal gimmick that seldom survived the season. A few days after Easter, the garbage cans around the nation began to fill up with brightly colored deceased chicks, overhandled or neglected. But in Alfred's care, Nickel had thrived, and as she grew, her feathers elongated and the blue dye stretched out and grew fainter until after a few weeks you couldn't tell her from a chicken that had started life in a conventional fashion. Anyway, Alfred was indulged in some ways and brutalized in others, just a bit more evidence demonstrating for Danny that the world was an unpredictable mixed bag.

"What happened to your hand?"

This question came from the crotch of a roadside oak. It was Abigail Arnold, occupying her favorite spot, and as usual she had a book in her hand. She was a year older than Danny, and quite precocious in academics but not much on getting dirty. Danny wondered why she bothered coming outside if it was only to read. He himself preferred reading inside with a good chair under him. He had tried it outside but there were far too many distractions.

"I fell off my bike."

"That surprises me," said Abigail.

"Lightning hit the bridge!" Alfred blurted.

Now this was a factor that had slipped Danny's mind. As usual, he had been concentrating only on his failure as a bicyclist, forgetting that there had been mitigating circumstances.

"There was lightning?"

Abigail climbed carefully down from her perch, adjusted her glasses, and walked toward the boys. She was a pretty little girl with blonde hair and a peachy complexion, and she gave the impression of being resolute. Danny was more or less indifferent to her, but she made Alfred nervous. A person who read books for any reason except by a teacher's command was immediately suspicious to him. Danny was careful to keep his own pleasure reading out of Alfred's sight. When Alfred saw Abigail climb down, he mumbled something about getting home and forged ahead.

"Tell me about the lightning," Abigail said.

"No big deal," Danny said.

"Well, you don't seem to have been very much charred," she remarked.

Danny was glad that Alfred was not there to hear that statement. The high-toned phraseology would have set his teeth on edge, but Abigail's observation started Danny considering the possible consequences of admitting that he'd been near a lightning strike. It was bound to make the adults nervous, and no good could come of that. In Alfred's case, it might mean even more restrictions.

As it was, the boys had spent many afternoons sitting around waiting for Alfred's mother to decide that the weather was clear enough to give Alfred permission to go swimming at the Sulphur Springs Pool. The weather forecast was of no consequence in the Ryan household. If a lightning storm came up, Danny's parents expected him to get out of it. Alfred's parents apparently did not think he had sense enough to come in out of the rain, and Danny had to admit that on the surface he might give this impression, but Danny knew that Alfred was really a scary kid and would never stay in the water when there was lightning. Besides, the lifeguards wouldn't let you! That was the thing that most made the Bagleys' position ridiculous. Furthermore, there was water everywhere you looked in Nowhere. The Bagleys seemed to think that the pool had some special properties that drew lightning. This business of lightning having struck a bridge in Sulphur Springs when the boys were near it was likely to create extremely undesirable results.

"Alfred made up the lightning story," Danny said. "It didn't happen."

"What?"

"You know Alfred. It was just something to make the story more interesting. Like the cigar in the mouth."

"What?"

"Like when Alfred asks somebody what he would do if a big black cigar suddenly appeared in his mouth."

"He never asked me that."

"Yeah, well, I gotta go. See you later."

Danny hurried off, leaving Abigail standing there ruffling the pages of her book. He knew he had been rude, but the most important thing now was to get to the Bagley house before Alfred messed everything up. By the time he arrived, Alfred was already inside. The jalousie windows were open and Danny could hear what was being said in the kitchen.

"Al's Swap Shop?"

"Yes, ma'am."

Danny knew he had to move fast. He knocked loudly. Mrs. Bagley answered the door. She was clearly troubled. Her receding chin was twitching, and her brown eyes, sorrowful under the best of circumstances, were moist. No doubt she was contemplating the pain in store for Alfred when Mr. Bagley found out about his son's boundary violation.

"Alfred's busy," she said.

"Yes, ma'am, but he didn't want to go over to the Springs. I asked him to help me."

As he said this, Danny thrust his hand up toward her.

"What happened to that?" she asked.

This boded well. Apparently, in his fever to get his trespasses off his chest, Alfred had not told the whole story, only the damning parts, which was good news for Danny because it gave him a cleaner slate with which to work.

"You better come in," Mrs. Bagley said.

Alfred was sitting miserably at their kitchen table, staring at a large glass of iced tea, the standard beverage at the Bagley house. No coffee was allowed, too much the stimulant. Danny had heard his mother say, "I'm surprised they allow tea. I understand it has some caffeine in it."

"Would you like some tea?" Mrs. Bagley asked Danny.

"Yes, ma'am. Thank you."

While she was pouring him a glass out of a big icy pitcher, Danny tried to catch Alfred's eye, but he was staring fixedly down at the Formica table top.

"You hurt your hand and Alfred helped you?"

"I was riding along with my fishing pole over near the Springs. We wanted to take a look at that gator in the storm pipe. But I ran the pole against something, and it snapped just like it had been struck by lightning."

At this Alfred raised up, his face full of wonder.

"So, I fell off my bike and tore up my hand on the pavement. Alfred wanted to go to somebody's house for help, but I thought it would be better to go across the bridge to the barber shop, where I get my hair cut. My parents don't like me to go into strange houses."

Mrs. Bagley was following attentively, and Alfred was in a state of high excitement. Danny's tale had a certain amount of truth in it, quite a bit actually, but it sounded so different from what he remembered. Alfred was now uncertain himself of what had happened.

"Alfred wanted to stay inside his boundaries, but he saw the blood coming off my hand, and he couldn't let me go by myself. He's too good of a friend."

This was pushing it, but Alfred looked down modestly, and Mrs. Bagley's expression remained sympathetic.

"But how did you wind up in the swap shop?"

Alfred looked up. The fear was back in his eyes.

"We were on our way to the barber shop, but once we were inside the arcade, I started to remember how rough that barber is when he puts the tonic on my hair, and I got a little scared. So, I took off one of my socks and closed my fist around it, and I thought I could ride home like that."

It suddenly occurred to Danny that he had the sock in his pocket, so he pulled it out and placed it on the table, still pink in spite of all the water that had run through it. Mrs. Bagley gasped and quickly moved the sock to the sink, where she stood washing it with detergent while Danny continued.

"So we had to cross the street to come home anyway, and I stopped for a minute to look at the diving suit outside of the shop, and Mr. Gallagher saw my hand, and he bandaged it for me, and he sent us right home."

"The swap shop man put that bandage on?"

"Yes, ma'am. Mr. Al Gallagher."

"Is that right, Alfred?"

"Yes, ma'am!" Alfred said fervently.

"You boys wait here."

Mrs. Bagley disappeared into her bedroom. She was a heavy woman yet moved lightly around her house. The boys traded significant looks. They heard a rustling of paper, followed by the sound of the phone being dialed.

"May I please speak to Mr. Gallagher. It is? My name is Mrs. Charles Bagley. I have a young man here who says you bandaged his hand. No, I'm the mother of the boy who was with him. Yes, Alfred. He did? Well, that sounds like him. I just wanted to thank you for tending to Danny. He says you sent them right home. About what time was that? It was? I'm sure Mrs. Ryan will appreciate what you did. They have sickness in their house. It's not easy for them right now. Yes. Goodbye."

Mrs. Bagley reentered the room without saying a word and sat down at the table with the boys. Her homely face was full of concern. They sat there for fully five minutes, saying nothing. Only the occasional gulp of tea broke the silence.

"Mr. Gallagher says you asked him what kind of car he drives."

"Yes, ma'am."

"What kind?'

"He doesn't drive a car."

"That seems strange. I guess he's like me."

This was another peculiar thing about the Bagley family setup. Mrs. Bagley could not drive a car. Just why this was, Danny could not be sure. Mrs. Bagley was quite capable of doing other things. She cleaned, cooked, sewed, and tended the yard, and she certainly had sharp eyes. Just let Alfred get into some mischief, and Mrs. Bagley was on it like a radar beacon.

"No, ma'am. He drives a truck," Alfred answered.

"Oh," Mrs. Bagley said distractedly, greatly disappointing Alfred, who had obviously had high hopes for this choice joke.

"A Chevy," he added hopefully, but Mrs. Bagley was not listening.

Danny could see that something unprecedented was happening. This was the first time he could recall seeing Mrs. Bagley thinking. Normally, she went about her routine in a matter-of-fact way, monitoring her surroundings and answering questions properly but never giving the impression that any deep part of her brain was involved. Now, her face was awash in contradictions. One moment, she would knit her brows, and the next her eyes would grow wide, and the next they would narrow, and then she would appear to be concerned with something in the corner of the room.

Danny started to feel creepy. He tried to make eye contact with Alfred, but the boy was staring with fascination at his mother, so enthralled that he did not notice when she reached over and took his hand.

At her touch, Alfred leaped up, shouted "Oh my God!" and immediately covered his mouth. Nothing could be seen of his face except his terror-filled eyes. Danny recognized the earth-shaking overtones of this event. The word "God" had come out of Alfred's mouth in an ungodly context. The Bagleys were very strict about language. Once, when Danny had called Alfred a "lucky dog," Mrs. Bagley had said that he should call him a "lucky duck" instead. Danny never got the distinction, but he knew that in the

Bagley world, what Alfred had just said was verging on blasphemy. Surprisingly, Mrs. Bagley did nothing but take Alfred by the shoulders and gently encourage him back onto his chair.

"Don't say things like that, son," she said mildly, "and take your hand away from your mouth. It doesn't look nice."

Alfred lowered his hand, but he was still afraid. Mrs. Bagley took out the hanky that she always carried in the pocket of her apron and wiped her eyes.

"You boys have had quite a day," she observed, replacing the hanky, "and I think the best thing to do is forget all about it."

What little color Alfred had remaining in his face drained away, leaving him completely ashen. He seemed incapable of speech; however, Danny seized the moment.

"Yes, ma'am."

Mrs. Bagley got up, went to a cabinet near the breezeway, and came back with a plastic box from which she took a pair of scissors and some bandaging materials.

"I don't mean you're going to lie. Danny, give me your hand. What happened today is that Danny fell off his bike and hurt himself, and that's the truth. I'm bandaging his hand, and that's the truth. That's as much as we need to say about it."

The three of them sat there in a profound silence while Mrs. Bagley rebandaged Danny's hand. Alfred sat stunned, but Danny's mind was racing, wondering if Mrs. Bagley had the wit to pull off this deception, inexperienced as she must be. For some reason she was going against her husband, but that was not the end of it by any means. Each evening at dinner, the Bagleys sat around the table and discussed the day, and the conversation involved a lot of questions by Mr. Bagley about what his family had been up to. In some ways, he was like a priest in a confessional, seldom satisfied with a generality. If Alfred were subjected to the probing of his father, he was sure to break down. But apparently Mrs. Bagley had been thinking of the same thing.

"Alfred, you don't look good," Mrs. Bagley said.

This was no lie. Alfred looked as if he had suffered a concussion.

"I'm giving you an early supper. You'll rest in your room until tomorrow, and you won't come out until you have my permission."

Alfred gave a vague nod. Mrs. Bagley finished her bandaging and let go of Danny's hand. As she did, she looked him square in the eyes. This was a day for being looked at searchingly by adults, first Al Gallagher and now Mrs. Bagley. The world was a different place this afternoon; that was for sure. The full meaning of Mrs. Bagley's look, Danny did not understand, but he knew it was important.

"You better go home now, Danny. You can see Alfred tomorrow when he's feeling better."

"Yes, ma'am."

Danny made his way to the door. When he opened it, he saw that the afternoon was fading fast, but there was still a shaft of sunlight on the roof of the Ryan house across the road. His father would be home from work soon. Who could tell what that would bring? It might be all right. It frequently was.

5

As Danny stood on the front steps of the Bagley house, looking across into his own yard, he felt good about his lies, but he had to depend on higher authority to determine how God felt about them. His thoughts about sin were guided by a helpful page in the catechism book he had studied for his first confession. It contained three illustrations. The first was of a child standing in a prayerful attitude. He had a shining, unblemished heart shape on his chest representing the purity of his soul. Behind him was his beautiful guardian angel, staring down lovingly at the child. This child was in a state of grace, sinless after confession and at one with God.

In the second illustration, the heart shape had some black spots on it, the effect of venial sins; the youngster was in fair shape but would spend some time in purgatory, temporary hell, because of those venial sins. In the third illustration, the heart shape was entirely black and in the lower right-hand corner, a salacious-looking devil was rising up, surrounded by flames. This child had committed a mortal sin and would go to hell if he didn't get to confession before he died.

Danny assumed that his own soul was currently peppered with black spots, and he had resigned himself to time in purgatory. There were so many venial sins that unless you were confessing twenty-four hours a day, you could not beat them. He was pretty sure he could stay away from mortal sins. Some of them, like killing somebody or worshipping a false god, were out of the question for him.

Other mortal sins were possibilities in his world. Knowingly eating meat on Friday, for example, or willfully missing mass on Sunday. He knew kids who did these things, but he couldn't understand their philosophy. It was tiresome remembering not to eat meat, but the act itself was nothing. You had some fish or buttered noodles. Who needed meat badly enough to imperil his soul? The same with mass. He knew he should enjoy it more, and that lack of enjoyment was probably a venial sin, but at least he was there. It was a small price to pay in order to avoid eternal suffering.

There was one danger area for Danny. He didn't care all that much about living. It had its good points, but it was a lot of work, and there was always some cloud hanging over your head. He would never commit suicide—he was too dutiful for that—but he didn't mind the idea of dying. So many things would be solved. He knew this was a bad attitude, but no amount of prayer or emphasizing the positive could completely erase his feeling that being dead was not such a bad deal. In combating this feeling, he hoped for help from his guardian angel. He sometimes addressed a plea for help to his angel, but he was not certain how much he got. There seemed to be a lot of complex rules governing when angels could intervene.

However, he was sure that his angel could not be very upset about today's spate of lying, unless he was really sensitive about venial sins. On the other hand, there was the lady in the barrel. He had a feeling she could lead to a serious sin of some sort, but he was not clear on all that was involved. He suddenly remembered the young woman he had seen on the trail that morning, and the way he had felt when she put her hand on his shoulder.

Yes, there was definitely something along those lines that he was susceptible to. He hoped that when the nature of the threat became clear his angel would get cracking, but that was in the future. For the time being, he was pretty sure that if he died, he would go to purgatory, not hell.

As Danny walked across the sandy street toward the Ryan house, his pace was slowed by the usual buildup of dread before entering. From the outside, the little block house didn't look so bad, but it was a mess in many ways. The home had been designed like a house trailer, with all the rooms in a row, starting with a bedroom at the west end, followed in a straight line by the living room, the kitchen, and lastly, an unfinished "back room" where the bathroom was located. The bedroom was the tidiest and most pleasant room. The living room was okay, the kitchen marginal, and the bathroom a disgrace—little more than a toilet, sink, and concrete shower stall, so badly put together that the plywood floor was slowly rotting from escaping water.

The back room was in many ways the most important room in the house because that was where Mr. Ryan spent most of his time, with the door closed. This door must be approached with great caution when he was holed up. Danny often stood in the kitchen with his ear to the door, fearing to knock because the knock itself might set off an incident. If all seemed quiet, he opened the door, not so quickly as to startle his father, but not so slowly as to suggest spying.

Danny would have avoided this troublesome door altogether, except that he had to go through it to get to the bathroom. What he saw upon opening that door was the haven of the bathroom a few feet in front of him and two washtubs in an alcove on his right. This was all he would see if his father were present, because looking left would suggest an unseemly interest in what Mr. Ryan was up to. If his father was not home, Danny could look to his left safely and survey the back room, the largest space in the Ryan house, an unfinished area of raw wood, something like a cross between a sleeping porch and a storage room. It contained a double bed, an old dresser, and an unfinished closet. The windows had never been installed, so the only barrier between the back room and the outside was some screening material stapled over the openings. In winter, the room was cold. You could get into the back room from the outside by way of a dilapidated door, but Danny's father seldom used it.

Danny had mulled over the layout of the Ryan house many times, and he could see no sense in it. Even if every part of the house had been properly finished and in good working order, it would have been a failure. Why would anyone design a house in which someone who woke up in the west bedroom with an urge to pee had to walk through the living room, the kitchen, and the back room to get to the bathroom? This was especially dicey for the Ryans, because the sane members of the family had to creep through one end of Mr. Ryan's lair to get to the toilet. When his father was home, Danny usually held his water for as long as he could and then hoped for the best as he scuttled to the bathroom. Most of the time nothing bad happened, but the threat was always present. If the house was in a state of emergency, Danny peed outdoors.

This, then, was the house Danny observed with a sinking feeling as he walked across the street from the Bagleys'. As much as he would have liked to stay outside and ponder its deficiencies, he knew he had to go in. His first stop was the bedroom. Ruth was lying in bed, looking out the window at the mulberry tree near the corner of the house. It was full of berries. These had been of interest to Danny until he bit into one and discovered half a worm. The other half, he presumed, had made its way into his stomach after having been ground up by his teeth. This was an unpleasant thought, and he didn't like the mulberries well enough to minutely examine each one, which was what he would have to do to neutralize the worm threat. Alfred came over and ate them as often as he could, untroubled by the worms.

"I don't taste them," he said.

"Would you eat poison just because you couldn't taste it?" Danny had asked.

"Worms aren't poison," Alfred had answered, missing the point as usual.

Ruth did not immediately realize that Danny had quietly entered the room. She was tired and distracted these days because she was on some mysterious therapy. Mr. and Mrs. Ryan had been required to sign a paper releasing the doctors from responsibility. Ruth referred to it as an "atomic cocktail." Danny knew about the atomic bomb, which he understood might be dropped on him at any time. Every Saturday at noon the air raid siren blew in downtown Tampa, just to let people know it was in working order. You could hear it for miles, even out in Nowhere. Danny would always look up, expecting the clever Russians to time their attack for noon on Saturday, so nobody would pay attention to the alarm. Yes, he knew about the bomb, but an atomic cocktail was a mystery.

"Oh, Danny. How long have you been there?" Ruth asked.

"I just came in."

"Your hand!"

Ruth stretched out her arms. Danny walked dutifully forward for his hug. He was not comfortable hugging Ruth. Her puffy neck made him feel strange, and he was afraid he would hurt her. It always took him a minute or two to get used to being with her, but then it was all right.

"What happened?"

"I fell off my bike. No big deal. Mrs. Bagley put a bandage on it."

Ruth rubbed her finger lightly over his bandaged palm, a look of concern

on her wan face. She loved Danny and was always patient with him, unlike
Loretta, who sometimes found Danny irritating and had no qualms about
telling him so. Danny took a secret look at Ruth's neck. It didn't seem any
better to him; if anything, she was worse. His parents and the doctors were
of the opinion that the treatment was sapping her energy, which accounted
for her fatigued aspect, but Danny had a funny feeling that Ruth was only
half in this world—not that she didn't make perfect sense, just that she
seemed to be speaking from far away. He never told anyone about this. It
would sound silly if put into words.

"This is an awfully big bandage. How badly are you hurt?"

The last thing Danny wanted to say to his ailing sister was that his palm
had been peeled back like a banana skin, so he lied. It was a day for lying.

"Just a few scrapes. It doesn't hurt. Would you like to do something?
Why don't we draw?"

Ruth could draw very well, and it was one of the things that she and
Danny could do together, even though she was frail. Their drawing sessions
were usually humiliating for Danny because his efforts were so inferior, but
Ruth was nine years older than he, which had given her a lot more time to
practice—at least this was what Ruth told him, though Danny felt that the
reason was probably deeper than that, something about talent. He went to
the chest of drawers and got out their pads. Ruth propped herself up on
her pillows and Danny climbed up on the bed beside her. When she flipped
through her pad, Danny admired the pages covered with charming little
drawings: a formal dress she had designed, a Christmas tree with trimmings,
all of them simple yet interesting.

Ruth stopped at a drawing she was working on as an illustration for a
satirical poem she had written about how the Ryan family could not get a
loan. The poem started with the lines, "Mr. Wilson's bank / Is bulging like
a tank" and went on to lament that the loan officer, Mr. Wilson, could not
see his way clear to part with a little of that money. The cartoon depicted
an official-looking edifice with the sides bulging as if under great pressure
and greenbacks sticking part way through the cracks in the walls. Ruth saw
Danny staring admiringly at her drawing and handed the pad to him.

"Why don't you draw one of the bills sticking out?"

Danny was doubtful about how well he could do this, but it certainly
seemed possible. After all, they were just little squares. He thought he might

be able to manage it, but everything looked perfect as it was, and besides, what kind of charity case drew on another person's work?

"Go on. I'd like to have you add something. Then it will belong to both of us."

Ruth's expression was so sweet and encouraging that Danny could not refuse, so he picked up his pencil and looked for a spot on the bank where another bill might fit in.

"How about here?" he asked, pointing to the least conspicuous spot.

"Why not the front door? I think it would be fun to have some sticking out there."

Danny looked pensively at the bank door. It was right in the middle of the drawing, where a badly rendered bill would be like a bullet hole, but Ruth was nodding encouragingly, so with his heart in his mouth, Danny put pencil to paper and drew the worst greenback in the history of art.

It was the wrong size, it was the wrong shape, it was at the wrong angle, it was stiff; in fact, it looked more like a brick than a bill. Danny was awe-struck. He knew he was bad, but until this moment he had never realized just how bad he was. However, Ruth was chuckling, and it had been a long time since he had heard her chuckle.

"You did that on purpose just to make me laugh!" she said.

It seemed to Danny that he had spent a good part of the day lying, but to have agreed with his ailing sister's misinterpretation of reality would have been unworthy. He didn't know whether she really believed it or was just offering him a way to save face, but it might have been real. She was just the kind of person who could laugh if her precious little brother had ruined her drawing as a joke. So, the situation called for delicacy, and a bit of humor.

"What's wrong with it? I think it looks pretty good," Danny said in-nocently.

"Seriously?"

"No. It's horrible, but that's the best I could do."

"Don't be silly. You can do much better than that. You have lots of talent, but you have to be more relaxed. Don't bear down on the pencil so hard. Don't try to make straight lines. Nothing is exactly straight, especially in a cartoon. Look at the other bills. They're bulging just like the bank."

Danny looked as Ruth instructed. It was true he had not taken the other bills into consideration, but as he compared his bill to the others, it dawned on him that the real cause of his failure was not poor observation but fear. He had been so afraid of destroying her drawing that he couldn't see it correctly.

"Erase that one and try again."

Danny didn't hesitate this time. Ruth's drawing was ruined anyway, so he drew a nearly perfect bill. It was rounded, it flared, and it gave the impression that it was being squeezed out of the bank like toothpaste out of a tube.

"Oh, that one is great! See?"

Yes, it was good, but Danny could still see the remnants of his poor work underneath. The ghost of his failure would linger there forever, but he could not dwell on this because Loretta came in.

"Hello, crew," she called. "Having fun?"

"We're drawing," Ruth said.

"I wish I could do that. Let me see."

Danny's heart sank as Ruth handed Loretta the pad. She stood studying it for a moment. Loretta was a seventeen-year-old knockout, without question the best-looking of the Ryan children. When this was mentioned, she would say mysteriously, "It's a curse." She had developed a breezy personality that was not quite natural to her, but it fooled casual acquaintances. In reality, she was moody and willful, and she was the only Ryan kid who would stand up to their father. This Danny both admired and abhorred. For him their father was a force of nature. You didn't try to go against it. You just hunkered down terrified and hoped that the passage of time would restore equilibrium. But Loretta fired back.

"That mean Mr. Wilson," Loretta muttered, passing the tablet back to Ruth. "But who can blame him? We're a crummy risk."

She went to the bedroom closet and began to change out of her work clothes. She had a summer job downtown at Woolworth's. Out the window, the shadows were longer. It was the iffy time of day and the room grew quiet.

"Here he comes," said Ruth.

She meant their father, moving down Florinda Street through the patches of afternoon sun and shadows. He took the bus to and from his job at Holsum Bakery, leaving the car with his wife in case it was needed for Ruth. In the sunshine, he seemed an unremarkable man in the white cotton clothes of his profession, a little over average height, balding. Loretta thought him handsome, but Danny couldn't see it. He was nothing like the leading men in the movies that Danny escaped to whenever he could, so how could he be handsome?

By now he had reached the front steps. Ruth and Danny exchanged significant glances. Loretta pretended not to care. In a moment the suspense would be over. If he was okay, he would either come in the room and greet them or they would hear him talking in a normal tone with their mother in the kitchen. That didn't happen. Instead they heard the clump of his step through the length of the house and the closing of the back room door.

"Well, now we know," said Loretta. "Sorry to leave you two to face the music, but I have a date, and I think I'd better meet him down at the end of the road."

As Loretta left the room, Danny collected the tablets and pencils. There would be no more drawing for a good while. If he and Ruth exchanged words, it would be in whispers. Nothing must filter into the back room that their father might think was directed at him.

"Well, hello. Who are you?"

What was this? Loretta was speaking in a normal voice in the living room.

"Does Danny live here?"

"Danny Ryan?"

"Don't know his last name. Cute kid about ten years old?"

"Well," said Loretta, "that might be my brother, but" (here she raised her voice so Danny would be sure to hear) "I don't know about the cute part!"

Both Danny and Ruth cringed when Loretta raised her voice. Their father must have heard it.

"You'll have to go out there," Ruth whispered, giving Danny an apologetic prod. "Do you know who it is?"

Danny shrugged his shoulders and walked into the living room. Instinctively, he looked toward the back room. What he saw was bad, his father's face protruding through the partially opened door like a disturbing mask. At the same time, he could see his mother working at the kitchen table, seemingly oblivious to the specter behind her. At times like this, Danny could hardly recognize his father. It was not that his face was angry or brutal, but the set of his eyes and jaw muscles gave the impression that something dark and devastating might emerge momentarily. Danny quickly cut his eyes away from the kitchen scene. If he had looked a fraction of a second longer, it would have been an invitation to disaster.

"Hey, Danny."

This greeting came from just beyond the screen door. Danny could not see who spoke, because Loretta was blocking the view, half in the house and half out, but he recognized the voice. It was Buddy. Danny pushed Loretta on through the front door and right into Buddy's arms.

"Oops!" Buddy said pleasantly.

"No great harm done," Loretta replied, disentangling herself but not too quickly.

"Lor-et-ta," Danny said with a rising intonation, which he hoped communicated everything about his father and what could happen if peace and quiet were not immediately restored on the front steps.

"Dan-neee," she answered pointedly, and then added in a normal voice, "Who's your friend?"

"Buddy, this is my sister Loretta."

"Hey," Buddy said.

"Loretta has to go someplace," Danny said.

"So, how did you meet Danny?"

Buddy looked at Danny, then at Loretta, and then at the screen door behind them, where an ominous shadow had appeared.

"Over at the Springs," he said carefully. "He took a little ride in my canoe. I hope that was okay. I came by to ask if he could come again, but I see that everyone is busy, so I'll go now. Maybe some other time. Bye, Danny."

Buddy turned abruptly to leave, but Loretta caught his arm.

"Wait a sec. We can go together."

The screen door flew open and Harold Ryan stepped onto the porch, glaring at Buddy. Loretta hung onto Buddy's arm and glared back. Danny could see his mother standing in the living room, supporting Ruth, who had struggled out of the bedroom. Danny's father moved closer to Buddy and Loretta.

"What do you want?" he asked.

Buddy was calm. For Danny, that was the most amazing thing. Mr. Ryan was towering over him, but Buddy just extricated his arm from Loretta's and took a step away from her.

"Nothing, sir," he said quietly. "It wasn't polite of me to show up like this. I'm sorry."

With that, he walked into the twilight. Loretta stood for a moment with her fists clenched at her sides. Danny was afraid she was finally going to fly at her father, but instead she turned her back to him. Slowly, she removed a bobby pin from her hair, twisted it in her fingers for a moment, and reinserted it. Then she strode away with elaborate slowness.

Danny was afraid to look at his father. He could only stand still and try to breathe normally, but he kept making a rasping sound. He knew that his rasping might ignite an explosion, so he held his breath. The cabbage palms in the front yard cast eerie shadows in the yellow light from the door. Everything was frozen.

"Harold, help me. Ruth has fainted."

And then his father was gone and Danny could breathe again.

6

Mrs. Ryan gave Danny and Ruth their dinner in the bedroom to keep the clinking of their silverware from being heard in the back room. There was something about that sound Mr. Ryan took personally. It cut through the stillness like nothing else, except maybe laughter. But nobody ever laughed.

Danny and Ruth ate in silence, heads hanging. Their mother stayed in the kitchen, ready to run interference if necessary, but she couldn't stay there indefinitely. In an hour she would have to leave for her job as a waitress for caterers who did parties on Davis Island, where the wealthy people lived. The family needed the money, so she had to go whenever there was work. And she would have to take the car because the buses didn't run near Nowhere in the wee hours when she finished work. In a little while, Danny and Ruth would be alone with their father, which filled them both with dread.

Why they dreaded it so much was a difficult question to answer. Their father had seldom hit or shoved anyone, and even when he did, his actions were not very harmful. Mr. Bagley did much worse to Alfred with his belt than Danny's dad ever did to anyone in or out of the Ryan family, yet in spite of that, Mr. Ryan could project a sense of menace with such a twisted emotional edge that it turned your stomach.

And on top of that, he managed to communicate quite clearly that you were the cause of it. If you had not spoken a certain way, or cocked your head a certain way, or set one foot ahead of the other a certain way, everything would have been fine. He would have remained the good-natured man God had intended him to be, except that you did that thing.

Of all the Ryans, Danny felt the greatest guilt over these blowups because he was the one most sensitive to the triggers that set them off. Why could he not convince the others to be more watchful? Somehow, he lacked the gift of making them see, and for that flaw he could not forgive himself.

"You should go to bed early," his mother said before she left.

Ruth wanted to study her shorthand for a while. She planned to attend secretarial school when she got well, so she was trying to get a head start with her subjects. Danny passed the time drawing some of the shorthand symbols on her pad. But their seeming normality was all pretense. At one point, Ruth gestured Danny close to her and whispered in his ear.

"I didn't really faint."

"Well, I almost did," Danny whispered back.

"I was afraid he was going to hurt somebody."

"You know he doesn't do that," Danny said, but he was remembering the wild ride his father had taken him on the day before.

"Do you think he's getting worse?" Ruth asked.

"I don't know," Danny said. "Let's stop whispering. He might pick it up."

Ruth nodded and went back to her shorthand. Danny picked up an old album and thumbed through it. He was bewildered by the fact that so many of the photos had been taken in situations that he knew must now be strictly avoided. There were even shots of his father taking part in an Abraham Lincoln look-alike contest long ago in Nebraska. Danny stared disbelievingly at those pictures and wondered what had happened.

He couldn't help thinking that he himself might have had something to do with the way his father was now. The oldest photographs showed a stable world with normal people in it, dressed in a slightly old-fashioned style, and in contrast to the present day, they seemed happy. The later photographs with Danny in them were okay at first, but soon after his arrival the family began to look tenser. In some of them, Danny thought he could discern the beginnings of his father's cynical sneer. Danny was an expert in noticing this expression. It could crop up at any time, but there were several circumstances Danny knew were especially dangerous. Highest among them was having anybody over to the house.

Yet he saw in the album many shots of his father with groups of people in what Danny understood had been the Nebraska family home. How different things were now! But Loretta and his mother often ignored this change. Loretta sometimes had her dates come to the house, and Mrs. Ryan, who of all people should have known better, was an even worse offender, most often through her attempts to do good works.

Once she had invited several charity cases for a big Thanksgiving dinner. Since the kitchen could not hold them all, the meal would have to be eaten in the backyard on a makeshift table comprised of a piece of plywood laid across three sawhorses. And there was more. The only sensible route to the kitchen from the backyard was through the back room, which would deny their father his private hole. The first time Danny had heard of this mad scheme, he couldn't believe it.

"What about Dad?" he had asked his mother.

"He'll be all right," she replied. "I told him about it."

This was the paradox that Marjorie Ryan never seemed to understand. When Harold Ryan was in his right mind, he was a pleasant, entertaining man, a bit quiet but well-spoken and with a dry wit; however, he could not be depended upon to stand by an agreement he had made when he was sane after he went crazy, which was inevitable if a bunch of needy strangers packed into the Ryan home.

The dinner was a disaster, of course, made all the more embarrassing by the way everyone tried to ignore the behavior of his father, who after sitting in a state of radioactive silence for a few minutes, barricaded himself in the back room, which eliminated the bathroom and required the food to be dragged through the front door and all the way around the house. Danny had suggested that they call dinner off and send everyone home, but his mother refused, and even chaperoned some of the guests on a skulking trip through the kitchen door to the bathroom.

To Danny's surprise, the day ended without any fatalities, but his father was in a dangerous mood for a week following the episode.

In a way, Danny was glad he had not lived in the world he saw in the photo album. Somehow it had clouded everyone else's vision. Only he saw clearly how his father should be handled. He looked once more at the photo of his father dressed as Lincoln, closed the album, and stared at the ceiling.

Around 8:30, Danny went into the living room to fold down the couch where he and Loretta slept. This was a difficult task to do quietly. First, the couch had to be moved out from the wall so that the back could fold down to make the bed. The moving could be done silently, but the folding-down procedure involved springs and catches that squeaked and clacked. Danny would have slept on the couch as it was, but Loretta would be coming in later, and she would have to have somewhere to lie down.

Danny was cautiously easing the back of the couch forward to release the catch when he heard the coughing. This was something new and confounding. His father had started having long periods of coughing, sometimes ten or fifteen minutes at a time. These fits were not caused by a cold or flu. They started without warning, and there was seemingly no stopping them, even though Mr. Ryan had taken to consuming cough drops at a tremendous rate. On this night, the coughing was helpful in covering the sound of the fold-down procedure, and Danny quickly flattened the couch after retrieving the bedclothes from the compartment under the seat.

In a moment or two, he had the couch made up, including the humiliating rubber sheet in case he wet the bed. He turned the lights out, and even though Loretta was not in the bed, he faced the wall and pushed himself up against it to make plenty of room for her. He had gotten good at sleeping in that position, hardly shifting the whole night through. It made him feel sort of invisible, wedged in like that, and if he had an accident, Loretta didn't get wet. He listened to his father cough for a long time and then stop as mysteriously as he had begun. It was quiet then, but Danny continued to listen devotedly until he fell asleep.

He woke in the morning with a strong desire to go to the bathroom, amazed that he had not wet the bed. Loretta was asleep. He thought of going outside, but he disliked peeing in the yard unless it was absolutely necessary. He climbed off the end of the couch without worrying too much about waking Loretta, who was a notoriously sound sleeper, and tiptoed down to the kitchen door, cracking it just a bit. The slightly moldy smell of the back room came through the crack, but there was no sound from inside. He peered around the corner and saw that his mother had gone to his father's bed last night after she had come home from work. These days, she usually slept in the double bed with Ruth.

Danny was glad she was with Dad. Her presence there usually meant that things had calmed down and that his father would probably be pleasant when he got up, as if nothing had happened. Danny decided that it would even be okay to flush and hurried into the bathroom.

After the great relief of a morning's pee, he tiptoed around the kitchen and poured a bowl of cold cereal. He often fended for himself, and today he wanted to get out of the house before the family started stirring. It would be restful walking through the woods in the early light. His family would assume that he was off fishing or something. He finished his cereal, pulled on dungarees and a T-shirt, and quietly let himself out the front door.

There was a mist in the air, and his feet were cold on the dewy ground, but he knew that was temporary. In a short while the sun would be out, and he would be glad that he didn't have his shoes on. He cut through the woods, stopping at the spot where he and Alfred had met the cigar girl. There was no trace of her, but Danny stood for a few minutes imagining the details of the scene. She had been very like some of the Latin women he occasionally saw in movies at the Springs Theater. So often they were looking upward with their eyes flashing, just as the girl had done yesterday, and these movie girls put an unsettling emphasis in their speech that hinted at much more meaning than their words were expressing. This was just one example in a world full of secret signs that Danny did not understand.

Heaving a sigh, he moved on, following the creek downstream. When he reached the Hillsborough, he stood watching the clear creek water create an undulating border where it met the brown river. After staring at this effect for several minutes, Danny began to feel strange. He tried to tear his eyes from the mingling water, but it was hard. Very slowly, Danny raised his head and looked across the river.

There was a new house over there today, one that seemed to have appeared of its own accord. It was like one of the bungalows in Ybor City, with a bright yellow stucco finish and a roof over the front porch. Danny sat down on the bank and noted a small dog sleeping by the steps. Then the porch door opened slightly, causing the dog to jump up and wag its tail. A hand came through the door and pulled on its ear, and then the person connected to the hand emerged. It was the girl from the trail, carrying a steaming, mustard-yellow cup. She was wearing a housecoat tied at the waist with a fringed sash.

The girl stretched, careful not to spill her coffee, and took a seat in a wicker chair. The dog came over, and she placed her hand idly on its head, then put her feet up on a nearby table. She leaned back. A streak of sunlight cut across the porch floor and illuminated her faded red slippers.

Danny had the feeling he was watching something he shouldn't, but could not look away. The scene before him was more like a movie than anything from life as he normally lived it. The river flowed slowly by, lapping at the steps of the house. The girl stroked the dog's head. The sun rose higher. He could imagine the coffee disappearing from the girl's yellow cup as she put it to her lips.

Slowly, the tension went out of Danny's shoulders, and the knot in his stomach untangled. He sank back against the cushiony riverbank. The moss was damp but soft. He squinted his eyes, which made the house seem to waver and grow dim. Then something happened that caused him to open them fast. The girl slowly turned her head and looked across the river. She continued to hold her cup in both hands. Danny felt an impulse to run away, but something had frozen him. The girl continued to stare and then seemed to focus her attention on the spot where Danny was lying. Her head moved slightly as if she were trying to clear her vision. He watched with fascination as she started to raise her hand.

"Danny."

Danny hardly heard his name spoken. At some level he knew it had happened, but he continued to look at the girl. She seemed to be moving ever more slowly. He wished she would hurry.

"Danny, what's wrong?"

Danny felt a strong hand clamp down on his shoulder. He whipped his head around and saw Buddy kneeling behind him.

"How many times am I going to have to pull you out of the river?" Buddy asked.

"What?"

"Look at yourself."

Danny cast his eyes downward and realized that he was halfway into the Hillsborough. His lower torso was completely submerged, but the bank was not very steep. Danny had sat in the same spot many times and had never slid an inch.

"How did that happen?" he muttered.

"You tell me," said Buddy, grabbing Danny's arm and urging him up. "What's that bandage? It's soaked."

Danny didn't answer. He just stood dripping, looking at Buddy, who stared back at him with a neutral expression.

"What's over there?" Danny asked, gesturing across the river without looking.

Buddy took a look and shook his head. Danny turned and saw the house was gone.

"Did you see anything over there?" Danny asked slowly.

"You really want to know what I see?" Buddy asked.

Danny nodded.

Buddy walked closer to the river's edge and stood gazing intently over the water. He picked up a small stone and skipped it across the surface.

"I see somewhere I could go if I had a canoe."

This sounded like a reminder that Danny had caused Buddy to lose his canoe. His tone was not mean, but a tone could change in a second.

"That's what I wanted to talk to you about last night," Buddy said. "I thought you might like to build that canoe."

Danny looked back across the river. The bank was back to normal, just a tangle of plants in the sun. It was hard to believe how real the little bungalow with the dog and the girl had seemed. Hard to believe and frightening. This was the sort of thing his father did, seeing things that were not there, not just for fun but because he couldn't help it.

"Don't look so serious," Buddy said. "Why don't you come and see what you'd have to do. It's not that much. No sweat if you decide not to."

What was to be done about Buddy? Danny was in no position to be making new friends. He could hardly handle the few he had, and he certainly had no room in his life for people who showed up on the front steps with no warning, but at this moment he was too frightened to be alone. He could cut it off with Buddy later. Right now he needed someone to keep him from seeing more visions.

"Okay," Danny said.

"Good deal," Buddy replied. "Got your bike?"

"Nope."

"You can ride with me, but we'll have to be careful of that hand. What happened?"

"Nothing."

Buddy shrugged, walked over to the weeds, reached down, and raised up a stripped-down bike. Danny's heart sank. There was nothing but a frame, handlebars, and wheels. He would have to sit on the crossbar. It would be an uncomfortable ride.

"It's not that far," Buddy said, as if reading Danny's mind.

Danny heaved a sigh, which seemed to amuse Buddy, but somehow Danny was not hurt by his attitude. He was probably just taking pity on a pudgy little nobody. That's what people were supposed to do, be helpful, but it was hard to be on the receiving end. You couldn't depend on charity. You had to fend for yourself.

"Hop on."

Danny reluctantly took his place on the crossbar. It immediately started digging into his behind. He could imagine what the sensation would be after a few minutes of riding.

"Here we go," Buddy said cheerfully.

Danny was tense from the start, experiencing his familiar discomfort at being a passenger. He knew he should be looser, but how? Danny could hear Buddy muttering under his breath. Shortly into the ride, Buddy began to have control problems, which worsened as they started around a sharp curve in the road.

"Oh, shit!" Buddy said.

Danny was scandalized by this language and abruptly turned around to give Buddy a reproachful look, but he forgot to keep his feet up, and his pant leg caught in the bike chain, yanking him out of balance. Buddy said "Shit!" again and barely managed to steer the bike into a bank of weeds before everything fell apart.

"You still with us?" Buddy asked.

"Yeah."

"Tear your pants?"

"Yeah," Danny replied morosely.

"Look here for a minute," said Buddy.

Danny turned and saw that Buddy was holding out his right hand for inspection. Its index finger was bent back at nearly a right angle. Danny gulped.

"Nothing I can't fix," Buddy said mysteriously.

He grasped the bent finger with his left hand and pulled it smartly into line.

"Nobody's fault," Buddy said. "It goes out like that every now and then."

"Oh," said Danny.

"Come on. Why don't we walk the rest of the way?" Buddy picked up the bike, which was unharmed, and gestured down the road. It's not too far."

As they walked, Danny contemplated his torn pants and the repair that would be required. His mother would use a denim-colored iron-on patch. She didn't have any time to devote to sewing, but a new pair of pants to replace the torn ones would be too expensive, so he would have a hated iron-on patch to mark him. He had never seen another kid with one of these patches, but his mother had a genius for coming up with strange stuff; the patches were just the tip of the iceberg.

To save time on ironing, she used pants stretchers, adjustable wire rectangles that she inserted into Danny's pants legs while they were still wet from washing. When they were removed after drying, his jeans had a crease and no wrinkles. Unfortunately, as their name suggested, these stretchers did more than neaten up his jeans. They also stretched them. Danny thought it unfair that his pants started out as "huskies" and then his mother made them bigger. Mrs. Ryan dismissed his concerns, saying that creased jeans looked nice, and even if the legs were a little bigger than normal, she didn't think the difference was noticeable. Danny loved his mother, but he had no respect for her ability to judge the size of pants legs.

"You think a lot," Buddy said.

"I guess so."

"How old are you?"

"Ten."

"You think a lot for ten."

Buddy made this seem more of a compliment than a criticism. Either way, Danny would not have been surprised. He had heard similar comments many times. He thought it must be something about the expression on his face because he assumed that everybody was thinking all the time. Alfred, for example, could drift off into a reverie, but somehow you knew he was dreaming of driving a pickup truck full of junk. With Danny, it was different. Loretta often kidded him, calling him "The Thinker." Anyway, Danny knew his demeanor made some people uncomfortable, so he tried to keep his thinking to a minimum when he was in company. Teachers loved it, though.

"I bet you're good in school."

"Huh?" Danny replied, stunned by the aptness of Buddy's comment. "Never mind. We turn here."

They had covered a couple of miles up toward the dam, but the road had veered away from the river. Here the houses were few, and no wonder. It was scrubby land, not far from the city dump, which Danny knew from experience could smell bad. However, the road that Buddy was indicating did not smell bad. Danny had been down many such tracks through the palmettos. There was seldom much of interest to be seen along such a way, and later in the day it would be hard for a barefoot boy to negotiate. The sand would get burning hot, but the spiky palmettos growing thickly on both sides of the road would not allow him to walk anywhere else. Very likely, he would wind up skipping from one little fragment of shade to the next while the hot sun beat down on his head. He stared with an air of melancholy down the road.

"What are you so worried about?" Buddy asked.

"Nothing, I guess," Danny replied.

7

A quarter of a mile up the road, they came to Buddy's home, a small Airstream trailer on cement blocks. Danny liked Airstreams. They always looked better than the cars that were pulling them. However, Buddy's Airstream was not going to be pulled anywhere soon. It was surrounded by things that seemed to have been there for some time, like the old outboard motor leaning up against one end. Near the door, there were several lawn chairs in a semicircle with an orange crate sitting in front of them. On the crate were an ash tray and a pack of Kools. Buddy walked to the door of the trailer and looked through the screen into the darkened interior.

"Dad's asleep," he commented, turning back to Danny. "Come over here."

Danny followed Buddy to a large shed behind the trailer. It was open on one side and covered over with a metal roof, perhaps fifteen feet high. There were pieces of lumber and fabric stored in the rafters. On one wall was a large electrical box surrounded by a variety of odd-shaped items hanging on hooks. Against another wall was a set of cabinets and a big workbench. The floor was just sand. There were several heavy tables scattered about.

"Dad wants to build boats here," Buddy said.

"Neat," Danny replied.

"Yeah. Here's what we use for the canoe."

He directed Danny's attention to a pile of wooden forms that reminded Danny of his mother's pants stretchers. They didn't look like anything to do with a canoe, but Buddy explained how they were set up with the biggest form at the center and increasingly smaller forms at intervals on each side. Pieces of one-by-two were stretched around them, secured at the ends, orange crate slats nailed to the one-by-twos, canvas put over that, and then waterproof airplane dope painted on the canvas. Then you had a canoe. It certainly sounded simple.

"Hey, boys."

Danny turned around and saw a skinny man in a robe and pajama bottoms leaning against one of the tables. He had a long face and a cigarette between his fingers. His voice was gravelly.

"What's going?"

"My friend Danny and I are about to get started on a canoe."

"Another canoe?"

The man looked around.

"Where's the other one?"

"Sank," Buddy replied.

The man took a drag on his cigarette.

"Well, they do sink," he said at last. "I might help you with it later."

"That'd be great," said Buddy.

The man nodded and went back toward the trailer. He was none too steady.

"That's my dad," Buddy said. "He was a mess sergeant on a submarine during the war."

Danny nodded. He never knew what to say to kids whose dads had been in World War II. His own father had never been called because of having three kids. But Buddy didn't wait for comment. He was already busy setting up the canoe forms, securing them to one of the long tables.

"Where were you going day before yesterday?" Buddy asked.

"Huh?"

"Out on the water lilies before the dam opened. You looked like you had something in mind."

"You were watching me?" Danny asked.

"I was upriver waiting for the dam to open, and I saw you heading out into the middle."

"He was like the famous chicken," said Buddy's father, who had lingered near the corner of the shop.

"What do you mean, Dad?"

"The one who crossed the road to get to the other side. Sounds to me like Danny wanted to get to the other side."

"That's funny, Dad."

"You'd be surprised how much it explains," Mr. Connolly concluded, leaving the scene.

Danny was glad Mr. Connolly had interrupted. Buddy's questions had been making him nervous. But Buddy continued.

"So what were you doing?"

"Just like your dad said. Crossing over."

"Why?"

"I thought I saw something."

"Like today?"

"Where does this go?" Danny said, picking up one of the canoe forms.

"At the end of the table," Buddy replied.

There was very little talk after that. The boys worked until lunchtime, when Danny felt he should go home. As he passed the trailer on his way out, he heard his name called, stepped to the screen door, and saw Mr. Connolly sitting on a bunk inside.

"Yes, sir?"

"You smoke, Danny?" Mr. Connolly asked, taking a drag on his Kool.

"No, sir."

"Ever think about it?"

"No."

"That's a lie. Anybody in your family smoke?"

"My dad smokes cigars sometimes."

"Cigar man," Mr. Connolly said reflectively. "Well, Buddy doesn't smoke, either. Guess you boys know your own minds. You two might get along."

Mr. Connolly leaned back and closed his eyes. Danny thought their talk was probably over, but he stayed at the door just in case. After a minute, Mr. Connolly began to snore, so Danny walked away. The sand on the road was not yet hot enough to inhibit walking, so he made good time, entering the woods on a well-used trail that wound toward the Ryan house from the south.

As he climbed the gentle rise up from the creek, he noticed something out of the corner of his eye. In the brush a few yards away, he saw a burst of purple. Danny rubbed his eyes. Was this more imagination? He paused for a moment, inclined to run away, but with a little request to his guardian angel for protection, he moved off the trail and wound his way through the foliage trying to make as little noise as possible.

"Is that an elephant I hear?"

There was no mistaking Abigail Arnold's voice or tone. Danny was not in the mood for a dose of her superiority, but it would have been cowardly to turn back. Instead he kept coming and did an impression of an elephant trumpeting.

"Have you caught a cold?"

Abigail never gave an inch. Or maybe she couldn't recognize an elephant. Several months before, he had shown her his drawing of a submarine, and she had guessed it was a water heater. That hurt. But he wasn't much of an artist, so maybe it did look like a water heater, except what water heater had twin propellers? Danny arrived at what seemed to be an impenetrable thicket. He could see the purple color through the branches, but Abigail's voice was coming from lower down.

"You can't get in here."

"Oh, brother!"

Girls had some stupid ideas. Abigail might be a better reader than Danny, but she could not possibly be his equal at thicket busting. Danny passed a practiced eye over the problem and had to admit the puzzle was deeper than he had assumed. Abigail seemed to be on the other side of a continuous tangle of branches.

"No elephants allowed."

These elephant comments were galling. Was she making reference to his weight? She had never done that before. Besides, he was not chubby enough to be compared to an elephant, not by someone as creative as Abigail. Well, he would solve the thicket problem or he would bull his way through, never mind the scratches. However, that was not necessary. He found the entrance at his feet, a tunnel similar to a rabbit run. It was kid-size, but Danny was a husky. He smelled humiliation in the air. Whether he left the scene, tore through the branches, or attempted the tunnel, he would lose. With a heavy heart, he decided to try to snake his way through the tunnel.

From the beginning, he was in trouble. You had to be at least six inches narrower than he was to get through cleanly. Danny set up such a shaking and tearing of brush that Abigail was in hysterics by the time he stuck his head into the clearing at the heart of the thicket.

What he saw when he cleared the rubbish away from his face was shocking indeed. Abigail was sitting daintily on her handkerchief in nothing but her underpants and camisole. Thank goodness she had a book in her lap.

He tried to back up, but the tunnel seemed to have tightened down. He was caught like a crab in a trap. Danny wondered what effect this was having on his guardian angel. Probably his wings were aflame.

"So you made it," Abigail said, once she had stopped laughing. "Don't you think you better bring your back end on through?"

What was she thinking? Had she forgotten she was in her underwear? He was caught in the bushes with a half-naked girl. His mind reeled as the word "naked" entered his head. He had to remind himself it really did not apply. He saw his sisters frequently in their underwear, but they at least had the decency to yelp and duck behind something. Abigail showed no such inclination. Yet he had asked for it. He had been determined to show off. This was what the priest meant by "Pride goeth before a fall." He had never understood it before.

Yet, even as he was ducking his head and pretending to brush things out of his hair, he couldn't help casting sideways glances at Abigail. And there it was: another sin on his soul. Who knew how seriously God took the act of finding a girl in her underwear too interesting? This smacked of the barrelly-covered lady in the swap shop, except Abigail was real. He could be facing years in purgatory.

Danny would have said, "Put some clothes on!" except she might have gotten up and done it, and he found her far too unnerving just sitting there. If she got on the move, there was no telling what would happen. His best course was to pretend everything was normal while he worked out an escape.

"What are you reading?" he asked.

"*The Mystery at the Moss-Covered Mansion*," she replied, riffling the pages. "It's a Nancy Drew mystery."

"Okay."

Danny twisted around so that he was facing away from Abigail and gained his feet. He saw that the thicket was open on the side that bordered the creek. He had tramped through there a couple of times, but he had never stumbled on any scantily clad girls. He turned away from the creek but avoided looking at Abigail, who continued sitting and staring at him. He observed that the purple item that had first caught his attention was a pair of shorts draped on the branches of a bush. Abigail's whole outfit was there.

"What are your clothes doing up here?"

"My mother doesn't like me to get them dirty."

It was true that Abigail was always crisp. He had noted that her underpants were bleached to a blinding shade of white. His own briefs were clean but did not reach anything like that level of whiteness. Now he was comparing his underpants to hers! He had to get out. Without turning toward Abigail, Danny started down the creek bank. He would find an exit point upstream, where his soul was less in peril.

"Don't go down there!"

Abigail's tone of voice had changed. Danny stopped.

"Why not?" he asked, without turning.

He heard Abigail get up and move to his shoulder.

"Look there."

Danny kept his eyes on the tip of her finger and cast his gaze where it led him. At first, he saw nothing, just the narrow creek channel. But then amongst the soft green of the bottom, he saw the outline of an alligator turtle far too big to be in such a small creek. Most turtles in Nowhere were harmless, but alligator turtles were of a different sort, plated, prehistoric-looking, and bad-tempered. Normally, they lay in wait for small fish, coaxing them with a fleshy thing in their mouths, but if a human were unlucky enough to get a toe or finger near that mouth, it might be snapped off. This specimen was as big around as a washtub, nearly spanning the bottom of the creek from one side to another.

"Gosh!" Danny said.

The sight of the giant turtle pushed all else from his mind, and he pivoted to thank Abigail for the warning. She was smiling, but the reality of his situation came crashing back on him. He looked at the sky, made a 180-degree turn, and headed down the bank.

"I'll hop over him," he said, making a flying leap to the opposite bank, where he scrambled into the brush.

"You're hilarious" was the last thing he heard Abigail say.

Danny made his way through the woods and eventually popped out at the south end of Florinda Street. He stopped for a moment and tried to figure out how much trouble he was in with God. He hadn't seen much. And he had done the right things in averting his eyes and running away. However, he had to admit that what little he had seen was far too interesting to him. There was definitely something wrong with that.

None of what had just happened made much sense to him. Abigail's trying-to-keep-tidy explanation was hard to fathom. Couldn't she sit on a handkerchief with all her clothes on? Well, he couldn't keep going over it. He would have to thrash it out during his next confession. There was no predicting how many Our Fathers and Hail Marys would be visited upon him, maybe even the time-consuming Stations of the Cross. However, he was fairly sure that he had avoided committing a mortal sin, and with that reassuring thought in his mind, he walked the rest of the way home. When he got there, he went to the bedroom door and saw that Ruth was asleep, so he padded to the kitchen where his mother was washing dishes at the sink.

"Ruth already ate," she said without turning. "You can make yourself a sandwich."

Danny went to the fridge and took out a couple of pieces of bologna, which he slapped between slices of white bread and spread with plenty of catsup. He sat down at the table but did not touch the sandwich. In a minute or two, his mother turned and looked him over.

"How come you're so dirty?"

"I . . ."

"Look at your feet! Good Lord, they're covered with scratches."

She was right. Danny had not noticed. His mother wet a cloth and gave his feet a good wipe. None of the scratches were deep, but there were a lot of them.

"I tried a new way coming home. It didn't work out."

"Where were you?"

This was tricky. He wasn't sure whether his mother needed to know about the canoe project.

"I was at a new kid's house. His dad is a boat builder."

"Why won't you wear your shoes?" she said, spreading out Danny's toes.

"They don't fit."

His mother gave his foot a squeeze and stood up. She knew very well that Danny's shoes didn't quite fit. They were half a size too small, but that was as close as they could come from what was available at the Goodwill store. Danny could bear to wear them for church, but they were impractical for tramping in the woods, and the Ryans were in one of their periodic money crises.

"Why don't you wear your tennis shoes? Go get them."

Danny went to the hall closet and brought out his sneakers. His mother held them up and looked regretfully at the holes in the soles.

"Suppose I put some cardboard in the bottoms?" she asked.

"It just gets wet in the woods. I don't know why, but I get poked with more things through those holes than when I'm barefoot. I like going barefoot anyway. Even if I had new sneakers, I'd still rather go barefoot."

"That's some comfort, I suppose," she said, handing the shoes back to Danny. "Maybe we can get some new ones at the end of the month. You'll have to have them when school starts, anyway."

"I can put the cardboard in for school."

"I don't think that will be necessary, but you're a good boy to suggest it."

"The tops look okay."

Danny didn't mind the cardboard for normal activities. It wore away pretty fast, but you just put some more in and you were fine for a while. Actually, he felt quite a sense of accomplishment when he cut a piece of cardboard that fit exactly in the bottom of his shoe. But he knew the shoe situation was bothersome to his mother. She felt as if she couldn't provide properly, but from Danny's point of view the money shortage was not difficult to bear. There was usually fifteen cents for the special Saturday morning kids' movie at the Springs Theater or a quarter for the pool. The Ryans didn't have TV, but Danny liked the radio, and he saw TV over at Alfred's sometimes. If his sister hadn't been sick and his father so moody, life would have been quite bearable. He might even feel different about Nowhere.

The catsup on the bologna sandwich had soaked the bread enough to create the pudding-like texture that Danny enjoyed so much. The time for philosophy was past, but as he raised the sandwich to his lips, he heard a brisk knock. From his position, Danny could see Abigail Arnold standing on the other side of the screen door. In an instant, Danny was across the kitchen and out of sight, startling his mother.

"What happened?" she asked.

"Don't tell her I'm here," Danny whispered.

"Tell who?" his mother whispered back, leaning down to look more closely at Danny's concerned expression. "What's wrong?"

"Abigail. She's at the door."

"The little girl from down the street?"

"Yes. Just say I can't come to the door."

"Why not?"

"Puhleeze!"

The knocking had started again and was going nonstop, so Danny's mother went into the front room. Danny heard the screen door squeak open, followed by some mumbling. He opened the refrigerator and stuck his head in just in case his mother brought Abigail into the kitchen. He heard the door squeak again and braced himself.

"What are you doing with your head in the fridge?"

It was his mom. Danny peeped over the top of the door and saw that she was alone.

"Looking for catsup."

"More catsup? Why don't you just drink it straight from the bottle?"

Danny picked up the bottle and pretended to drink.

"Very funny. Wipe off the lip of that bottle before you put it back," she said, throwing him a dish cloth. "I guess you'll be happy to know that Abigail did not ask to see you."

"What did she want then?" answered Danny, his voice full of dread.

"She dropped this off for you."

Danny's mother tried to hand him Abigail's copy of *The Mystery at the Moss-Covered Mansion*. Danny turned red and went to his seat at the table without accepting the book. He took a bite of his sandwich but found it difficult to chew.

"What made her think you'd want to read Nancy Drew?"

"I don't know. It's probably a joke. She likes to make fun of me."

"She didn't seem like that. She's a grown-up little thing."

"I'm going out. I'll take the sandwich with me."

Without waiting for a comment from his mother, Danny bolted from the room, pausing only to glance out the door to see if Abigail was lurking outside. When he was sure the coast was clear, he headed over to Alfred's house. That was one place he knew Abigail would never go. He found Alfred sitting in the breezeway with Nickel, who was orbiting around hoping for a cockroach snack.

Alfred was filling a jar with seeds from the crab's eye vine. They were hard little red beads with a black spot at one end, and they had the attractive characteristic of being deadly poisonous, though Danny was pretty sure Mrs. Bagley was not aware of that. Supposedly, they were sharpened and used by assassins in India. That was the kind of fact that got around among the neighborhood boys, who immediately tried to find an animal to kill using the technique. As far as Danny knew, no one had succeeded.

But Alfred was doing exactly what you could expect of him regarding deadly seeds, putting them in a jar because he thought they looked interesting. As he watched Alfred place the crab's eye seeds in a maddeningly slow manner, Danny let his mind drift back to thoughts of Abigail in the thicket. This was no good. If Alfred could offer no more distraction than seed art, Danny would have to leave. He finished his sandwich and was about to go when Mrs. Bagley saved the day.

"Would you boys like to make some butter?"

Here was an activity that promised more action and was something that both Danny and Alfred could enjoy. The Bagley family bought milk in a state unknown to Danny before he met Alfred. It was not a uniform white fluid. They preferred their milk in two parts: thin bluish stuff on the bottom and thick yellowish stuff on the top. When they wanted regular milk, they mixed the two together. However, on occasion, Mrs. Bagley would let Danny and Alfred drain off the thick stuff and put it in a separate jar. With enough shaking, it made the fascinating change from liquid to solid, an irregular mass of butter slowly emerging like something in a monster movie.

"Neat," Danny said immediately.

Alfred looked longingly at his seed project.

"C'mon, Alfred," Danny said.

"Answer me, son."

"Yes, ma'am," Alfred said.

"Don't be so slow when your mother asks you a question," Mrs. Bagley said, returning to the kitchen.

Danny sat looking at the floor. He felt bad about Alfred's rebuke. Nickel cruised over in case Danny might be looking down at a roach. Alfred kept placing seeds, but with the butter project looming, he tried to rush, and he spilled several onto the floor. In a twinkling, Nickel pecked them up and stood peering around for more.

"Alfred!"

Startled, Alfred dropped several more seeds on the floor, but Danny grabbed Nickel by the neck before she could eat them. Alfred's eyes grew big.

"What are you doing to Nickel?" he asked.

"Don't you know those things are poison?"

"I never heard anything about that!"

"Well, they are. Gee whiz!"

"Don't say that! Mama might hear."

Danny had forgotten that in the Bagley family, "gee whiz" was profanity. Here he was holding a poisoned chicken by the neck, and he wasn't even allowed to say "gee whiz." But today he couldn't quibble. Something had to be done about Nickel, who was struggling and threatening to decapitate herself. Danny let her go for the time being. He tried to think of some remedy, but nothing came to mind. You couldn't hold a chicken upside down or pat it on the back or put your finger down its throat. At that point, Mrs. Bagley arrived with a jar of cream.

"Mrs. Bagley," Danny asked as innocently as possible, "what might make a chicken puke?"

"Don't say 'puke,' Danny. Say 'throw up.' Did Nickel throw up?"

"No, ma'am. We were just wondering what would cause it if she did."

Mrs. Bagley looked at the boys with mild alarm, but she could not figure out what was improper about the question. She stood turning the jar of cream in her hands for several seconds before she spoke.

"I don't believe I've ever seen a chicken throw up. To tell you the truth . . . ," and here she glanced around to see if anyone was within earshot, "I think everything goes through them so fast, there isn't any need for throwing up."

Alfred burst out laughing. He had probably never heard his mother say anything so racy before. Mrs. Bagley looked pleased and left the room after handing the jar of cream to Danny. Alfred regained his composure as Danny began stealthily crawling toward Nickel, who was clucking softly in a corner. She was showing no ill effects other than an intense wariness. Alfred caught Danny by the foot.

"Don't bother her."

"Well, we should do something. Maybe we should feed her a bunch of stuff. It might water down the effect."

"What stuff?"

"What do you usually feed her, besides the roaches?"

"Chicken feed."

"Well, get it."

Alfred disappeared into the garage and returned with a coffee can full of hard corn. He threw a handful on the floor and Nickel was off to the races, her recent tribulations forgotten. Danny sat on the window sill, gently shaking the jar of cream while Nickel consumed one handful of corn after another. Finally, Alfred stopped throwing it on the floor and just set the can down for her. She pecked like an engine until Alfred finally took it away.

"Could she eat herself to death?" he asked Danny.

"They're pretty stupid. Maybe we should let it go at that. She ate a lot."

They stood observing Nickel walk stiffly around the breezeway. Danny wondered if the poison might be taking hold. Mrs. Bagley came in and noticed the can of corn in Alfred's hand.

"What's that for, Alfred?"

"We're giving Nickel some extra, Mrs. Bagley," Danny piped up.

"I asked Alfred, Danny. Don't answer for him."

"We're giving her some extra," Alfred said.

"You're not trying to make her throw up, are you?"

"No, ma'am!" the boys said together.

"Well, don't overfeed animals. It's bad for them. How's the butter coming?"

Danny looked down at the jar he had been shaking and was surprised to see that the cream had turned almost entirely to butter.

"That's good work," Mrs. Bagley said, "but you'll have to run along now, Danny. Alfred has some things to do."

Danny knew from experience that this pronouncement was not negotiable. Alfred was always having to give up doing something fun because of mysterious other "things to do." So, with one last glance at the ill-fated Nickel, Danny left the Bagley house.

8

As Danny wandered regretfully away from the scene of Nickel's flirtation with death, he could hardly believe it was only midafternoon. That was the way with Nowhere: some days empty, some days full. His mind drifted back to the way the day had started, with his vision of the bungalow, the dog, and the girl. He had been frightened, but after working on the canoe with Buddy and his adventure with Alfred and Nickel, that seemed silly.

Perhaps he had fallen asleep and dreamed the scene across the river. The more he thought about it, the more sensible that explanation seemed. He felt he should go back and visit Hanna's Whirl, just to settle the matter, so he headed that way. During his approach, he kept his gaze away from the opposite bank of the Hillsborough, concentrating instead on the creek. This near to the river, the creek that ran behind his house joined with the one where he had seen the giant turtle. He preferred to think in that fashion, divorcing the creek from any image of Abigail Arnold. Danny stopped for a moment to stare at the creek's sandy bottom with its population of healthy green plants and darting minnows. It was so different from the cloudy river. Abruptly, he glanced upward.

Across the Hillsborough, he saw just what he had hoped, nothing more than the usual riverbank. He plopped down and swept his eyes over Hanna's Whirl, much less cluttered since the dam had been opened but still ringed by a band of green hyacinths. Danny shook his head, thinking how Buddy would probably consider the sight beautiful, but Danny's heart was closed to the Hillsborough. It was not his river. He was a foreigner here, born a long way away and brought against his wishes to this place, though he had only sketchy memories of his origins. That was one of the things that made him feel so bad. He knew he didn't belong in Nowhere, but he had no real claim on anywhere else.

He looked across the slowly flowing river and remembered the family's trip across the country to Florida three years before. The train had been packed with strangers trying to be too familiar, and it scared Danny to go from one car to another. In the passageways between cars, there was such a grinding and lashing of metal that his ears hurt, and the plates under his feet vibrated and jerked sideways as if something were trying to throw him down and crush him. It was the first time in his life that Danny had sensed bad intentions in his surroundings, and it had been the start of a horrible decline. Even on the banks of the peaceful Hillsborough, he seemed to feel the vibration of the train, and the longer he sat, the more he shook until he finally leaped up and ran his hands over his face and shoulders.

That made him feel stupid, so he turned around and walked away without looking back, but he continued to be uneasy. He decided to check on the canoe. Halfway up the road to Buddy's place, he turned a corner and found himself face to face with Buddy's father, still in his robe and pajama bottoms.

"There you are," the man said.

Danny didn't know how to reply.

"I thought I was headed wrong. Let's get going."

He grasped Danny by the shoulder, turned him around, and started walking him in the wrong direction. Danny went along for several steps, bearing the man's uncomfortable weight. There was something scary about him, not that he was mean, but he gave the impression he might do something bad by accident. He was already hurting Danny's shoulder, yet Danny was reluctant to pull away and seem unfriendly.

"The shop's back up the road," Danny said.

"Damn right," Mr. Connolly replied but with no change in direction.

"Back there," Danny said, turning to point.

The man's hand slipped off Danny's shoulder, causing him to come slumping down on Danny with his full weight. The two fell to the ground with Buddy's father on top.

"Jesus Christ, what the hell happened?" Mr. Connolly sputtered.

The man was wallowing around, grinding Danny into the sand. Danny heard a car coming and feared the two of them were going to be run over, but the engine stopped and a door slammed. Danny was not in a position to see who had arrived, but he recognized the voice.

"What are you doing down there, Bart?"

It was Al Gallagher. In a moment, Bart was off Danny and in the seat of Al's Chevy pickup. Once he had safely stowed Bart, Al turned his attention to Danny, who was staring at him in disbelief. This was not Sulphur Springs. What was Al of Al's Swap Shop doing on this back road?

"How's the hand?" Al asked casually.

"Okay," Danny replied, still slightly disoriented.

"What's your connection to Bart?"

"I know Buddy."

Al studied Danny for a moment and then motioned him into the cab of the truck.

"You better come along. Straighten Bart up, will you?"

This was new territory for Danny, straightening up adults. Bart had gone to sleep and was leaning precariously out the truck door. Danny pushed at him gently. Bart turned his head slightly. Al laughed.

"You'll have to do better than that. Give him a good shove. He deserves it. I'll pull from this side."

Together they got Bart upright and the three of them headed up the road to the Airstream. As they pulled in, Buddy appeared from the shop in back. He smiled at the sight of Al's truck, but he shook his head sorrowfully when he saw his dad.

"Bart's been on the loose, Buddy," said Al. "He was on top of Danny here when I drove up."

"What happened, Dad?" Buddy asked.

"We were on our way to work on the canoe," Bart said. "I think I lost my footing."

"The shed's not in that direction," Buddy said. "Are you okay, Danny?"

"Sure."

"He said that's where it was," Bart commented mildly, cocking his thumb at Danny.

Danny was scandalized. He had said no such thing. He looked at Buddy and Al with such indignation that they both broke out laughing.

"Stop lying, Dad," Buddy said, helping Bart out of the truck.

"Well, that's what I thought he said."

Bart threw himself down on one of the lawn chairs, lit a Kool, and looked at Danny.

"I must have gotten it wrong."

"Yes, sir. You did," replied Danny, his voice full of indignation.

"Don't be prissy, son. A man can make a mistake."

"I better take off," Danny said, turning and heading back down the road.

He had been humiliated earlier by Abigail and now again, but this was worse because it had taken place in the presence of Buddy and Al. He had not asked either of them to pay attention to him. They had done it on their own and now he was in the middle of something uncomfortable. And they had laughed when Bart had called him "prissy"! Behind him, he heard Bart say, "What's his problem?"

"You hurt his feelings, Dad."

"Does he think he's the only one with feelings?"

This was impossible. People were discussing him behind his back. Danny broke into a run and continued running until he was out of breath. Once he had gotten his wind back, he walked toward home. The sun was low in the sky. Danny's spirits were low as well. The scene with Al, Buddy, and Bart had been dreadful, but it had been instructive. He had to stay out of other people's business and keep them out of his. That was the only way he could get along. He was glad that Alfred Bagley came from a family that wanted to keep the Ryans at arm's length. This was a great benefit of being Catholic in Nowhere, people thought you had plague in your system.

As he entered the Ryan house, Danny wondered if his father was home. His heart sank when he saw his mother and father sitting at the kitchen table, talking. His father wasn't mad, but he didn't like the low tone. It sounded like one of those serious conversations that never brought any good. He turned left and went into the bedroom, where he found Loretta and Ruth sitting quietly on the bed.

"What's going on?" he whispered.

"We're not sure," Ruth whispered back. "Daddy might be sick."

"What else is new?" Loretta said far too loudly.

Danny ducked his head, and Loretta patted him on the shoulder.

"They didn't hear me," she said. "They wouldn't know what I meant, even if they did."

Danny knew this was true, but he also knew that their father did not respond to meaning alone. His motives could not be fathomed, so it was best to send as few signals as possible. Loretta could not swallow that simple fact, but she kept quiet for the time being.

While they sat listening to the ominous drone of conversation from the other room, Danny gazed for the millionth time at two framed photographs on the bedroom wall. They seemed entirely out of place hung at the Ryan house in the middle of Nowhere. One was of Roy Rogers and the other was of the Sons of the Pioneers, Roy Rogers' musical group. Even more incredibly, they were both signed to Ruth and Loretta Ryan. The story that went with the photographs was just as fascinating to Danny as the photographs themselves. Like the snapshots of his dad dressed as Lincoln, these pictures were evidence of a time when things were different. In California, his dad had run a small service station, and one of the Sons of the Pioneers had brought his car in for gas. His father had asked if he could get an autographed picture for his kids, and the man had obliged by bringing in the two photos the next time he came to the station.

This, then, was the world the family had lived in before Danny arrived on the scene, a world in which movie personalities dropped in and gave you autographed pictures. Danny had actually been born into that world and spent some time there but had been torn out of it. However, the friendly face of the King of the Cowboys was always up on the wall to remind him of past golden times, and when he saw a Roy Rogers movie at the Springs Theater, it gave him a queer feeling to know how close he had once been to the real thing. Danny's thoughts were interrupted by his mother's arrival in the bedroom. She came in and calmly sat down on the bed, but her expression was strained.

"I have a little bit of bad news," she said.

Loretta fell back on the bed and stared at the ceiling. Ruth clasped her hands. Danny continued to stare at Roy, hoping for strength.

"Daddy is going to have to quit his job."

"Did they fire him?' Loretta asked.

"No, not at all. Daddy is an excellent worker."

"What's wrong then?" Ruth asked.

"You know how he coughs. That's because he's breathed flour into his lungs. If he keeps working at the bakery, he'll breathe in more, and he could get seriously ill."

"Is he going to die?" Danny asked.

"No, no. He's going to get another job and everything will be fine."

"Who," Loretta asked with great significance, "is going to hire him?"

"Daddy has always been a good employee. There is no complaint against him."

"I guess he saves it all up and dumps it on us. Aren't we lucky?"

"Shh. He might hear you."

"So what? You think he doesn't know? Why does he think we're huddling in here like Anne Frank? Why don't you divorce him and do us all a favor?"

With that Loretta stormed out of the room. A moment later the front door slammed violently.

"I have some dinner for you two," Danny's mother said.

Ruth and Danny both gave her doubtful looks.

"Daddy's tired and is lying down in the back room," she said, standing up.

"Mom," Danny whispered. "Are you sure he didn't do something at work?"

"No, no. He's valuable at Holsum. They always put him on the wrapping machine at Christmas to wrap those little souvenir loaves. Nobody else can handle it. This is just bad luck."

The three went into the kitchen and ate silently. Danny thought Ruth and his mother clinked their plates too much, but he minded his own business. Afterward, Ruth started to wash the dishes with Danny drying, but she got too tired and Danny finished up. Their mother disappeared into the back room, and when Danny heard more mumbling through the door, he fled to the other end of the house. Back on the bed, Danny spoke to Ruth in a low voice.

"Why won't Mom divorce him?"

He felt bad asking the question. He loved his father, he guessed, but he couldn't help thinking that having him around was too scary to endure when there was a way out.

"Catholics don't get divorced," Ruth said quietly.

"But Dad isn't even Catholic. He never goes to church."

"We're Catholic, though."

"But this is an emergency!"

Ruth patted him on the head.

"It won't always be this way," she said. "Things will get better. Let's listen to the radio."

She turned on some music, but Danny couldn't concentrate. Ruth had said that things would get better, but what evidence was there to back her up? He kept thinking of his father lying in the back room with his lungs full of flour. It seemed crazy that it couldn't be removed somehow so he could go back to work. Danny wondered bitterly why, if they could make an atomic cocktail for Ruth, they could not make an atomic lung cleaner for her dad. He hated to think it, but the worst thing about his father's illness was not that he was sick but that his presence in the house would be unpredictable if he wasn't employed. He might burst upon you at any time.

By bedtime, Loretta had not returned, so Danny helped his mother prepare the couch, including his rubber sheet. He prayed he could stay dry tonight when everything was in such a delicate state. His mother finished making the bed and went in to sleep with Ruth. Danny lay down and wedged himself against the wall. He thought about the Christmas celebration at Holsum Bakery. On the roof of the plant, they put up a big representation of Santa's sleigh with Rudolph in the lead. His nose lit up red. Long lines of people formed to tour the facility and eat warm bread fresh from the oven, cut into thick slabs and slathered with butter. Everyone received a gift bag containing various things, but its greatest prize was a little loaf of bread about six inches long, wrapped just as the big ones were, in shiny orange paper with "Holsum" in white letters on the side. His dad wrapped those loaves. He hadn't known that.

Later he was awakened by the sound of his father emerging from the back room. Danny began to breathe very lightly so as not to do the slightest thing that might be inflammatory. His father came into the living room and sat down in a nearby chair and lit a cigar. Danny could hear him clacking a cough drop against his teeth. Soon the room was filled with the smell of a King Edward cigar.

His father seldom smoked, but when he did it was King Edward. Sometimes he was seized with a pressing need to smoke and would send Danny running a half mile to Halper's neighborhood store, the closest place where a cigar, or anything else for that matter, could be bought. Once Mr. Halper had said, "This is about the best cigar you can get for ten cents." Danny nodded as if he had understood and had repeated the comment to his father, hoping it would please him.

"He's probably right" was all his father had to say.

The smell of cigar smoke was not unwelcome to Danny. His father had never gone screwy while smoking. Sometimes when he went with his father to pick up his mother after she worked a party on Davis Island, Danny would lie down in the back seat of the car to sleep and his father would blow clouds of cigar smoke over him to keep the mosquitoes away. This was the King Edward at its best from Danny's point of view. Tonight, however, Danny was haunted by the image of his father's lungs, already heavy with flour, also carrying a load of cigar smoke. That could not be good. If his father grew sicker, he might never leave the house again. But Danny could not stay awake to worry. With the smell of smoke in his nostrils, he drifted off to sleep.

At five in the morning, he was awakened by the sound of his father closing the door on his way out to work. He would finish the week at Holsum and that would be all. Danny was happy to find that his bedclothes were dry. This was not really surprising. He always woke up when he wet the bed. Maybe the cigar smoke had done the trick. Loretta was not in the bed and had apparently never been. She came in shortly after Mr. Ryan left.

"Where were you?" Danny asked.

"Walking around."

"All night?"

"I couldn't stand to be in the house anymore," she answered. "I would rather sleep in a tree."

"Are you going to fight with Dad?"

"No. But I'm going to do something that will make things better."

Danny hung his head. Loretta's ideas about what would make things better were highly suspect. He watched her go into the kitchen and get some leftovers out of the fridge. She sat down at the table and ate them cold. Then she went into the bathroom, and a moment later Danny heard the shower. Loretta had not lit the water heater and waited ten minutes as was usual. This was disturbing. She was not the type for cold showers. In a few minutes, Loretta came back through the house wrapped in a towel. She went into the bedroom. Danny busied himself making up the couch.

"Do you have to go to work early?" he heard his mother ask.

"No," Loretta said.

"Why are you getting dressed up?"

"I am going to look for a place to live."

"You're too young for that."

"Then come and get me, but bring a doctor because I will slit my wrists before I spend another day in this atmosphere. I just wish I could take Ruth and Danny with me."

"Couldn't you try . . ."

"No! I am doing the only thing I can do. If I don't go, I will take a baseball bat to Dad and spend the rest of my life in jail for his murder."

"You wouldn't do that."

"I don't know what I might do. I only know it is best if I am out of here. At least there will be one less body in this coffin."

"Is that the way you think of us?"

"Don't try to make me feel guilty. You could get us out of this, but you won't. I think letting this go on is a much bigger sin than divorce."

"Have you lost your faith?"

"I can't talk about it. I'm so mad I could say anything. Just let me get out of here. I'll sneak back when he's not around and get my stuff."

"We won't be a family anymore."

"I'll give you whatever extra money I can make. Don't worry."

"That's not it."

"I don't care what it is."

At this point Loretta emerged from the bedroom wearing a skirt and blouse. She looked at Danny and noted his stricken expression.

"Cheer up. You'll have the couch to yourself."

Danny didn't know what to say.

"Oh, come on. It's not the end of the world. You're always telling me to shut up when Dad's around. Now you won't have to worry."

"Where will you go?"

"I have a secret plan."

Danny suspected she had no plan and was about to say so when she held out her arms. He got up and gave her a hug, after which Loretta strode out the door. In the other room, he could hear his mother and Ruth crying. He knew he should want to comfort them, but in his heart, he knew Loretta was right. He loved her, but she was always about to explode. Everybody was better off with her out of the house, yet it would seem traitorous to say so. At the same time, he couldn't go in the bedroom and lie about it. In the end, he skulked out of the house leaving his mother and sister weeping.

It was grey morning before sunup, everything in mist. Across the way, there were lights on in the Bagley house, but it would be hours before he could go over there. He felt chilly but could not bring himself to go back into the house for a long-sleeved shirt. He looked up the road. Loretta was out of sight, somewhere in the fog on Florinda Street. Danny envied her, but he knew he could not follow in her steps. He had read stories of boys running away from home, but he was too practical to believe it ever worked out well. If he tried it, he would be brought back in humiliation, and things would be worse than before.

The only encouraging possibility was that someday he would grow up, though he had no concept of how even grownups got along in a world so full of traps. Something must happen to toughen you up. That's why Loretta could leave. She had reached the point where she had no more fear, like Roy Rogers.

Danny sat down on the front step and reflected on the nature of Roy Rogers. Whatever complication was thrown at Roy, he was always up to the challenge. There was no doubt about his ability to rope his enemies and bring them into town. They might still be snarling, but they were out of gas. It must be wonderful to be like that.

"Come in and have your breakfast."

Danny looked up and saw his mother standing in the doorway. She had regained her composure and was holding the screen door open for him. He got up and went inside. Ruth was still crying in the other room. She seemed to feel things deeply, maybe because she was so sick. Danny watched his mother walk into the kitchen rubbing her hands together. He listened to the sniffling from the other room. He looked at the couch and realized that he had left a corner of the rubber sheet sticking out from under a cushion. He turned and ran out the front door.

9

So now he was out of the house in the early morning with no breakfast and a bad taste in his mouth. He wished he had brushed his teeth, but that was unfeasible when bolting from a room. He wandered into the woods and picked his way to the creek. The water was especially cold in the chilly morning. He knelt down to put his mouth in the stream, trying to keep his bandaged hand from getting wet, but he managed to get it muddy, which was worse than wet. In the end, he had to plunge the bandage into the water to clean it up. He was disgusted with himself, and he still had the bad taste in his mouth.

With time on his hands, he decided to go over and see if the big alligator turtle was still where it had been yesterday. He got to the spot in just a few minutes and warily approached the creek bank. The turtle was gone. At first he was glad, but the more he thought about it, the more concerned he became. This turtle was a monster. It was probably best if you knew where the monsters were located. Now he would have to be thinking about this creature roaming around. He was probably lucky not to have lost his hand earlier when he was getting a drink.

The sky was lighter now, but it was still much too early to visit Alfred. Danny couldn't bear to go back to his own house, so he wandered in the direction of the fish hatchery. The ladies who worked there arrived early, and he thought he might see the girl from the trail. Why this idea was so appealing, he could not say, but he walked cautiously to the water plant processing building and peered through the open door. The women were hanging up their purses and other effects on wall pegs. Some of them had already donned the rubber aprons they wore to keep dry while handling the wet plants. The room had an intense aquarium smell that Danny found pleasant, but he wondered if the ladies felt the same, having to breathe it every day.

At the other end of the building, he spotted the girl. She had already put on an ugly black apron, but it did nothing to quell her radiance. Danny stared at her, but he was reluctant to move any farther into the work space. He watched as the workers settled down, some bringing big pails of plants from tubs of bubbling fresh water and placing them on a big central table. The women sat around the table, picking through the plants. In this work, the girl was deft, her fingers flashing through the plants, separating the vigorous specimens from the droopy ones. Danny had never found this process so interesting as when he watched it being done by the girl. She was new, but she did her job at a supernatural pace. The women chattered in Spanish while they worked. The girl said little, but she was not aloof.

"Hey, Donna! You got a boyfriend." Suddenly this English phrase popped out of the Spanish, but for a moment Danny didn't understand that it had anything to do with him. When the girl looked up, he realized what it meant, and he blushed. This brought a burst of laughter from the ladies. Danny felt paralyzed.

"Do you like her, little boy?" one of the ladies asked.

Danny could not answer. He took a step backward. This proved he could move. He might have run away, but he had to maintain some dignity.

"I think you do!" the lady said.

"Be quiet, Rosa. He's a friend. We like to talk."

"I think he would like to do more than talk. Would you like to kiss her?"

Danny didn't even blush at this. The idea was too ridiculous.

"No, ma'am," he said.

"What's wrong with you? She's so beautiful!"

"I don't go around kissing people," Danny said.

"Then I am sorry for you!"

This brought a great laugh from the ladies. The girl laughed too.

"You'll find out how nice it is!" the lady said, puckering up her lips.

The water was getting too deep for Danny. He stood in the doorway for a moment, thinking. The ladies all looked at him. The girl gave him a kind little smile.

"Excuse me," he said, bowing from the waist. "I have some other business."

This brought an explosion of laughter from the ladies. Several of them clapped their hands. Danny walked away feeling better about himself.

By this time the air was bright, but the day was still too young for visiting. Danny decided to go back to the Ryan house and check the atmosphere. If the mood was endurable, he could have something to eat, maybe even drum up the price of entry into the Sulphur Springs Pool. Maybe Alfred could get permission to go if the weather forecast looked promising.

He entered the house through the back door and glanced at his father's carefully made bed. He was neat for a crazy man. The bathroom was unoccupied, and Danny gave his teeth a good scrubbing. Afterward, he felt encouraged enough to poke his head into the kitchen. From the other end of the house, he heard an ominous mumbling. His mother and Ruth were talking in low voices. What a depressing sound.

On the kitchen table, Danny found Abigail's copy of *The Mystery at the Moss-Covered Mansion* and, much more importantly, two quarters. His mother had anticipated his return. Danny grabbed a slice of bread and butter and went out to the back steps to pass an hour. Desperate for some distraction, he took Abigail's book with him. The cover seemed promising at first glance. Three figures were dramatically illuminated by a lantern on the ground. A girl in a blue dress was wielding a shovel. Over her shoulder could be seen an ominous grey two-story house with a yellow moon shining in the sky beyond it. Another girl, this one in a red dress, seemed to be putting some greenbacks in a tin can. The third figure was looking on interestedly, a short-haired girl in a mannish jacket.

He turned to the first chapter, where he found a black and white drawing of a young girl making an awkward escape from a second-story window. She had apparently knocked over a ladder that could be seen falling away in the lower portion of the picture and was having to leap for a tree to save herself. To make matters worse, the girl was wearing a dress. Danny could not think of a worse garment for climbing around on ladders. There were all sorts of things against it. If anyone should have been climbing on a ladder, it was the mannish girl from the cover.

He closed the book in disgust. People in dresses having adventures—the concept was ridiculous. Danny knew from the movies that the proper role for females was to cower in a corner while the hero fought the villain. When women tried to help, they inevitably hit the hero over the head with a vase.

He put the book under his arm and headed off toward Abigail's house. With any luck, he could leave it where she could find it and be gone without notice. If he then avoided her for a few days, he might be spared any questions about how he liked the book, not to mention a humiliating reminder of the thicket episode. Danny forged smartly ahead and in no time was at the back border of the Arnold property. With great stealth, he made his way through a unique aspect of the grounds, a grove of banana trees behind the house. This grove would have been much more interesting if the plants had actually produced good bananas, but they stayed green. Alfred had gotten diarrhea from eating one. He had tried again with the same result, after which he gave up on the Arnold bananas.

Danny dodged through the grove and crept to the back entrance. Here he was confronted by a long screened porch. His plan was to crack the door and slide the book inside where it would be out of the damp, but before he could do that, he would have to make sure the porch was unoccupied. He crouched at the edge of the porch and slowly rose up to peer inside. It took a moment for his eyes to adjust to the shadowy interior, but when they did he found himself staring at Abigail Arnold, standing on the porch staring back.

"Didn't you see enough yesterday?"

Danny considered this remark unnecessarily cruel, though he had to admit he had placed himself in a bad light. Abigail was giggling. He turned, intending to walk away with a dignified air.

"Danny Ryan, you stop right there."

Danny halted. He felt he had to face her.

"I want to talk to you," Abigail added.

"I just came to bring your stupid book. I wouldn't be here if you hadn't left it at my house."

"What, you don't like mysteries?"

Danny held up *The Mystery at the Moss-Covered Mansion* and pointed disdainfully to the front cover.

"Not this kind. Excuse me, I have things to do."

Danny felt he had acquitted himself pretty well. With one stroke, he had expressed himself on the subject of Nancy Drew books and gotten himself out of a sticky situation. The more he thought about it, the better he felt. However, as he walked back toward his house, he discovered to his disgust that he still had Abigail's accursed book in his hand. Was there no escaping it? He thought about tossing it in a ditch, but that could lead to trouble. The last thing he needed was Abigail coming to his house at the wrong time looking for her precious novel. Why was it so hard for him to make headway in the world? He badly wanted a dose of Alfred Bagley to cheer him up and was pleasantly surprised when he spotted him out by the Bagley garage.

Alfred was too absorbed to notice Danny's approach. He was watching the ant lions again. Alfred enjoyed monitoring the little traps that the ant lions set, funnel-shaped depressions in fine sand. If an ant fell in, it would slide down the sides of the funnel and into the jaws of the ant lion lying buried at the bottom of the pit. A meaner boy would have seized an ant and put it in the pit for the purposes of entertainment, but Alfred was content to let nature take its course. Danny felt sorry for the ants.

"Hi, Alfred," Danny said. "How's Nickel?"

Startled, Alfred jumped a foot, then collected himself and fished in his pocket.

"Hold out your hand," he said.

Danny did so, thinking that Alfred might produce some treasured memento of the deceased Nickel, perhaps a downy feather. Instead, he deposited five crab's eye beads in Danny's left palm. Danny stared at them for a moment.

"So?" he asked.

"That's them," Alfred said with a huge smile.

"What?"

"That's what Nickel ate. They didn't kill her."

Danny stared down at the five beads, struggling to comprehend the means by which they might have come into Alfred's possession. As he slowly came to the inevitable conclusion, he rotated his wrist and let the beads fall to the ground. Then, holding his hand out in front of him like a dead fish, he walked to a spigot and turned it on full force, letting the stream of water beat on his palm for a minute. Finally, he took some sand and scoured it to a bright shade of red.

"Thanks, Alfred," he said. "I have one hand torn up and the other polluted forever."

"It's only Nickel," Alfred said. "I washed them off. I bet you've picked up a lot worse without knowing it."

"I'll never understand you, Alfred. It's good manners to tell a person when you're about to put something in their hand that has passed out of a chicken's behind. If it's nothing, why don't we go show these to your mother?"

Alfred's face went white. Danny was immediately sorry.

"I'm just kidding. I wouldn't do that."

Alfred relaxed somewhat, but as was his practice after a moment of intensity, he began peering about in mild desperation. His eyes fell on *The Mystery at the Moss-Covered Mansion.*

"What's that?" he asked.

"Abigail's stupid book. She left it at my house."

Under normal circumstances, Alfred would not have been interested in a book, but today he picked it up and began examining the cover. Danny waited for him to toss it aside, but against all expectation, Alfred continued to ponder the cover art. Finally he looked up.

"What are they doing?" he asked.

"Digging a hole in the middle of the night," Danny replied.

"Where did that money come from?"

"I have no idea."

"Who lives in that house?"

Danny shrugged his shoulders. Alfred turned his attention back to the book. He opened it and found the illustration for the first chapter.

"Is she sneaking out?" he asked.

Danny could hardly contain his amazement. Clearly something in Alfred's makeup had been touched by this ludicrous book, probably because the poor kid was not allowed to go to the movies or have comics. Alfred had once mentioned something about having seen a movie at church, but Danny could not conceive of what sort of movie might be shown at El Bethel Baptist Church over on 15th Street. It was bound to be deadly dull.

Now, Danny was seeing firsthand the effects of Alfred's deprivation. It had turned him into a boy who was fascinated by Nancy Drew, girl detective! Still, there might be a silver lining.

"Alfred," Danny said casually, "you can keep the book to look at if you'll return it to Abigail."

Alfred looked longingly at the picture of the girl sneaking out at night. He bit his lip and glanced toward the kitchen.

"You could keep it someplace out here in the garage and look at it when no one was around."

Danny was afraid he had stepped over the line. Alfred was visibly shaken by this idea. Danny thought it was a silly reaction. Kids had secrets and that was that. They were fine as long as they weren't sinful secrets, and there could be nothing really sinful in that book, although Danny thought the artist might not have made the girl's dress cling so tightly to her legs when she jumped for the tree.

"Can I keep it at your house?"

Danny realized that he had tried to be too clever and was paying the price. This accursed book was now against all odds tangled up with Alfred, who had always considered books his worst enemy. What perverse magic did it possess?

"Let's forget it," Danny said, reaching for the book.

Alfred looked so sorrowful that Danny had to take pity.

"All right, but just for a couple of days."

Alfred nodded vigorously, and was turning back to the book for another look when he spotted his mother coming through the breezeway door. He hastily shoved the book back at Danny.

"What's that?" Mrs. Bagley asked suspiciously.

"Just a book," Danny said. "I was showing it to Alfred."

"What's in it?"

"I don't know. I haven't started reading it yet."

"May I have a look at it?"

"Yes, ma'am," said Danny.

He wished Alfred would stop skulking like a dog about to be whipped.

"*The Mystery at the Moss-Covered Mansion*," Mrs. Bagley read slowly. "This looks like a girl's book. Is it?" she asked, turning to Danny.

"It's about a detective," he answered.

She opened the book and examined the illustration at the beginning of the first chapter.

"Are those high heels?" she asked, presenting the book for Danny's scrutiny.

He accepted the book with some confusion. Perhaps high heels were another of those odd preoccupations of the Bagley household. Danny's mother and sisters had some high heels. Danny saw them in the movies all the time. They looked uncomfortable, but he couldn't see anything else wrong with them. Yet there seemed to be something at stake. He looked at the illustration.

"I guess so. That's probably why she's falling off a ladder."

Mrs. Bagley looked concerned.

"She isn't wearing high heels in the other picture," Danny said helpfully.

Mrs. Bagley returned to the dust jacket illustration.

"Which one is she?"

Danny had guessed the girl with the shovel only because she was the most prominent. He assumed an authoritative air and pointed to her, and then to her shoes.

"A girl detective," Mrs. Bagley mused. "And she's the one who solves the mystery?"

Danny was once again struck by how dull adults could sometimes be. Everything was staring her in the face, but she was acting like a zombie.

"Yes, ma'am."

"That's very interesting," she said, handing the book back to Danny, who thought it was about as far from interesting as anything could be, but he sensed an opportunity.

"Could Alfred come swimming at the Springs today?"

"Maybe after lunch," she replied, turning away, and then added, "if it doesn't look like rain."

Alfred watched his mom walk away and then, seemingly having forgotten about his interest in *The Mystery at the Moss-Covered Mansion*, he motioned conspiratorially to Danny to follow him into the garage, where he stopped in front of two large burlap sacks stacked in one corner. They smelled strongly of tobacco, which was shocking because the Bagleys thought smoking was a quick road to hell, right up there with dancing.

"What this for?" Danny asked.

"Fleas."

"What do you mean, 'fleas'?"

"You can use tobacco stems to drive out fleas," Alfred said. "We put them in the goat's stall."

"How does the goat like it?"

"He eats them."

"Is that good for him?"

"Hasn't hurt him yet. Look here."

Upon saying this, Alfred drew out a stem that had most of the leaf left on it. This Danny found interesting. Here was another case of something being improperly represented. Someone had certified this as a bag of stems, but here was a nearly perfect leaf nestled like a diamond among the scraggly discards. He held it up and took a sniff. Alfred laughed uproariously. Danny lowered the leaf and stared in disdain at Alfred, who demonstrated for the millionth time that he was impervious to disdain. Rather than being put in his place, Alfred pulled out a cardboard box containing fifteen or twenty of the intact leaves. At first Danny thought this must be one of Alfred's endless collections, but there was more to this. Alfred was trying to wink at Danny. He had no experience in winking and the effect was grotesque.

"Stop that, Alfred. You look stupid."

"Would you smoke it?" Alfred asked, his voice atremble.

"Got matches?"

Alfred lifted up the tobacco leaves to reveal six safety matches dipped in paraffin wax to keep out the damp. Danny guessed that these had come out of Alfred's Cub Scout kit. Luckily for Alfred, a scout troop met at the Bagleys' church, so he was permitted to participate.

"Let's go, then."

The boys crept out into the weedy part of the Bagley property. When they were well away from the house where they could not be seen, they cleared a place and set up shop.

"You have to roll it up," Alfred said excitedly, turning the box over to provide a flat surface.

"My dad smokes cigars," Danny said, assuming a superior air. "I think I know more about it than you do."

Alfred immediately saw the good sense in this and sat back on his haunches to watch. Danny removed his penknife and began trimming the leaves away from the stems.

"I only want to smoke the good stuff," he said.

Alfred nodded admiringly. Danny continued cutting until he had several half-moons of brown leaf. He studied the materials, trying to decide how best to roll them. He picked them up and turned them this way and that. Alfred was beside himself. He could hardly keep his hands off the leaves. Finally, Danny decided that Alfred was really the man to neatly roll up a bunch of dried leaves.

"Alfred," he said, "why don't you roll 'em and I'll smoke 'em?"

Danny could tell by the expression on Alfred's face that this arrangement was tremendously attractive, but he shrank back.

"I better not."

"All right. I'll do everything."

Danny took the leaves and purposely rolled a scraggly, disreputable-looking cigar. This was too much for Alfred. If Danny was going to finally smoke a cigar, Alfred could not stand to have it be this travesty. Danny held his pathetic cigar out enticingly, and Alfred took it in trembling fingers, unrolled it, laid the leaves in a clever pattern, added more where needed, and rolled an amazingly cigar-like product, nearly collapsing the cardboard box in his effort to get it as tight as possible.

"Alfred, that is great," Danny said, taking the cigar and holding it out admiringly. "The Bagley Special!"

Alfred blushed a deep shade of pink.

"Light me up, Alfred."

Alfred clearly had reservations about further participation, but the chance to put a flame to his creation was too enticing to pass up. He scratched a match on the sole of his shoe and lit the Bagley Special. Danny puffed furiously and blew out a cloud of noxious smoke. Alfred burst into delirious laughter. Danny struck various smoking poses, each one of which drove Alfred to an increased level of hysteria. He was rolling in the weeds like a madman, so convulsed that Danny snubbed out the cigar and sat motionless. Still Alfred rolled and howled until they heard the voice of doom.

"Boys, what's going on out there?"

10

Alfred went stiff at the sound of his father's voice, his uncontrollable mirth replaced by dry fear.

"Come out of the weeds," Mr. Bagley said. "Walk this way," he added, using one of his favorite phrases.

It was a command that could not be ignored. Alfred rose up and proceeded like a robot toward his father. Danny raced ahead to do damage control.

"Hi, Mr. Bagley," he chirped. "Do you know where we could find some fleas?"

Mr. Bagley eyed him suspiciously and rattled his key chain.

"Fleas?" he asked.

"We want to see if we can kill them with tobacco stems. Alfred said you could, but I don't believe it."

Mr. Bagley shifted uncertainly.

"Tobacco stems won't kill fleas," Mr. Bagley said, looking over Danny's head at Alfred, who was moving toward them ever more slowly.

Danny wished Alfred was quicker on the uptake, but he had been undone by the magnitude of his crime. Tobacco and matches together. To Alfred's way of thinking, nothing could possibly stand between him and his father's belt.

"See, Alfred, I told you. Fleas don't care about tobacco stems."

"Huh," Alfred said, still some distance away and slowing by the second.

"You're wrong!" Danny shouted.

"Don't raise your voice, Danny," Mr. Bagley said. "People might think you were angry."

"Yes, sir. Sorry."

"Tobacco stems don't kill fleas, but they do drive them away. Do you mean to say that you boys were out in the weeds looking for fleas?"

"Yes, sir!" Danny said loudly, hoping Alfred would pick up on his clue. "We left the stems back in there. Want me to go get them?"

"No. We can do without those tobacco stems. Don't you two have anything better to do than look for fleas? If that's the case, I think Alfred could spend his time studying the Bible in his room. What was so funny?"

Danny was much relieved now that Mr. Bagley was coming to the point. Apparently, he had not seen or smelled smoke; rather, he had heard suspicious mirth coming from the weeds, and for Mr. Bagley, where there was mirth there was a good possibility of ungodly behavior.

"We have fleas at my house," Danny said.

"Is that so?"

Danny could see that Mr. Bagley's interest was piqued. This was excellent. Now to go back and soften the lie.

"We've seen a couple."

Mr. Bagley was crestfallen but not completely.

"Where there are two, there can be many more," he said. "And Alfred was laughing at the fleas in your house?"

"He couldn't control himself."

"Is that right?" Mr. Bagley asked Alfred, who had arrived on the scene in a glazed-over state.

"Yes, sir," he answered automatically.

Alfred could be counted on to answer ninety percent of his father's questions with "Yes, sir." Danny felt that things were falling into place nicely, and he iced the cake by assuming the melancholy demeanor of a kid with flea problems. Mr. Bagley looked him over reflectively.

"You're welcome to have lunch with us, Danny," he said after a moment. "Come inside, boys."

With that, Mr. Bagley moved off toward the breezeway. The looking-for-fleas-in-the-weeds story was patently ridiculous, but adults believed kids to be capable of incredible stupidity. Danny often depended on that fact of life.

"What happened?" Alfred whispered.

"You laughed at the fleas," Danny said through clenched teeth.

"The fleas?" Alfred replied too loudly.

"Anybody can have fleas," Mr. Bagley said over his shoulder.

"I didn't know you had fleas," Alfred whispered and started to giggle.

"Alfred!" said Mr. Bagley sternly.

Alfred shut up immediately, and the boys followed Mr. Bagley into the house where Mrs. Bagley was laying out the lunchtime meal in the dining area adjacent to the kitchen. If Mr. Bagley had not come home for lunch, as he often did not, the meal might have been sandwiches, but today she had fixed slices of ham, lima beans, greens, and fresh biscuits. As always, there was sweet iced tea in wavy glasses with silver threads running through them. Mr. Bagley took his favorite seat, with his back to the kitchen so he could look out the window.

The moments just before a meal at the Bagley house were always agonizing for Danny because everyone had to hold hands while the blessing was said, usually by Alfred. Every now and then, Mr. Bagley would delegate the chore to his wife or would do it himself. Danny cringed when Mr. Bagley did it. He was an impressive man, too portly, but with strong features and a wealth of dark curly hair. His voice was commanding, and when he lit into the blessing, it was enough to send a chill down your spine, altogether too much religious fervor for a simple midday meal.

Occasionally, Mr. Bagley would ask Danny to say the blessing. This was awkward because the Catholic Church was very specific on the subject of whether or not Catholics should pray with Protestants. The correct answer to that dilemma was "not." So, just being in the room while Protestants were praying was a dangerous situation, and when you acquiesced to the hand-holding, you were probably increasing your time in purgatory. Danny figured if you actually agreed to pray yourself, the ante shot up considerably, and he could not go that far. Besides, it irked him that Baptists had a "blessing" and Catholics had a "grace." If a guy asked for a blessing, would it be polite to provide a grace? There were endless confusions in the matter of religion.

Today, however, Alfred got the call, and in his usual unaffected way ran through a quick recitation: "Lord, we thank you for this food, in Christ's name, Amen." As he was doling out the food, Mr. Bagley made conversation.

"I found the boys out in the weeds, Mrs. Bagley."

Danny was amazed that the two addressed each other so formally. He assumed it was done for his benefit. Surely when they didn't have a stranger in the house, they lowered the tone a bit. His own parents often called each other "Mama" and "Daddy," which, he realized, probably sounded strange to Alfred. Abigail's parents called each other by their first names, Dick and Louise. Why couldn't people get together on these things? It was like they were conspiring to make it confusing for kids.

"It's getting hot, Mr. Bagley. Danny and Alfred were probably cooler out there."

"That's probably it," Mr. Bagley said, winking at Danny and Alfred.

"I thought they might go swimming later if it doesn't rain."

Mr. Bagley looked at Danny.

"Should Danny go with that bandage on his hand?"

"I wouldn't get it wet," Danny said.

This was a complete lie, but there was no reasoning with adults in these matters. He had already had the bandage muddy and wet that very morning with no ill effect, but nothing could be gained by pointing that out. He would only seem careless. However, while Mr. Bagley was looking him over, Danny had a brilliant inspiration. He scratched his arm as if suffering from a flea bite. Mr. Bagley looked away.

"If his mother gives Danny permission, Alfred can go with him. Just to the pool and straight back."

"Tell your father thank you," Mrs. Bagley said.

"Thank you," said Alfred.

"Thank you what?" asked Mrs. Bagley.

"Thank you, sir."

"That's all right, son. Be careful," Mr. Bagley said.

The rest of the meal passed with Danny and Alfred on their best behavior so as not to provoke a change in the swimming decision; however, there was one singular moment. Midway through lunch, the biscuits were exhausted, and Mrs. Bagley got up to get more. While she was up, Mr. Bagley noticed his glass was empty, and, without bothering to turn around, he held the glass up over his shoulder and said sternly, "Tea!" Mrs. Bagley was fumbling with the biscuits and did not come running with her usual speed. "Tea!" Mr. Bagley repeated after five seconds, and after five more, he added, "Woman, walk this way!"

"I'm coming, Charles. Give me a moment, please."

A combination of disbelief and anger crossed Mr. Bagley's face, but in the next second, his glass was full, and he lowered it to the table in a state of confusion. Meanwhile, Mrs. Bagley settled into her chair.

Danny wondered if Mrs. Bagley might get the belt later that day. The remainder of the meal passed without incident. Afterward, Danny agreed to meet Alfred in an hour. Under no circumstances would Mrs. Bagley let Alfred leave for swimming less than an hour after eating. It was no use to argue that it took twenty minutes to pedal over to the Springs. She would not be swayed. What with the waiting for the food to settle, and for the weather to show itself favorable and figuring in Alfred's strict deadline for returning in the afternoon, they would probably have only three hours at the pool, which was hardly worth the money, but Danny wanted to swim. He went home to get his trunks.

Danny was happy to find that things had settled down in the Ryan house. His mother was washing something in the back room, and he hoped he could get in and out without having to talk to anyone. He went into the closet between the living room and bedroom and found his trunks on the shelf where his things were kept. He closed the door and put his trunks on in the darkness. As usual he would ride over in just his trunks and a T-shirt. That would save the extra money needed for a locker in the changing area. Alfred might bring more stuff. He got very cold when he swam.

When Danny stepped out of the closet, Ruth called him, so he went into the bedroom. She was lying there with the covers up to her neck. Her eyes were still red from the morning's crying. It was depressing to see his sister so upset. Normally, she faced her own problems and those of the family with a saintly calm. He steeled himself.

"Hi," he said.

"Are you going swimming?"

"I think so," Danny replied. "Alfred's mother still has to okay the weather," he added, rolling his eyes.

"What about your hand?"

"It'll be fine."

"Let me look."

This was just the sort of thing Danny had hoped to avoid, but there was nothing to be done except move to the bedside and let Ruth carefully undo the bandage. The wound looked generally better, but the flap of skin that had been torn off his palm had turned a whitish grey.

"That should come off," Ruth said.

"Why don't we let it come off on its own?" Danny said hopefully.

"It's in the way, sweetie. It won't hurt if we cut on the white part. Really, it should be taken off to promote healing."

Danny did not feel that he could argue with his sister on matters of healing. He looked on with his teeth clenched as Ruth tugged at the flap, which proved to be stuck down on the raw flesh underneath. Danny shivered.

"Go get a damp cloth so we can soften it up."

Though it was the last thing he wanted to do, he went into the kitchen and dampened a cloth. Luckily, his mother was out back hanging clothes on the line, so he did not have to explain himself.

"Bring some alcohol!" Ruth called.

She couldn't be thinking of putting alcohol on it! He considered fleeing, but something compelled him to grab a bottle of rubbing alcohol from the bathroom cabinet and go back to his sister. He found her arranging items on a tray in her lap. These had come from the nightstand, where she stored all sorts of medical things. She looked up and Danny handed her the washcloth.

"This is one of the clean ones, right?"

"Yeah."

"Just hold it in your hand for a while."

Danny sat on the edge of the bed with the damp cloth in his hand and watched as Ruth stuck a pair of curved nail scissors into the neck of the alcohol bottle. He gave himself over to a building sense of dread. It was like standing in the line for the confessional. You knew you were in for a humbling experience, but there was no point in running. Sooner or later he would have to face this skin flap thing. It might as well be with Ruth. She knew about doctoring, or at least she had seen a lot of doctors. After five minutes, she put Danny's hand down on the tray, opened it, and removed the cloth.

"Don't make a claw, sweetie. Open your hand wide."

Danny had been looking away and was not aware he was making a claw, but he saw she was right. He stretched his hand open and was happy to see the skin flap slide free. Ruth took the curved end of the nail scissors and lifted the edge. It came up and she grabbed it gently between her thumb and forefinger.

"See where it's pink?" she asked, indicating an area near the base of the flap. "We wouldn't want to cut there because that's still alive."

Danny nodded vigorously in agreement.

"Cut way up!"

"Not too far. You'll be surprised."

Danny wanted to say he was already as surprised as he could stand. Poor Ruth! Doctors had been doing this sort of thing to her for so many years that she could no longer get the creeps.

"Are you ready?" Ruth asked.

"Okay," Danny said, looking away.

He felt a tug, which sent a wave of fear through him, and then nothing. After a moment, he peered around.

"All done," Ruth said cheerfully.

She was examining his hand. The flap of skin was nowhere in sight.

"Oh good. It's nice and clean, but we'll put some peroxide on it."

She poured a little liquid on it and watched intently as the wound foamed faintly.

"It's not boiling much at all. Very good."

The rest was easy. She squeezed a big dab of ointment onto the raw area, but Danny felt little discomfort as she spread it gently over the surface, then applied some gauze, and a nice tight bandage over that. She used plenty of hardy adhesive tape all the way around his hand.

"You should keep this dry," Ruth said. Danny opened his mouth, and she added, "Don't bother claiming you won't get it wet. I know you will. But don't play with the rocks, okay?"

Ruth was referring to the occasional chunks of cement that could be found on the bottom of the Springs Pool. Adventurous swimmers liked to dive for them.

"Okay."

Danny kissed Ruth goodbye, waved to his mother through the back window, and shouted, "Pool!" She waved back. He held up the quarters from the table and added, "Thanks!" She waved again. He picked up his bike and pushed it over to Alfred's house, where he found Alfred in the front yard staring at the sky.

"Looks pretty good," Danny said.

"What about those clouds?" Alfred said nervously.

"That's nothing," Danny replied, but he knew that nothing could turn into something very quickly on a Florida afternoon.

"If it rains, the book will get wet," Alfred said casually.

He was talking about Abigail's book. Danny had forgotten it in the drama of being summoned by Mr. Bagley. He had left Nancy Drew out in the weeds.

"Why didn't you get it?" Danny asked.

Alfred just shrugged his shoulders.

"Chicken," Danny muttered as he went into the weeds, but he couldn't blame Alfred.

Danny knew that he himself was chicken about a lot of things, and he certainly understood being afraid of your dad. Like everyone else, Alfred was a puzzle to Danny. He wouldn't go off the high board at the Springs, but he would chase fish up under a ledge in the creek with his hands and capture them. Danny would not think of groping around with his naked hands under a creek bank. He thought of the alligator turtle and shivered. In that way, he was a bigger chicken than Alfred.

Danny arrived at the cigar-smoking spot and looked around. He found the remains of the cigar, which he buried to conceal the evidence of their crime, but the book was gone. He thrashed in the weeds, but he knew it was useless. If it was there, it would be in plain sight. He returned to Alfred.

"I put it where it will be okay," he said.

Alfred nodded, and Danny marveled once again at the magnificent way Alfred accepted the improbable. He had no interest in what safe place Danny could have found during his two minutes in the weeds. Sometimes this characteristic was exasperating, but today it was welcome. That missing book could destroy their chances for a good time if Alfred suspected his dad had found it. But if *The Mystery at the Moss-Covered Mansion* was going to cause trouble for Alfred somewhere down the road, there was nothing to be done about it. If it wasn't, why bring it up? It was certainly no reason to spoil a trip to the pool.

"Alfred, I think it's going to be clear," said Mrs. Bagley from behind the screen door. "You can go on with Danny now, but be home by five-thirty."

"Yes, ma'am."

Alfred got his bike, and soon the two were flying down the river road toward the Springs. Fifteen minutes of hard pedaling took them to the entrance of the pool. Inside the foyer, Danny paid the admission charge and walked through the changing area without stopping. Alfred got a locker, but Danny didn't wait for him. He waded through the shallow trough of disinfectant at the locker room exit and emerged into the bright sunlight.

The Springs Pool was composed of two main areas, the walled-in spring and the short spring run that emptied into the Hillsborough. Some of the water from the spring left the pool by way of two slides that swimmers were allowed to go down. The rest of it was emptied by an artificial waterfall between the slides. From an exalted throne over the waterfall, the lifeguard watched the swimmers in the main pool. Every part of the pool was ten or more feet deep, so any young kid who wanted to swim in it had to pass a test, which consisted of swimming confidently from one side of the pool to the other, a distance of thirty yards. After one such performance, the lifeguards remembered you or pretended to.

The spring run was a short river of crystal water, its bottom covered with waving green plants. Close to the spring, the spring run took a turn and formed a wide bend. In this bend was a sunbathing raft. Swimming out to the raft was another big step in mastering the Springs. Beyond the bend was a much tamer stretch with a sand beach and a gently sloping bottom where it was safe for little kids to play. Danny had played there when he first started coming to the Springs, and Alfred still preferred it. He could happily sit in waist-deep water for long periods of time, watching the minnows nipping at his toes. If Danny approached him and disturbed the minnows, Alfred would look up reproachfully. Danny had asked his dad why minnows congregated around people's feet and had been told they were after the dead skin being shed. Alfred was unfazed by this information.

"They can have it" was all he said.

Alfred was not a strong swimmer and did not like the big pool, so today Danny didn't wait for him. They would get together later, but first Danny wanted to immerse himself, and not in Alfred's timid way of wading out to his knees and slowly lowering himself down. Danny wanted a quick and total experience. As he approached the pool's edge, he steeled himself for the shock of diving into the spring. On a hot day, the water felt icy at first, but after a period of adjustment, it was great.

The pool was not crowded, but an unusual number of people were standing at the edge, peering into the water. Danny ignored them and took a flying leap into the pool.

Once under the surface, he spotted something fascinating: a diver with an air tank was circling the boil of the spring. Danny had heard about these inspections but had never seen one, so he descended for a closer look, engrossed by the bubbles rising out of the diver's regulator. When he was a few feet away, the diver turned over and stared up at him. This was very gratifying, but at that same moment Danny felt a hand grasp his hair from above, and he was roughly forced upward. He tried to free himself, but he got water in his mouth and started to choke. By the time he broke the surface, he was in bad shape and had to be towed like a baby to the edge of the pool, where he lay gasping for air. A lifeguard stood towering over him.

"I said 'Nobody in the pool!'"

"He didn't hear that," said a voice from the crowd.

"I blew the damn whistle!"

"When?" Danny sputtered.

"When you jumped in the damn pool!" the lifeguard shouted.

Danny knew that he had done something wrong, but he wondered why the lifeguard was so mad. He looked around questioningly and saw the diver pop to the surface only a couple of feet away.

"You're gonna have to stay out because you can't pay attention!" the lifeguard growled.

"Simmer down, Frank," said the diver. "He's okay. I know him."

Danny felt sure he was not acquainted with any divers and immediately feared this mistake would somehow increase his guilt. He shook his head, but the lifeguard was looking at the diver.

"Okay, but he's your responsibility."

With that, the lifeguard strode back toward his perch. Danny was withering under the stares of the onlookers, and he blushed at the thought of how he must have looked, flopping like a fish on the pool rim. He was about to flee the scene when the diver heaved himself up next to Danny and pushed back his mask. It was Al Gallagher.

"You're a good swimmer," Al said, blowing through his mouthpiece and sending a spray of mist outward.

Danny glanced around and noticed how the crowd's attitude had changed from pitying to envying. A moment before, he had been an ineffectual rule-breaker, and now he was chums with a frogman. He watched as Al looked over at the lifeguard, raised his arm above his head, and made a couple of circles in the air with his index finger extended. The lifeguard blew his whistle, and the patrons began jumping back into the spring.

"You gave Frank a scare," Al said.

This was news to Danny. Frank had looked anything but scared.

"He was scared?"

"That he'd drowned you. He roughed you up for no good reason. Now he's seen what can happen. It's a valuable lesson for him."

Al looked around at the remaining bystanders.

"Good thing this kid is so tough!" he said. "Might've had a bad situation otherwise."

II

~~~

Al shrugged out of his air tank, then slipped off his fins and handed them to Danny.

"How about carrying these for me?"

Danny took the fins and watched as Al heaved his tank over his shoulder for the short walk to the locker room. Danny walked along, trying not to feel important, but he did anyway.

"You left in a hurry yesterday," Al said. "How come?"

"I don't remember."

"That surprises me," Al replied. "We were sorry to see you go. Buddy and I could have used some help with Bart. He was in one of his moods."

Danny stopped walking. He wanted no more of this conversation about a father in a mood. Al turned around and looked at him inquisitively. Danny didn't know what to do next, but he didn't have to do anything because Alfred ran up, shivering with excitement.

"You've got an Aqua-Lung!"

"What makes you think that?" Al asked.

"That's it right there!" Alfred said, pointing to the tank.

"Well, look at that," Al responded.

"Can I breathe through it?"

"That can be arranged," Al said. "Come to the shop sometime and I'll show you how."

Al took his fins from Danny and started toward the locker room.

"Where did you learn?" Alfred asked, desperate to delay Al's departure.

"Picked it up during the war," Al replied. "See you boys later."

"Are you going to the swap shop now?" Alfred asked.

"In a while," Al said, disappearing into the building. Danny could almost hear the clanking of Alfred's mind, weighing the pros and cons of a visit to Al's Swap Shop. It would be a second violation of his boundaries in three days. He had miraculously escaped the consequences of the first. If he were caught a second time, a whipping was inevitable. On the other side was the enticing promise of breathing canned air through a rubber mouthpiece. Never in his life had he faced so hard a choice.

Danny felt he must act. With all the tension in the Ryan house, Danny could ill afford to be without Alfred's distracting company, so he found himself in the unusual position of supporting the boundaries he usually despised.

"Let's swim today," Danny said. "The swap shop will always be there."

Alfred looked doubtful. This was an Aqua-Lung, after all. Danny could see that Alfred's lips were still blue from having sat in the water so long.

"You look chilly," Danny continued. "Why don't we go over and get some of that delicious sulphur water?"

"Okay," Alfred answered, after an agonized pause.

Danny congratulated himself on this brilliant stroke of distraction. As always, Alfred's mood lifted as they approached the little gazebo where the sulphur water gushed up in a thick column. Surrounding this fountain was a circular bench where people were presumably meant to sit between drinks. However, though the gazebo was a charming structure, it was seldom visited by patrons of the Springs Pool. Sad to say, the sulphur caused the immediate area to smell like a sewer. Most people turned back halfway up the path and fled with their fingers clamped over their noses. If the freshwater spring and its run were a bit of heaven, the sulphur spring was a bit of hell, but prettily packaged.

Danny watched with amusement as Alfred climbed the bench and leaned in to gobble several mouthfuls. He turned to Danny and smiled, sulphur water dripping off his chin. Then he took another mouthful and spit it at Danny, who jumped back and watched it sink into the ground.

"Nice move, Alfred."

"I could have hit you if I wanted," Alfred said.

Even though he knew this was true, Danny looked off into the distance as if in disbelief, but what he saw there knocked all pretense out of his head.

Alfred saw Danny's eyes widen and swung around to observe the cause. Near where the spring run emptied into the Hillsborough, there was a footbridge spanning the run. Standing on the bridge, looking out over the river, was Buddy, which for Alfred meant nothing, but what did impress him was the person standing next to Buddy. It was Donna, the cigar girl.

"That's her!" Alfred whispered.

As the boys watched in fascination, she reached over and lightly touched Buddy's cheek.

"What's she doing?" Alfred asked.

Danny shrugged, but both of them knew something funny was going on. The girl kept her fingers there for only a moment, and then she and Buddy walked across the bridge to the other side of the spring run.

"Let's go see where they're going," Alfred said, setting off toward the bridge.

Danny hung back. Accidentally seeing people on a footbridge was one thing; creeping after them was another. He wondered if his guardian angel would approve. But Alfred was off and running, and Danny felt responsible for him. What's more, in his deepest heart, he wanted to see what would happen next.

By the time the boys got to the bridge, Buddy and the girl were on a spit of land bordered on one side by the spring run and on the other by the Hillsborough. It was a grassy area with many trees and a few picnic tables. This part of the springs complex didn't have much to do with swimming, so Danny seldom spent time there. On the weekends, families ate meals on the tables, but on weekdays it was popular with older teenagers. Danny had never understood why.

The boys slowed to let the couple disappear around a bend and then scampered across the bridge. Here they proceeded with more stealth, and the stealthier they got, the worse Danny felt. Darting from one bush to the next brought them to within fifty feet of the couple, who had stopped to sit on one of several benches facing out on the Hillsborough. Danny had once sat on that bench for about ten seconds but had deserted the spot out of a conviction that nothing would ever happen there. Now something was happening, but neither of the boys could tell exactly what.

The couple sat quietly, looking out over the river. Donna had her arm around Buddy's shoulder. This was odd. Danny knew from the movies that it should be the other way around. Danny noticed how different they were. Buddy was blond and ruddy. The girl was dark-haired, with silky olive skin. She raised her hand and stroked Buddy's hair. Buddy shivered.

"Let's get out of here, Alfred," Danny whispered.

"No. I want to see."

"They're not doing anything."

"I don't care!"

Danny could hardly believe that soft-spoken Alfred had raised his voice, but he was not the only one who had heard. The couple on the bench turned around and stared at the spot where the boys were hiding. Danny and Alfred retreated toward the bridge at top speed. When they had crossed to the other side, they looked back, but no one was following. Danny glanced questioningly at Alfred, but he walked off on his own without saying anything. Danny followed behind and watched him wade into the shallows and plop down in disgust.

Danny wandered back to the main pool, hoping Alfred would recover his good humor if left alone with the minnows. He thought about getting into the line for the high dive, but several older guys were doing flips, and he did not want to look stupid by comparison. Frank was still sitting in the lifeguard's chair, and Danny tried a little wave in his direction. To his surprise, Frank waved back, and not in an unfriendly way. Danny started to feel better.

He decided to dive for rocks, so he inhaled and exhaled several times and plunged into the pool, streaking for the bottom where he found a chunk of concrete the size of a bread loaf. It was heavy, but Danny thought he could worry it to the surface. He cradled it in his arms and struggled upward. About five feet from the surface his lungs began to heave, but he managed to control himself. He caught on to one of several ladders located around the pool and pulled his head into the air just as he involuntarily exhaled. It was a close call, and Danny was pleased with himself.

After he got his breath back, he decided to try an even more dangerous trick. This one involved eliminating his buoyancy by expelling all the air from his lungs. In this state, he would release his hold on the ladder and allow the rock to carry him at great speed to the bottom. The ride would be exhilarating, but once on the bottom he would have no oxygen reserve, so he would have to act quickly. He would immediately drop the rock, of course, but even having done so he would not float without air in his lungs. If he did not use muscle power to fight to the surface, he would drown.

This procedure required some exacting tolerances, and Danny was always in distress by the time he broke the surface and got a good gulp of air. He had never confessed this activity to anyone because he knew it would sound insane. He was not sure why he did it, except that he felt good afterward.

Danny began his routine by seating himself on the bottom step of the ladder with the rock in his lap. Then he took several deep breaths in succession until he began to feel a little lightheaded. At this point, he exhaled as forcefully as possible, finishing his purge with a pumping action in his mouth and throat that drew out so much additional air that he could feel his lungs contract. With that, he slipped off the last rung of the ladder and plummeted downward. His feet hit the bottom with a muffled thud and he stood for a moment, his lungs already starting to register mild distress.

On this day, Danny ignored that signal and did something unusual. He did not immediately drop the rock and head for the surface. Instead, he tried walking like a deep-sea diver. After a couple of steps, he looked up and could see the sun shining in the water above him.

At that moment, his lungs began to heave. Danny dropped the rock and pushed off the bottom, but he was moving in slow motion. He knew that if he stopped pulling and kicking, he would drop to the bottom and drown. The feeling in his chest was the worst he had ever experienced. The shiny surface was close. His right hand went through, but the last two feet were coming hard. His left hand went through. He kicked more violently. The crown of his head was out. It was horrible to be so close yet still in danger. When Danny finally lost control and took his desperate breath, his mouth was barely out. He breathed in a spray of water and began coughing violently but he managed to grasp the rim of the pool, where he lay gasping. For the second time that afternoon, Danny drew a crowd.

"What the hell am I supposed to do with you?"

Danny looked up and saw Frank towering over him once again. Even if Danny could have spoken, he would have had nothing to say in his defense. As it was, he turned his head away and wheezed. Frank blew his whistle and dispersed the onlookers.

"You've had it," he said. "Go kill yourself somewhere else."

Danny looked up and saw Frank pointing toward the exit.

"I wasn't hurting anybody."

"Take a hike."

"Can I come back?"

"Not today."

"But sometime."

"Yeah, yeah. Just try to stay under control, for God's sake! Show some sense."

Danny got to his feet and walked toward the beach to tell Alfred what had happened. He hadn't gone far when Frank blew his whistle.

"I said 'Out!' "

"I have to tell my friend."

"Out!"

Danny changed course and went toward the exit, a big revolving gate. Luckily, his T-shirt was nearby. He picked it up and pushed his way out. When Danny was on the other side of the fence, Frank went back to his chair. Danny stood hanging on to the chain-link fence for quite a while, hoping Alfred would come into view, but after a while the sun beating on his head drove him away. He went to the front entrance and asked if he could get a message to someone inside.

"You the kid who got thrown out?" the attendant asked.

"I guess so."

"Did you get thrown out or didn't you?"

"Yes, sir."

"I'll have to ask the manager," the attendant said. "Hey, Bud. Kid who got thrown out wants me to find somebody for him."

"No can do!" said a voice from another room. "We got a rule. Tell him not to get thrown out."

"You heard it, kid."

Danny walked out into the sunlight. The heat from the asphalt parking lot burned his feet. Beyond the fence, the pool grounds swam in the heat like a cool mirage. Danny felt his back burning and put on his T-shirt. If only he could go home . . . but he was captive. If Danny left abruptly, Alfred might feel hurt. Even worse, his parents would want to know why the boys had split up. When they found out, they might be disinclined to let Alfred go to the pool again with the type of kid who got thrown out.

Danny plodded around to the fence where he could see inside. Though he despised the idea, he thought perhaps he could persuade some passerby to find Alfred for him. Danny didn't like approaching strangers, but maybe a friendly adult would inquire about his welfare if he looked pathetic enough. Danny walked to the fence and hung on it as if he were on the edge of collapse. He stared longingly into the distance. He placed his left hand so that his bandage showed to good advantage. Pretty soon, he began to feel as pathetic as he looked. When his tongue started to protrude, he decided to give it up.

He figured it must be nearly four, which meant that Alfred couldn't stay inside much longer. He went to the front desk again and got a pen and paper with which he wrote a note: "Waiting by the Springs Theater. Come there before you go home. Danny." He stuck it on Alfred's bicycle and rode over to the theater. This late in the day, there was plenty of shade under the marquee. Danny amused himself by looking at the posters for the coming attractions.

He was especially interested in one called *The Creature from the Black Lagoon*. It looked scary, the type of movie Danny anticipated with a shiver, but after he had seen it, wished he had not. It usually took several days to shrug off the fear. In the middle of the night he would awaken and stare at the window, expecting to see a monster appear in the moonlight. Even with Loretta on the couch with him, he would be terrified. She was brave, but so what? Against the type of monsters Danny feared, bravery didn't count. You were no problem to them. They just destroyed you and went on with their business.

This reminded him that Loretta would not be there when he got home, and that thought brought him back to the many other vexations that had cropped up lately. They seemed innumerable. He began to shake his head and rub his scalp vigorously. Then he let out a yell. In an instant, the movie attendant came out of the theater, looking around in alarm. She saw Danny.

"Did you do that?"

Danny nodded.

"For heaven's sake, why?"

Danny wasn't sure himself, but he knew he could not get at it without giving his life's history. That was out of the question, so he just gestured at the *Creature from the Black Lagoon* poster. The attendant looked thoughtful.

"Did that scare you?"

Danny shrugged his shoulders.

"It's just a movie."

Danny nodded.

"You're okay?"

Danny nodded again.

"Can you speak?"

"Sure."

"Young man, I think you should go home and talk with your mother about shouting. It upsets people."

Danny nodded again.

"Go on now. I'm a little worried about you."

"Yes, ma'am."

Danny left the front of the theater and went around to the side where he could keep an eye out for Alfred. In a few minutes he saw him pedal up to the ticket booth, exchange a few words with the attendant, and ride toward where Danny was hiding.

"Alfred!"

Alfred swerved and stopped, looking at Danny in a queer way.

"Everybody's talking about you," he said. "What happened?"

"I don't know. I didn't do anything very different."

"They threw you out of the pool!"

"That lifeguard is real strict."

"And the movie lady said you screamed."

"Everybody is paying way too much attention to me. I can't make a move without somebody complaining."

Alfred nodded. Danny was talking his language now. The two boys stood there for several moments looking at the ground.

"Let's go to the swap shop," Alfred said at last.

"That's no good."

"Why not?"

"I don't want you to get in trouble."

"I won't!"

"Come on! You're always saying how somebody might report on you."

"We could go around back," Alfred suggested, rubbing his toe in the dirt.

"We can't get in through there."

"I'm going," Alfred said, pedaling about twenty feet and then stopping.

He looked back expectantly. Danny could see that Alfred was in a funny mood. He might cave in if Danny refused, but on the other hand he might not, which would put him on his own in a shady enterprise. He was sure to foul it up.

"Okay," Danny said, "but it's getting late."

"Just for a few minutes!" Alfred shouted and headed down one of Sulphur Springs' residential streets.

The rear of Al's Swap Shop could be approached by going down a little-used alley. Behind the shop was a small yard enclosed by a chain-link fence. In the yard were some outdoor items and Al's truck. There was a gate, but it was locked, and there was no way to get to the front door of the shop from the back. Danny didn't know what Alfred had in mind, but it would probably fail, and that would be the end of it. By the time Danny caught up, Alfred was already climbing the fence.

"Alfred! That's trespassing."

"No it's not. He said to come over."

"He didn't mean like this."

"You don't know that."

"I didn't hear him say 'Climb into my locked yard.'"

"He doesn't care. He likes us."

By this time, Alfred had reached the big back door of the swap shop and had banged loudly on it. After a short wait, he banged again.

"He can't hear," Danny called. "Let's go."

Alfred ignored this plea, went to a nearby stack of lumber, picked out a short length of two-by-four, and started striking the door rhythmically. He continued until the door began to slide open. Then he stepped back and waited. Al Gallagher stuck his head out quizzically. He looked down at Alfred, who said, "Hey, Mr. Gallagher!" Then he looked past Alfred at Danny, still standing respectfully on the other side of the fence. Danny shrugged his shoulders. Al looked back down at Alfred. He was quiet for an uncomfortably long time. It began to dawn on Alfred that he might have gone over the line. He took a step back.

"You," Al said ominously, pausing to glance again at Danny and then back to Alfred, "can start calling me Al," and with that he threw the door open.

Alfred plunged in, hoping to find himself in the secret back room, but no. There was only a large receiving area and another door leading to one arm of the main shop.

"Where is everything?" Alfred asked.

"Where it should be," Al answered, walking out to open the gate for Danny.

Alfred followed along behind.

"Al," he asked," what would you do if a big black cigar appeared in your mouth right now?"

Danny cringed.

"That's easy," Al answered, rattling the key in the padlock on the gate, "because a big black cigar does occasionally appear in my mouth."

Alfred was awestruck.

"What do you do?"

"Well, it would be pretty silly of me to put a cigar in my mouth and not smoke it."

"Oh," Alfred said, obviously disappointed.

"I guess you would prefer me to eat it," Al observed, herding the boys toward the shop.

Alfred burst into maniacal laughter. Danny wished for a moment he was Alfred. It must be wonderful to be so easily diverted, but then he remembered all the restrictions in Alfred's life and put aside his wish. It would be good to be somebody other than Danny Ryan, but as long as he was wishing, he would set his sights higher. Al took the boys into the shop and called to his assistant.

"Bruce, take down that old French rig. Little Al's going to look it over."

Alfred was off like a rocket to pester Bruce. Danny walked slowly into the shop and stared around. The shop had momentarily lost its tang. He heard Alfred ask, "What's that?" and Bruce reply, "That's the regulator. If you tried to breathe out of the tank without that, you'd blow up!" Alfred laughed loudly. Danny heaved a great sigh.

"You're kind of a drip today," Al said.

"I guess so."

"That's not the right answer."

"What?"

"You should tell me to mind my own business."

With that, Al moved off toward the small crowd that had gathered around Bruce and Alfred. Bruce had fitted Alfred with a mask and flippers. Since Alfred was too small to support the weight of the two tanks, Bruce had rested them on a stool and was standing behind Alfred to make sure they didn't tip. Alfred was breathing loudly through the mouthpiece, making swimming motions with his arms. The spectators were much amused, especially an old gentleman.

"Just like my grandson," the man announced gleefully. Alfred extracted his mouthpiece and flapped over to the display window, causing much laughter. He grabbed his kaleidoscope and flapped back.

"Maybe your grandson would like this," he said, holding it out.

"What is it?"

"You look through that end," Alfred explained, pointing.

The man held it up and looked through. Alfred waited patiently as the man turned the kaleidoscope and discovered the slide that brought the different materials into view.

"I like the beans," Alfred said.

"The beans is pretty," the man said without conviction. "What's it worth?"

Alfred stared out from beneath his mask and noted the frayed cuffs on the man's trousers.

"Six cents."

"I notice it ain't all there," the man observed, displaying the broken container.

"A nickel," Alfred said.

"That there's a fair offer," the man replied, fishing in his pants pocket. He extracted a nickel and, with a wink at Al Gallagher, put it in Alfred's palm. Alfred removed his mask and stared down at the shiny coin, but he had hardly had time to enjoy it before Al plucked it out of his hand and replaced it with four pennies.

"Dealer's commission," he explained.

If anything, this increased Alfred's glee.

"I sold it," he said. "Would anyone else like to buy something?"

Danny thought this was just like Alfred, to push a good thing, but several shoppers picked up items and tried to present them to Alfred, who looked up at Al Gallagher.

"Put him behind the register, Bruce."

For the next hour Alfred sat working the swap shop's big turn-of–the-century register, reveling in the sound of the bell whenever the drawer opened. And he made change flawlessly in spite of having gotten a D in arithmetic in the fourth grade. Danny was amazed, and without his noticing it, all his woes went to the back of his mind as he watched Alfred keep store. Danny even helped a lady carry her packages to her car. He came back into the store with a smile on his face. The lady had tried to tip Danny a dime. He had refused, but he felt good about the offer.

"Commerce is an excellent tonic," Al observed, "but we are coming up on closing time."

"What?" Danny asked.

"We open in the morning, and we close in the afternoon."

"What time is it?"

"A little after five."

"Alfred has to be home by five-thirty!"

"The phone's over there. Just call and say you'll be a little late."

Danny ignored this suggestion and rushed over to Alfred.

"We gotta go! It's after five."

Alfred paused with his finger in the air over a cash register key. He turned white, sprinted to the back door, and tried to open it. Locked! He spotted the big latch near the top of the door and began to jump up, pawing at it. Danny raced over and tried to give him a boost, but Al arrived and put a stop to this plan. He turned the boys around and knelt down.

"What's wrong?" he asked.

Neither one would answer. Al studied their faces, then shouted over his shoulder.

"Bruce! I'm going to run Alfred and Danny home."

"What about our bikes?" Alfred asked.

"You may recall that I drive a truck."

Alfred's eyes lit up and the boys bolted for the backyard.

12

~~~~~

Soon they were barreling along Nebraska Avenue with the boys' bikes rattling in the back. Danny was giving directions. Alfred was huddling out of sight on the floorboard.

"What's that all about?" Al asked.

"Alfred gets queasy in trucks," Danny answered.

"I do not!"

"You explain it then," Danny sniffed.

"Never mind," Al said, slowing the truck.

"How come we're stopping?" Alfred asked, starting to rise up.

Danny pushed him down.

"We're picking someone up," he said.

"Who?"

"You'll see later. Just stay out of sight for now."

There was some noise at the rear of the truck and someone hopped on the bed. Alfred could not contain himself. He squirmed upward and peered through the rear window.

"It's him!"

"Okay, now get back down!"

Alfred reluctantly dropped under the dash and resumed watching Al shift gears.

"Go left on Sligh," Danny said.

A few minutes later, they were close to home.

"Could you pull in there?" Danny asked, pointing to an overgrown lot.

"In the weeds?"

"Yes, sir. Behind those tall ones. What time is it?"

"Five twenty-five," Al answered, glancing at his wrist watch.

"You can make it!" Danny said to Alfred.

"They like me to be early," Alfred replied glumly.

By this time, Al had stopped the truck. Danny threw open the door and herded Alfred out.

"Just get back on time and keep your mouth shut. Say, 'We had a good time and stayed as long as we could.'"

"We had a good time and stayed as long as we could," Alfred repeated.

"Try not to say anything else. If they want more, tell about the sulphur water and the minnows. You got cold."

"I *did* get cold."

"That's what I said. Now let's get going."

"Hey, Danny."

The boys looked up and saw Buddy standing by the truck. He had unloaded their bikes for them.

"I saw you two at the pool today," Buddy added.

Danny blushed and looked down.

"My name's Alfred Bagley. What's yours?"

"Buddy Connolly."

"Get going!" Danny shouted at Alfred, bringing him to his senses.

"We had a good time and stayed as long as we could," Alfred muttered, speeding off.

Once Danny had gotten Alfred started, he didn't know what more to say.

"Thanks for the ride, Mr. Gallagher."

"You're welcome, Mr. Ryan. Glad I could help out."

"I was hoping you'd come back and work on the canoe," Buddy said. "Dad won't be a problem."

"I don't think he likes me."

"The funny thing is that he does. He keeps asking, 'Where's that kid who took me down the road? He's got potential.'"

"You're lying."

"No. He wouldn't say anything at all if he didn't like you. Dad has a strange sense of humor. Also, when he drinks, he's in another world."

"What?"

"He sees things. He didn't mean anything yesterday. Come in the morning. He's almost never up before noon."

Danny looked toward Al, but he had climbed back in the truck.

"Okay. I'll come tomorrow."

"Great."

Buddy got in the cab of the truck with Al, and they drove away. Danny could see them talking and laughing through the rear window. He couldn't blame them. The way he and Alfred had been acting must appear strange. He didn't think he'd mind explaining things to them, if an explanation were possible, but the situation was too complicated to sort out. When you put it into words, it sounded stupid, as if everybody involved was an idiot.

He rode slowly home, where he found two banana stalks standing next to the front door. He went in the kitchen. His mother looked up from stirring a pot on the stove.

"Where did the banana stalks come from?" he asked.

"Oh, Abigail left those when she brought your book back."

Danny looked at the table and saw *The Mystery at the Moss-Covered Mansion* lying on it. So Abigail had been spying on them and had picked it up when they left. It was clear he would have to read this accursed book or else she would be trailing him for the rest of his days, leaving it under his nose. She really was something.

"What about the banana stalks?"

"Those are for our flea problem," Mrs. Ryan said. "Supposedly, you leave them in a room, the fleas jump on them, and then you throw the stalk out, fleas and all. And," she added, turning toward him, "that is just one of the ways we can rid ourselves of our fleas. Mr. Bagley came by earlier with a bag of tobacco stems and several helpful suggestions on how to use them. Apparently it is all around the neighborhood that the Ryan house is flea central. I wonder how they got that impression?"

Danny could hear Ruth giggling in the other room.

"Well?"

"I don't know."

"Danny. Your eyes tell me you're lying."

His eyes had let him down again. When would he learn that absolute denials simply did not work? Besides, this flea manipulation was something about which he could level with his mom. She would understand.

"Okay, you caught me. Here's what happened."

"Oh, come in the bedroom," Ruth called. "I want to hear."

Danny and his mother joined Ruth and sat on the bed. Danny thought Ruth was looking paler.

"So what did you tell people about our fleas?" she asked, snuggling down in the covers.

"Well, Alfred and I were out in the weeds smoking a handmade cigar."

"Let's back up," said Danny's mom. "Where did you get the cigar and why did you want to smoke? We let you try a cigarette that time and you hated it."

"I wasn't really smoking. I was just fooling around because Alfred gets such a big kick out of it. One of his favorite stupid questions is 'What would you do if a big black cigar appeared in your mouth?' "

Ruth laughed, and Danny's mom rolled her eyes.

"I think it's cute," said Ruth.

"After a hundred times you might get tired of it," Danny commented.

"Was it one of Daddy's cigars?" Ruth asked apprehensively.

"Nope. The Bagleys put tobacco stems in the goat's stall to drive out the fleas."

"At last, the fleas," Danny's mom said.

"Yeah. And sometimes a lot of leaf is left on a stem, so Alfred saves it, and today he asked me if I would roll a cigar out of those leftover leaves and smoke it."

"And naturally you had to say, 'Yes, Alfred. That sounds like a good idea,'" Danny's mom said.

"It was something to do. Anyway, that's how we wound up in the weeds, but while I was smoking, Mr. Bagley shouted, 'What's going on, boys?' "

"Oh, my goodness," Ruth said. "Did he see you?"

"No. I was afraid he saw the smoke, but he just heard Alfred laughing."

"I'm sure that made him suspicious," Danny's mother said. "They don't go in for laughing over there. But how did the Ryans get fleas?"

"I had to run out to talk to Mr. Bagley before Alfred spilled the whole thing and got a whipping, so I said we were trying to find some fleas to test the tobacco stems on."

"Did you have to say *we* had fleas?"

"He was trying to make the story more believable," Ruth said.

"I know that, dear, but the neighbors already think we are ungodly Catholics, and now we are supposedly infested with fleas. I'd like to preserve what little reputation we have."

"Danny will tell them he was wrong," Ruth said confidently.

Danny winced.

"Couldn't we just pretend we got rid of the fleas?" he asked.

"No. I'm afraid you are going to have to go to the neighbors and say you were fibbing."

"But I did see a flea in the house."

"A flea on the cat does not count, Danny," Mrs. Ryan replied.

Sometimes Danny was astounded by his mother's discernment. Why couldn't she show that insight with her husband? Danny turned his attention to damage control.

"Who do I have to tell, everybody for miles?"

"I don't think our infamy has spread quite that far. I'll tell you what, since you have put on your most convincing mask of sorrow, I'll be satisfied if you just tell the people who are personally involved: Mr. Bagley and the Arnolds."

Danny slapped his forehead.

"How about just Mr. Bagley? He'll tell everybody else."

"No. I've given you my best deal. The sooner you get it over with, the better you'll feel."

"I'll never feel better after this!"

"Don't be silly. I'm sure you will find some clever way to do it. But I want to be very clear about one thing: when you are finished, there must be no doubt in their minds that we have never had a house full of fleas, not even a minor infestation. Do you understand?"

Danny nodded.

"I hear Daddy," she said, and left the room.

Danny let himself fall melodramatically across the bed. He lay there looking at the ceiling.

"At least this gives you a chance to see Abigail again," said Ruth. "I think she likes you."

"What!" Danny said, sitting up.

"Yes, of course."

"She likes me to make fun of," he said.

"Oh no. She speaks very kindly of you."

"You talked to her?"

"Yes, for quite a while this afternoon."

"That's great," Danny sighed, getting up.

"Don't you want to know what she said?"

"No, thanks," he replied, and walked out.

From the living room, Danny could see his father sitting at the kitchen table reading the encyclopedia. The family had a set from 1925 that one of his mother's charity projects had given them. For Danny, this gift was at once frustrating and fascinating. Frustrating because when you tried to do a school project on "flight" you found the subject illustrated with a picture of a biplane. On the other hand, Danny had to admit that it was often fascinating to see what things were like thirty years before, an unbelievably long time in the past by his reckoning. This ancient encyclopedia was his father's favorite reading matter.

As he walked into the kitchen, he observed that his father was reading Volume A. Danny thought that he should have finished that one by now, but his father's reading scheme was not systematic. Danny nodded to his father, picked up *The Mystery at the Moss-Covered Mansion* from the kitchen table, and turned to leave the room.

"Son," his father said.

A chill ran down Danny's spine. He turned around.

"Yes?"

"Do you know what is unique about Arkansas?"

"Nope."

"It is the only place in the United States where diamonds have been discovered."

Danny nodded thoughtfully. His father went back to his reading.

"I would have guessed it was unique for its bad roads," Danny's mother said.

You could never tell how his father would respond to a joke, but his mother never learned. Luckily, Mr. Ryan did not get strange. He only remarked that roads had improved quite a bit since the war.

"Go keep Ruth company," Mrs. Ryan said to Danny. "Dinner will be ready in a little while."

Danny returned to the bedroom and found Ruth leaning back against

a stack of pillows with her eyes closed. He sat down on the bed thinking
that it would be better if Ruth were in the back room near the bathroom.
She was so tired all the time. But his father made that impossible. If only
they lived in a different house!

Danny opened Nancy Drew and started to read. The story began with
plenty of action. Three girls, Nancy, Bess, and George, were forced onto a
detour. The fact that one of the girls was named George gave Danny pause.
This was the first he had heard of such a thing, and he looked at the cover
illustration once again. He assumed the girl in the sports jacket was George.
Anyway, the car radiator boiled over and while Nancy and George looked
for water, Bess searched for a house where she could ask directions.

She wound up at a spooky moss-covered mansion and was frightened
by moaning sounds coming out of it. She took off running and found her
friends. Nancy Drew was all for investigating, so the three approached the
mansion, heard more shrieks coming from within, and were threatened by
a bearded man with a pistol, who ordered them off the property. When he
went back inside, the girls heard shots fired inside the house. Thus ended
chapter one.

It was better than Danny had expected, although there seemed to be an
unnecessary emphasis on golden hair and other such trivia. And Bess was
an irritating, skittish person of the sort who always finds a way to get into
trouble. It was only the first chapter, and she had already torn her linen
frock. Her cousin George was hardly better, having stepped into a lily pond,
ruining her stockings. But why was that important? What this book needed
was less about stockings and frocks and more about people with revolvers.
At this point, Ruth woke from her nap and looked at Danny.

"Is that Abigail's book?" she asked.

"Yeah."

"I loved Nancy Drew."

"You read this stuff?'

"Yes. When I was little, I wanted to be just like her."

"Did you read this one?" he asked, holding up *The Mystery at the Moss-
Covered Mansion.*

"I'm sure I did."

"What happens?"

"I wouldn't want to spoil it for you."

"You won't spoil anything. I just need a few details in case Abigail asks me about it."

"Why don't you two read it together?"

"No way."

"I think she's sweet."

"Get off that, would you!"

Danny stalked to the window and looked into the backyard. In the distance, he could see the chicken yard. His father was out there choosing some chickens to slaughter. These unfortunates would be taken to a corner of the house out of sight of the remaining chickens and put through a grim procedure. His father would wring their necks, cut their heads off, and hang them from a wire to bleed into the ground. The first time Danny had come upon this scene, he had run screaming in the opposite direction. Since both of his parents had been raised around farms, it never occurred to them that their son would be undone by such a commonplace event. They had never reproached him for his cowardice, but he had heard them say he was "sensitive."

"What happened with the chickens?" Danny asked. He was ashamed of having yelled at Ruth and wanted to make up.

"What do you mean?"

"Why did they have to be killed?"

"They didn't lay the way Daddy and Mom expected."

"Why not?"

Ruth looked at Danny for quite some time before answering.

"Daddy thinks . . ."

She looked away.

"What?"

"He thinks someone is poisoning the chickens."

"Who?"

"He doesn't know. He's suspicious of everybody, even us. You've seen him drive up to the store and grab a bag of feed from the bottom of the stack. That's so nobody can poison it."

"Why would anybody want to poison our chickens?"

"I don't know," Ruth said. "Actually, Danny, I don't think anybody does. I believe Daddy just imagines it."

"What's wrong with him?"

"I guess the things he imagines seem very real to him, but he's wrong a lot of the time. You know that."

"Is he insane? That's what Loretta says."

"I don't know what to call it. He's not normal. If I could just get well, things might be better. It's such a drain on the family for me to be so sick."

"You can't help it."

"You're a darling to say that. Give me a hug."

While Danny was hugging Ruth, the phone rang. Their mother answered. Then she said "Yes, Loretta," but after that she began talking too low to hear. The phone conversation went on for several minutes and was followed by some more low talking from the kitchen. Then they heard the door to the back room close forcefully. During this period, Danny and Ruth continued holding on to one another, both listening intently for any clue as to what new storm was brewing. Shortly, their mother appeared in the doorway with a stricken look on her face.

"I have some news," she began.

"Is Loretta all right?" Ruth asked.

"She says she is, but she won't tell me where she's staying."

"Oh."

"She could be camping out in the park for all I know. Danny, do you have any idea where she might be?"

"How would I know?"

"You get around."

"Not where Loretta goes. She hardly says a thing about it."

Mrs. Ryan looked pleadingly at Ruth, who just shook her head.

"She doesn't talk to me either. I think she's always been afraid we'd let something slip to Daddy."

At this point, their father suddenly appeared behind their mother, who whirled around when he touched her shoulder.

"You scared me, Harold!"

Their father said nothing, just stood looking at the three of them for an uncomfortable span of time. Danny could see that his dad was over the edge, staring sideways. There was no telling what strange meaning he was assigning to the events of the last ten minutes and especially to the secret conference he had stumbled into. Danny wondered if his father had heard

Ruth say the phrase "let something slip to Daddy." That would be the worst possible case.

The tension grew. Danny's mom scratched her arm nervously. Danny could have killed her. Why was she moving in a situation like this? You had to stay still! He watched with dread as his father slowly scratched his arm in the same place as his mother had scratched hers. There it was. Anything could happen now. Ruth started to cry.

"Danny," his father said.

What would come next? Danny began to tremble.

"Go get me a cigar."

His father placed a dime on the chest of drawers and left the room. Marjorie went to Ruth and put her arms around her. Danny slumped.

"Go on, Danny. I'll finish dinner. It will be all right."

"Mom, you can't go to work tonight," Ruth said.

"I'll call in. Get going, Danny."

Danny grabbed the dime, climbed on his bike, and took off for Halper's store. When he turned off Florinda onto Sligh Avenue, he wished he could do as Loretta had done, just keep going and never come back. It was impossible, of course, yet he might attempt it if he could be sure he would never again have to endure his father's stare, which was like being scrutinized by one of the robots he saw in science fiction movies at the Springs Theater. They just stood there clicking, processing the data that would tell them whether to ignore the humans or disintegrate them. Whatever the decision, it was based on an alien logic having nothing to do with the merits or intentions of the humans.

In a few minutes, he slid to a halt in front of Halper's. He was ignored by some older boys sitting on the bench in front, putting peanuts in their Cokes. This was a waste of money in Danny's estimation. He preferred to spend his money on a comic book from the selection of used ones in a box at the back of Halper's store. Whereas food could be enjoyed only once, a comic could be read repeatedly. Danny tore his mind away from this subject. He should not be thinking of comic books. He scampered into the store and asked for a King Edward.

"How about a Hav-a-Tampa instead?" said Mr. Halper, smiling. "You look like a man who might like to step up in class."

"Are you out of King Edward?" Danny asked desperately.

"What's wrong, friend? You're shook up."

"My dad wants a King Edward."

"Sure, sure. I was just kidding," he said, reaching into the case. "Here's one right here."

Danny plunked down his father's dime, but Mr. Halper didn't give him the cigar.

"Son, you're white as a sheet. Are you sure you're all right?"

"Yes, sir," Danny said, holding out his hand.

"Why don't you take a comic out of the box back there, no charge. A kid traded in some Disney ones this morning. Aren't those the kind you like?"

This was too much to bear. Danny's father was waiting at home ready to boil over, and Mr. Halper had chosen this worst of all possible moments to take an interest in him. Yet it was kindly intended, so Danny could not scream "Mind your own business!" even though he wished he could. He had to stay under control.

"No thank you, sir."

"No thanks to a comic! I don't believe it. Politeness can be taken too far. I treat all the kids every now and then. Today's your day. Go on now."

Mr. Halper pointed to the back. There was no avoiding this man's generosity. Danny rushed to the comic box and picked the first comic off the top without looking at it. He ran back to the front of the store and put it on the counter.

"Thank you," he said, extending his hand for the cigar.

"Are you sure this is the one you want?" Mr. Halper asked, displaying the comic book distastefully between thumb and forefinger.

Danny saw that he had chosen a horror comic. On the cover was a man's face, half melted away, his deteriorating skull and teeth visible. The source of his predicament was a cylinder of radium hanging in the air just above the remnants of the man's broiled hands. The victim's terrified eyes were goggling downward as his lower lids dissolved.

"Wouldn't you rather have Donald Duck?" Mr. Halper asked solicitously.

Danny opened his mouth as if to answer, but instead he began to laugh, and when he tried to stop, discovered he could not. He put his head on the counter and howled. He looked down and saw a pair of red wax lips in the candy case and found them hysterical as well. He looked up at Mr. Halper's shocked expression and laughed harder. The boys from outside were peeking in the screen door. Danny was on the floor now, writhing.

"You boys get away," said Mr. Halper, banging his palm against the screen.

He went to Danny and dragged him to his feet, but Danny was limp, still wracked by laughter. Mr. Halper shook him. Danny's laughter increased. Then Mr. Halper shook him so hard that his head wobbled.

"That's enough!" he shouted.

Danny's laughter tapered off, and he began to grasp what he had done. He blushed and stepped back out of Mr. Halper's grasp.

"What time is it?" he asked.

"Son, the time is the last thing we should be talking about."

"How long have I been here?"

"Maybe ten minutes."

Ten minutes was a long time. Danny saw the King Edward lying on the counter and grabbed it. Before Mr. Halper could react, he had bolted out the door, but one of the boys outside blocked his way.

"What's so funny?" he asked.

"Nothing," Danny said, moving past the boy to his bike.

He managed to get on, but the boy held it fast. He wasn't a mean boy, but he was showing off for his friends.

"Let me go. I have to get home."

"Don't give me orders!"

Danny could waste no more time. The kid was too big to fight, and he didn't have the time anyway. He got off his bike and started to run, leaving the boy still holding the handlebars. He never saw Mr. Halper come out of the store and never heard him call out, "I've got it, son! You can ride."

Danny could run only so far before he got a pain in his side and had to walk for a while. He alternated running and walking for ten minutes, which brought him near the corner of Florinda and Sligh, where he cut across the Arnold property to save time. He had just entered the banana grove when Abigail stepped into his path.

"Why are you running? Where's your bike?"

"None of your business," he said, brushing past her.

To his surprise, she caught up with him and ran alongside. This was embarrassing. He could have outrun her if he had been fresh, but he had to stop. His side was killing him. He stood gasping, doubled over. Abigail was observing him as if he were a lab specimen.

"You're in bad shape."

"Leave me alone."

"You look like you've seen a ghost."

"Can't you take a hint? What have I ever done to you?"

"Meaning?"

"Oh God," Danny moaned and took off again.

This time Abigail did not follow, and Danny limped the last block to his house without further incident. He had no idea what he would find inside, but he thought it best not to catch his breath. The worse he looked upon arrival, the more convincing he would be in making his excuses. He burst into the house with the cigar extended. His father was not in sight. The door to the back room was closed. His mother was in the kitchen, standing stiffly by the sink.

"Why did you take so long?" she whispered.

"Flat tire," he replied. "Had to run back."

His mother looked at him and took in his heaving chest and the sweat soaking through his T-shirt.

"You poor child," she said, giving him a hug. "I'll take this in to Daddy. You wait a few minutes and then sneak through to the shower. He won't notice."

"Yes, he will!"

"Well, get your swimsuit off the line and use the hose. Things will calm down soon."

Danny turned away, thinking, *That's what she always says.* He walked toward the bedroom to check on Ruth. She was sitting with a dinner tray on her lap but hadn't touched her food. When he entered, she looked up in alarm.

"Oh, Danny. I'm so glad it's you. Did you get the cigar?"

"No problem. What's for dinner?"

"Salisbury steak," she replied, and picked up some mashed potatoes on her fork.

Danny's spirits rose slightly. Salisbury steak was a canned item that he enjoyed, though Loretta called it "mystery meat" and wouldn't touch it.

Danny's mother usually tried to make something fresh for Ruth, but tonight was different.

"Would you like a bite?" Ruth asked.

Danny nodded and went around to the side of the bed. Ruth wiped the mashed potatoes off her fork and loaded it up with steak.

"Open up," she said, "and close your eyes."

This was a game she liked to play, so Danny obliged, and in a moment his taste buds were flooded with the dank goodness of warm Salisbury steak. It melted in his mouth, and for a few seconds life was worth living again.

13

Danny woke in the morning with a slight sunburn. His father had been up in the middle of the night, coughing and smoking his cigar, but he never came out of the back room. His mother had stayed home and tended to Ruth. After his father left in the morning, Danny heard some low talking in the bedroom. He got up, went to the bathroom, and then padded to the bedroom door, where he observed Ruth and his mother fast asleep. They had probably been awake most of the night. He went into the kitchen and fixed himself some cold cereal. He had not taken the first spoonful before Loretta tiptoed in. She held her finger to her lips.

"Bad night?" she whispered.

Danny nodded.

"I saw him go by with the stone face on. Mom and Ruth are dead to the world. How are you doing?"

Danny shrugged his shoulders.

"What about helping me get a few of my things together without waking them up?"

"Okay. What?"

"Get my stuff out of the bathroom. I'll take the closet."

In short order, Danny and Loretta had collected the things she needed and put them into some brown paper bags from the kitchen. She beckoned to him to follow her out into the dim morning. About halfway down the block, they came to a car on the side of the road. Behind the wheel Danny recognized one of Loretta's mysterious dates, a jaunty high-school graduate who had once shown Danny a card trick. He leaned out the window and waved.

"Hi, Sport!"

No doubt the boy did not remember his name, but Danny didn't remember his either, so they were even. Danny waved back but kept quiet. The trunk was open, so Danny and Loretta put the bags in there. The boy stayed in the car.

"Thanks for helping me make my escape," Loretta said.

Danny nodded and glanced at the boy in the car.

"Don't worry. He's harmless. Look, I'm going to give you my number, but under no circumstances will you give it to anybody else unless there is an emergency. I know I can trust you."

Danny took the scrap of paper and put it in his pocket.

"Is it his number?"

"Don't worry. I'm still sleeping on the couch. The only difference is this way I don't have to worry about your dirty feet."

Then she hugged him.

"I'll call Mom and Ruth every day or so, but I'll depend on you to call me if anything happens, or even if you think something is about to happen."

"Okay."

"Things might look up now that I'm out."

She stepped back and rumpled his hair.

"Oh, just a sec," she said, and ran to the rider's side of the car.

Danny followed and watched as she leaned through the window and took something away from the boy. She turned to Danny and presented him with a Donald Duck comic book. It was brand new, except for having been fingered by What's-his-name.

"Did you hear something about me?" Danny asked.

"What could I hear?"

"Nothing."

"Everybody knows you like Donald Duck. It's all around the neighborhood."

"Thanks," Danny said, "I . . ."

He stopped. Something was moving in the mist beyond the boy's car.

"What's wrong with you?" Loretta asked.

"Dad's there," Danny replied.

Loretta whirled and saw Mr. Ryan emerging from the gloom. He was carrying his lunch bag in one hand. His white baker's clothes looked eerie in the early light. He walked to the driver's side of the car and stood staring at Loretta's friend. The boy must have been too preoccupied to notice his quiet approach. After a couple of seconds he cried out and started the engine.

"Damn! Loretta! There's a guy out here!"

Loretta ran to the rider's side and jumped in, but Mr. Ryan moved to the front of the car and stood in its path. The boy revved his engine but the ghostly figure in front of the car, the bottom half of its body glowing in the headlight beams, did not move. The boy backed up and tried to go around, but the figure moved determinedly to block the way. The boy honked the horn.

"That's enough!" Loretta growled, opening the car door.

"Are you crazy!" the boy shouted. "Don't go out there!"

He tried to hold her arm, but she shook him off and came out of the car like a rocket, but by the time she appeared in the headlight glare, the figure was gone. She stood fuming.

"What are you thinking?" she shouted into the mist. "Why don't you blow your top and get it over with?"

There was no response. Loretta stood for a moment more before returning to the car.

"Who was that?" the boy asked.

"Nobody," Loretta replied. "A man from the neighborhood."

"He looked like he wanted to kill me."

That was the last thing Danny heard as the car pulled away. He tracked the headlights in the mist as they moved down Florinda and turned onto Sligh Avenue. Then everything was quiet, except for the sound of coughing in the distance. Danny stayed still. If his dad was watching, he didn't want to do anything to set him off. He tried to look as natural as possible, standing in the middle of the road with a comic book in his hand. He heard the coughing again. It sounded farther away, so he took a long breath and slowly headed for his house. What he had seen that morning was yet another event that he would have to keep to himself. It would do no good to tell his mother or Ruth. That would only increase their worry. He certainly would not discuss it with Loretta. That would just produce uncomfortable moments of vitriol.

Danny had many such secret memories, a good portion of them centering on his father. As he neared his house, he passed the spot where his dad had run over him with the car. That was actually a pleasant memory because the event had happened when his father was in a good mood. When they had first come to Nowhere, Harold Ryan had been much more stable and much more playful. In those days he had driven the car to and from work, and Danny sometimes met him in the afternoon at the corner of Sligh and Florinda. Danny liked to ride on the running board for the last block home.

In order to spice up the experience, he had asked his father if he could ride on the sloping fender and hang on to one of the teardrop headlights that stuck out of it. His dad had agreed but drove very slowly. After doing this a few times, the novelty had faded, so Danny had started hanging off the fender. This had increased the thrill factor considerably, until the day that Danny had lost his grip on the headlight and slipped under the car. Its rear tires had passed over his thighs.

At first, Danny thought he must be crippled for life but was surprised to discover that he could stand up and walk. The big balloon tires must have saved him. Limping only slightly, he made it to the Ryan front yard, where he saw his father on his knees, peering under the car. Danny walked quietly up behind him and said "Dad?" Mr. Ryan looked up slowly. Even in those early days, he was having episodes, and Danny was afraid that he had set one off. However, this time he had shown only concern, quietly explaining how serious the accident might have been if Danny's legs had happened to fall across a hole in the dirt road where they could have been bent and snapped like matchsticks. Danny saw the sense in this. Having determined that Danny was unharmed, Mr. Ryan ended their conference with a memorable statement.

"Son, let's not tell your mother about this."

Danny had also seen the sense in this, and he had never mentioned the incident, nor had he and his father ever discussed it further. Danny sometimes wondered if his dad even remembered running over him—not that Danny blamed him for doing it. Mr. Ryan could be blamed for many things, but not that. In Danny's estimation he himself had been entirely at fault, with his hanging behavior.

After the morning's excruciating confrontation, it seemed to Danny that a great deal of time had passed, but it was still too early to do anything. In an hour Halper's store would open, and he could go there to see about his bike. Then he would go to Buddy's to work on the canoe. At the store, he would have to face Mr. Halper and after him Buddy's dad. Also on the schedule was the flea clarification with Mr. Bagley and Abigail's parents. It would be a day of excruciating confrontations.

Danny had not felt so low since contemplating his first confession, but at least that had led to something positive, his first communion. As he walked into the house, he glanced at a little shelf in the living room on which was a picture of Danny in a white communion suit standing with his hands clasped together in a prayerful manner. To Danny's mind the most striking aspect of the picture was the object on a little table in front of him, a cake in the shape of a lamb.

Both the suit and the cake had put a considerable dent in the family budget. Danny had overheard his parents discussing the problem, and he had told them that he would be far more comfortable going to the altar in jeans, but that scheme had been rejected. His mother told him that first communion was no time to skimp. As to the cake, Danny understood the symbolism but had been uncomfortable when the lamb's head was served to him as a special prize. The ears had a lot of icing on them. The rest of the family made do with the forequarters, torso, and haunches.

Since today was going to be vexing, Danny thought he might as well make it a total experience, so he went in the kitchen and read more of *The Mystery at the Moss-Covered Mansion* while he finished his breakfast. Chapter two began with the girls running away from the mysterious mansion where they had heard moans and been confronted by a bearded man who might have been guilty of firing shots. As they drove along, they put forth all sorts of theories about what might be happening. Maybe the man was holding someone prisoner. Or perhaps the mansion was an insane asylum, in which case the bearded man might be a victim, having possibly been attacked by an inmate.

All this was of interest, but then, to Danny's disdain, they started talking about what Nancy Drew was going to give her father for his birthday!

And what was this gift? An oil painting of herself! These girls seemed every bit as disturbed over the fact that a chip of paint had flaked off one corner of the portrait as they were about the mansion, the moans, and the gunfire! Thus had *The Mystery at the Moss-Covered Mansion* gone from bearable to boring in six short sentences. Danny finished his last swallow of cereal and determined to abstain from further Nancy Drew.

At any rate, it was time to take on the day. His mother and Ruth were still sleeping, so he let himself out and headed to Halper's store to collect his bike. He arrived at the store just as Mr. Halper was unlocking the door.

"That's good timing!" Mr. Halper said when he saw Danny.

"Yes, sir."

"Looking for your bike?"

"Yes, sir."

"Go around to the back of the store. I've got it chained."

By the time Danny reached the back, Mr. Halper had emerged from a rear door and was removing a big lock from his bike. He stepped back and pretended to give the bike a once-over.

"Old Bess is none the worse for wear," he remarked, looking pleasantly at Danny.

Danny didn't care for the name "Old Bess," but he recognized that Mr. Halper was trying to be friendly. Like most adults, he didn't know what to say to a kid. On the other hand, maybe some kids would like their bikes referred to as Old Bess, but Danny didn't know any.

"No, sir."

"Well, here she is."

"Thank you. I was in a hurry yesterday."

"You were at that. Your name's Ryan, right?"

This was unsettling. Suddenly, Danny's head was filled with images of Mr. Halper at the Ryan front door trying to do good. However, there was no avoiding the question of his name.

"I guess so," he answered.

"Is there a doubt?"

"No, sir."

Mr. Halper looked at Danny for several seconds and then released his bike to him.

"Tell you what I'm gonna do, young man. You see this little button here? That rings a bell inside the store. From now on, if you need a King Edward fast, day or night, you ring that bell and I'll come with one. And if you need help of any kind, feel free to ring that bell."

Danny wanted to throw up, but he controlled himself.

"Thanks."

With that he pedaled away, leaving Mr. Halper shaking his head. Danny wished fervently that there was somewhere else he could get a King Edward cigar. They must have them at Sulphur Springs, but that was too far in an emergency. Then a thought hit him. He could buy King Edwards at the Springs and keep them at the house for an emergency. That way, he would never have to see Mr. Halper again. He would miss the second-hand comics, but that could not be helped. As for the occasional purchase his mother sent him to make at Halper's, he could handle that. Maybe Alfred would go for him. It could work out.

There would be an investment to be made, but one cigar would be enough, though two would be even better. All he would have to do is pretend to go to the movies a couple of times and use the entrance money to buy cigars. And there was always the possibility of collecting returnable soda bottles and getting the two-cent deposit. If he could find a few of those, he wouldn't even have to miss a movie.

He headed for Buddy's place, but when he passed the turn to Hanna's Whirl, he decided to stop for a few minutes of peace and walked his bike to his usual spot. He was a little nervous about what he might see on the opposite bank, so he kept his eyes cast downward. This proved lucky because it allowed him to spot a Nehi bottle in the weeds next to the creek, which seemed a good omen. He put the bottle in the wire basket on his handle bars and pushed his bike forward, keeping a sharp eye out for other bottles, but he spotted none and finally had to look across the river. There he saw a moss-covered mansion.

It was two stories of spookiness, situated close to the bank, a building more massive and solid than any Danny had previously imagined over there. Composed of stone and brick covered over with green moss and ivy, it was very like what Danny had pictured as he read Abigail's Nancy Drew book, but not precisely. This building was larger and grander than he had imagined, but it was frightful, perched precariously on the bank, looking as if it might at any moment fall into the Hillsborough and create a wave that would overwhelm Danny. He was so wary that he did not sit down, instead standing astraddle his bike in case a quick retreat was required; however, nothing happened.

The breeze across the river ruffled the ivy on the mansion, but no moans issued from it and no girl detectives appeared. Then the door swung ajar with a creak. Danny rode away in confusion, wondering what was happening to his mind. Imagining things on the opposite bank of the Hillsborough had once been a diverting pastime, but he had always been able to control his fantasies. Now, they seemed to have a will of their own. Was this the sort of thing his father was seeing? No wonder he was acting crazy.

As he rode along, he kept thinking of the vision across the river. What could it mean? He became increasingly frightened, but where could he go for help with a thing like this? His immediate family was out. Alfred was out. Maybe a priest in a confessional, but that was for sins. Besides, a priest might think he was possessed or something, and there was no telling where that might lead. One encouraging thing was that his imagination seemed to get out of control only at Hanna's Whirl. If he stayed away from there, he might be okay.

Soon he was at the turn for Buddy's house, and the prospect of seeing Mr. Connolly again knocked everything else out of his mind. Halfway up the road, Danny heard the sound of a power saw, which was worrisome because he couldn't imagine Buddy's dad sleeping through that noise. However, when he arrived at the trailer there was no sign of him. Danny found that Buddy had made progress on the canoe. He had secured the one-by-twos around the forms, creating the craft's outline.

Danny thought they might be ready to nail on the orange crate slats, but Buddy pointed out that the one-by-twos forming the bottom of the canoe were on at an angle and one corner would have to be flattened so as to create a surface on which to nail. This was to be done with a small plane that fit in the palm of the hand. While Danny was working with the plane, Buddy set about doing some prep work for the next stage of the operation.

Danny did quite well, pushing the plane in the direction Buddy had described as "with the grain." There was a great deal of satisfaction to be had in flattening that protruding corner. The shavings curled back over his hand neatly. When he had finished the left rail, he called Buddy over to examine it. After showing Danny a couple of spots needing refinement, Buddy stood back and nodded approvingly.

"Do the other one," he said. "You're showing talent."

Danny began to consider a career in canoe building. He approached the other rail with a practiced air and laid the plane on the corner. He sighted down the length of the rail and pushed the plane forward. Unfortunately, amidst all his posing, he had failed to note the direction of the grain. Instead of creating a pleasing curl of wood, the force of his thrust raised a splinter and drove it deep into his thumb. The first Buddy knew of this was when he noticed Danny kneeling next to the canoe staring downward in disbelief.

"What happened?" he shouted, rushing over.

Danny held out his hand. Buddy reached for it, but Danny jerked it away in horror.

"Okay, just let me look," Buddy said, putting his hands behind his back.

Danny held the thumb out, and Buddy leaned over with elaborate care. The splinter had entered Danny's thumb under the nail, penetrated all the way to the first knuckle, and broken off, leaving only a small stub protruding.

"Needle-nose pliers," said a voice from above.

Both boys looked up to see Buddy's dad, in his bathrobe as usual, standing over them. He had a small glass in his hand. Danny let out a low moan.

"Or you could go to the doctor."

Danny knew that a doctor was out of the question. Doctors were for atomic cocktails, not splinters.

"Okay, pliers," Danny said.

Buddy went to the tool drawer, while his father took a reflective pull at his drink.

"Danny," he said, "let me give you a piece of advice. When you're injured, make some noise. Nobody knows to help you otherwise."

Buddy returned with the pliers. Danny contemplated his throbbing thumb, and it dawned on him that he could never endure anyone's touching it, not even Buddy and certainly not Buddy's father.

"I'll do it," Danny said.

"That might be a mistake," Buddy's father observed quietly.

"Then I'll go home."

"You are a great one for hopping on your high horse and galloping off just when things are getting interesting," the man replied.

Danny stood up.

"That doesn't do any good, Dad."

"He's got to hear it sometime, son."

"I'll get my bike later," Danny said.

"You're a bull-headed piece of work," Mr. Connolly commented. "Give him the pliers."

Buddy handed Danny the pliers. He took them and with a final look at Buddy's dad, he turned to examine the task before him. The end of the splinter was protruding only an eighth of an inch beyond the nail. He would have to manipulate the pliers with his left hand, which was not ideal. The bandage on that hand would make it even trickier. He must perform correctly on the first try if he was to avoid the worst possible result, waggling the splinter rather than extracting it.

He brought the nose of the pliers up to the splinter and tried to grab the end, but the jaws slipped off. This produced a pulsing pain so awful that Danny felt he must get the extraction over with or die in the attempt, so he grabbed the splinter and yanked. It was a waggle of monumental proportions. Danny dropped the pliers and sat down.

"Told you," said Buddy's dad.

Danny was infuriated. He picked up the pliers and, ignoring the awful pain, dug the point of the jaws into his thumb until he had a secure hold on the splinter. Gritting his teeth, he yanked with all his might. It came free. A welcome warmth flooded Danny's thumb. He sat panting and looking at the splinter protruding from the end of the pliers. It was big.

"And sometimes being bull-headed is just as good as being smart," Mr. Connolly commented. "I tended a lot of minor injuries in the service, and many a grown man would have passed out during that procedure, let alone done the job himself."

Danny was suddenly fond of Buddy's dad. The warmth from his finger had spread to the rest of his body. Maybe a splinter in his thumb was what he needed. He tried to get up and fell back.

"But most of the time smart is better," Mr. Connolly concluded.

With that, he disappeared into the trailer. Buddy helped Danny to a lawn chair and brought him a drink of water. He took a sip and ventured a glance at his thumb. It looked remarkably good for having caused so much pain. A little blood was seeping under the nail, but that was the only evidence of the wound.

"Here," said Buddy, holding out a piece of ice.

Danny took it and touched it to his thumb, causing a big shiver to go through him.

"Put it on the fleshy side first," Buddy said.

Danny tried that approach and found he could stand it. In a few minutes, the throbbing had subsided enough for him to try the ice on the nail. The sensation was exquisite, not exactly pain but profoundly uncomfortable; however, he endured it, and a half-hour after the accident, Danny felt close to normal. His thumb was sensitive and achy, but he could almost ignore it.

"I don't think you should try to work with that hand today," Buddy commented, "but if you can ride your bike, we might get something out of the way."

"What?"

"I see you've got a bottle in your basket. Why don't we go to the dump and find some more? If we get enough, we can ride over to the Springs and buy a fresh can of dope for the canoe."

This struck Danny as an excellent plan, combining as it did the generating of cash and a trip to the Springs. If all went well, he might have at least one emergency cigar on hand by the end of the day. It made sense that there would be plenty of bottles at the dump, and with Buddy along the place might not seem so creepy. Danny looked down at his bare feet.

"I can loan you some shoes," Buddy said. "I outgrew them."

"Okay, but I need a dime for myself out of the bottle money."

"We should get enough bottles to pay for everything," Buddy replied, disappearing into the Airstream. He emerged with a pair of black sneakers. While Danny put them on, Buddy went around in back of the trailer. He reappeared with a small hand-made wagon that he hooked to two pegs on the back axel of his bicycle. He put some old towels in the wagon.

"This'll keep the bottles from rattling around and breaking," Buddy said.

"Good thinking," Danny commented, settling his Nehi bottle among the towels.

He sat down and removed the shoes Buddy had given him.

"They're a little floppy for bike riding," he explained. "I can put them on at the dump."

As the boys left the Airstream, Mr. Connolly came to the doorway. He raised his drink.

"Bon voyage," he said pleasantly.

14

It took only twenty minutes of easy riding to reach the dump. The boys entered from the side, leaving their bikes in the weeds and plunging in between two gigantic piles of garbage. In the distance, they could hear the rumble of heavy equipment, and they kept away from that. Some other parts of the dump were burning, and they avoided those areas also. But the place was so large that there were always parts that were abandoned for the moment and easy to pick through without being spotted. The main thing was to navigate the maze of bulldozer tracks and to remember where you had come from and thus how to get out.

They moved slowly toward the interior of the dump, finding a few bottles, carrying them for a while and then caching them when they got unwieldy. By Danny's count, they had accumulated around fifty cents' worth.

"How much do we need for dope?" Danny asked.

"Not much. A dollar and a quarter."

"That's a lot of bottles."

"I have mine in cash. We only have to find enough bottles for your half."

Danny started to feel like a charity case, but he forgot about that when he discovered a box full of NuGrape bottles, more than enough to furnish the necessary cash. Danny turned to Buddy in triumph, only to see him shaking his head as if he had something against NuGrape.

"Hello, boys."

Danny was startled by a gravelly voice. He looked over his shoulder and saw a man in a green suit, standing partially concealed behind an old refrigerator. The man stepped into the clear and walked toward the boys, stopping a few paces away. Danny saw that the man was not as present-able as he had seemed at a distance. His suit was dirty and an unpleasant sweetish smell was coming off him. He smiled and Danny could see that his teeth needed a good scrubbing.

"You boys got any money?" he asked.

"Not much," Buddy replied, taking a step toward Danny.

"Don't need much for some things," the man said, cupping his elbow. "What you boys doing here?"

"We're looking for deposit bottles," Danny explained, hoping it would satisfy the man, though he sensed that something besides information was wanted.

"Let's get going," Buddy said, taking Danny by the shoulder.

"You boys must be friends," the man observed slyly, stepping into their path.

"That's no good," Buddy said.

"Just don't be in such a hurry. Let's talk for a while."

This prospect did not appeal to Danny. He began to glance around for a way to escape, but he saw someone had come in behind them. It was a woman in a frowsy dress.

"We're not interested in anything you've got to say," Danny said.

"Those shoes are mighty big," the woman remarked to Danny, sticking her hip out.

"Can't lose nothing by talking," the man said to Buddy.

"We're done," Buddy replied, leaning over and grabbing the handle of a discarded tar bucket.

The man took a hard look at the bucket. Buddy was swinging it gently. The expression on the man's face was so sour that Danny took a step back-ward and fell on his behind. The man and the lady laughed.

"Suit yourself," the man said, grabbing the lady by the arm and escorting her around a big pile of trash. They did not look back.

"What did they want?" Danny asked.

"They just hang around the dump because they don't have anywhere else to go," Buddy said. "They bother people because it makes them feel big. Sometimes you just have to give them a taste of tar bucket."

Danny laughed and realized his knees didn't feel as weak as before.

"That's brave," Danny said, glancing at the tar bucket.

"It's not even brave," Buddy said. "You just feel things sliding downhill, and you know you have to do something. That's the way I felt when I saw you out in the river."

Danny ducked his head.

"I just meant you might drown," Buddy said, tossing the bucket aside.

"How do you know you're doing the right thing?" Danny asked.

"Just hope for the best," Buddy said. "But if you don't do anything at all, you feel bad. Let's go collect our bottles."

The two walked toward their cache of NuGrape. The box was in good shape and Danny carried it easily, but they hadn't gone more than a few feet when they heard a racing car engine. From behind a mountain of trash came a rattletrap automobile careening from one side of the dozer track to the other. Danny could see the man and lady behind the wheel. She was scooted way over next to him in the front seat. Their expressions were wild.

"Up top," Buddy said, pulling Danny by the shirt collar. Danny dropped his box and scrambled with Buddy up the nearest mountain of garbage. The car bumped harmlessly past them blowing its horn.

"Let's wait a minute," Buddy said. "They might come around again. They like to scare people."

Danny and Buddy sat quietly listening for the car engine. Danny wished he were in a movie, where somebody like Roy Rogers would ride up and take care of the situation. Buddy was doing okay, but could he keep it up? Roy Rogers always seemed so sure of himself. He could not remember Roy ever having to climb a pile of garbage to make an escape. While they were waiting, Buddy spotted something in the trash not far away from them.

"How could somebody throw that out?" he muttered.

Before Danny could spot what he was talking about, Buddy scrambled a few feet across the trash heap, did some minor excavating, and brought his prize safely back, a three-foot-long model of a World War II battleship.

"Somebody put a lot of work into this," Buddy said.

Danny could see that for himself. Every piece of the ship's equipment, however tiny, had been individually crafted. On the wooden base was a plaque that read:

My beloved Mighty Mo
She kept me safe in vicious waters.

"The *Missouri*," Buddy whispered. "Some guy honored his ship."

"Do you think he died?"

"Could be. Somebody should have kept this."

"Maybe there wasn't anybody."

"There's always somebody," Buddy said. "But I'll find a home for it."

"How about your dad?"

"Naw. We don't have room. Dad's a bubblehead, anyway."

"What?"

"Submarine sailor. It's a different breed. There's a lot of competition between branches of the Navy."

"Oh."

"Let's take it to the Springs and show it to Al. It could be worth money."

After a few more minutes of waiting, Buddy decided it was safe to clamber down off the garbage and take their booty back to the bikes. It was a big load and Danny put some of the bottles in his basket so there would be enough room in Buddy's wagon for the *Missouri*. Even so, they would have to ride carefully.

"Let's cash in the bottles at Halper's before we go to the Springs," Buddy said.

"But . . ."

Buddy was already on his way, so Danny swung in behind. Along the way, he tried to devise a strategy for avoiding Mr. Halper. What if he were to ride ahead to the Springs for some helpful reason? But no such reason came to mind, at least nothing that made sense, and he certainly didn't want to seem a fool to Buddy. Mr. Halper would probably have the tact to keep quiet about yesterday's debacle, but even so Danny was sure he would have to endure the man's inquisitive glances, and there was a very real possibility that somehow Mr. Halper would contrive to have a private word with him, which could only be mortifying.

All this ran through his mind as he and Buddy rode sedately down Sligh Hill, a feature of the road that usually provided an exhilarating increase in speed, but with bottles on board, you had to be careful. Halfway down the hill, Danny saw something confusing. Alfred Bagley and Abigail Arnold were standing beside their bikes near the intersection of Sligh and Florinda, apparently in deepest conversation.

In Danny's experience this was unheard of. Alfred and Abigail had no mutual interests, and sometimes Danny thought they had only minimal vocabulary in common. Still, they were head to head. Danny was so fascinated that he forgot to hail them, but the keen-eyed Alfred spotted Buddy's cunning trailer with an intriguing bundle poking out of one end, and in an instant he had deserted Abigail and was off in pursuit.

Danny looked back and saw him pedaling ferociously. Behind Alfred, Danny glimpsed Abigail on her purple bike. The white streamers on the ends of its handle bars were standing straight out, and she was gaining despite Alfred's best efforts. Abigail was the only kid in the neighborhood with gears. That must explain her speed. In a few moments, she had sailed by Alfred, not even pausing to jeer, and seconds later she pulled abreast of Danny with no hair out of place.

"What's going on?" she asked.

"Deposit bottles," Danny replied, hoping to stifle any further conversation but suspecting his effort would fail.

"Where'd you get them?"

"Dump."

Alfred caught up in time to hear the word "dump."

"You went to the dump! You lucky duck!"

Abigail did not condescend to comment, just pedaled slightly harder for a moment and pulled abreast of Buddy. Alfred lingered behind with Danny, hungry for more information.

"What was it like?"

"What do you think? It's a dump."

"Was there lots of stuff?"

"Mountains of it."

At this, Alfred nearly ran off the road.

"What kind?" he asked, swerving back.

"Just garbage mostly. I've told you this before."

"But you found something good, didn't you? I can see it wrapped in towels. What?"

"You probably wouldn't care about it."

"Yes I would!"

"Okay. A model ship."

This caused another swerve.

"Like a pirate ship?

"Nope."

"What?"

"Battleship from World War Two."

"Man!"

Alfred stood on his pedals and moved up next to Buddy where he could look more closely at the mysterious bundle. The model was completely obscured by towels, but Alfred stared avidly at it anyway. He couldn't have been happier if Danny had brought a real battleship out of the dump. At this point, the four of them rolled into the parking lot in front of Halper's store. Danny was relieved to see that none of the boys from yesterday was around. Buddy stopped, and Alfred stood his bike on its kickstand and ran to Buddy's wagon.

"Did you make that wagon?" Alfred asked excitedly.

"Yep," Buddy answered, fishing bottles out from around the model.

"Would you make me one?"

Danny could not comprehend Alfred's cheekiness. He would ask for anything.

"I'm working on something right now, but maybe after I finish."

"What are you working on?"

"Ask Danny."

"Can I see the model?"

"I guess so. But be careful. It has a lot of little parts."

Buddy unwrapped the model and handed it to Alfred, who immediately sat down and began a close examination. Abigail was more interested in Buddy.

"How old are you?" she asked.

"I'm sixteen . . . I mean seventeen."

"Which is it?"

"Seventeen."

Abigail thought for a moment. Danny could see she was going through some sort of analysis. He just hoped she wouldn't embarrass him by asking some tactless question. As it turned out, she said something Danny could not believe.

"You're good-looking," Abigail said.

This set Buddy to laughing. He didn't blush or anything, just laughed and gathered bottles.

"That's what they tell me," he said.

Danny admired the way Buddy tossed this comment off. He thought it must be wonderful to be able to say such a thing and not seem big-headed.

"You're good-looking, too," Buddy added, winking at Abigail.

He was smooth, like somebody in a movie. Danny could not fathom how people got that way. Abigail took off her glasses and put them in her pocket. Buddy laughed harder.

"Don't bump your nose."

"They're for reading mostly," Abigail replied.

"All right then. Help with some of these bottles. We brought back a lot."

Danny never thought for a minute that Abigail would deign to touch dirty bottles, but she took four of them and followed Buddy into the store. Danny crept in behind them.

"The mother lode!" Mr. Halper exclaimed. "You'll break me!"

"That's what we're aiming for, Oscar," Buddy said. "We have more outside."

"Good grief! The NuGrape people are going to have to put in overtime."

"I'll get the rest," Danny said, darting out the door.

He burst into the sunlight. Alfred was still sitting in the parking lot with the model. He had it over his head, examining the hull.

"It's mostly there," he said when he saw Danny. "This part fell off."

He held up a gun turret.

"It was loose."

"That's okay, Alfred."

Danny gathered up some of the remaining bottles and carried them inside, leaving them on the counter and ducking out again quickly. He made two more trips, and came in with the last of them just as Mr. Halper was saying to Abigail, "How about one of these candy lipsticks? They taste like cherry."

Abigail took one of the lipsticks and studied it. After a moment, she reached into her little purse, extracted a nickel, and handed it over to Mr. Halper. She licked the end of the candy and applied some of the color to her lips, turning them scarlet.

"That's the ticket!" Mr. Halper said. "Just like a movie star."

Abigail turned toward Buddy and puckered extravagantly. Buddy laughed.

Danny couldn't figure out what was going on. He put his armful of bottles on the counter, and Mr. Halper started counting them out loud with much dramatic emphasis, placing each one in a box on a table behind him. Eventually, there were fifty-one bottles in the box.

"That's a dollar and two cents," Mr. Halper said with a quaver in his voice. "Might have to go to the safe for that amount."

"Can I see the safe?" Alfred called from the doorway.

Buddy laughed as if this were a good joke. Alfred looked a little abashed, but you couldn't get mad at Buddy.

"Is it a vault like at the bank?" Buddy asked.

"Nope. Just this."

Mr. Halper brought out a cigar box, opened it up, and extracted a silver dollar. This was unusual enough to bring Alfred to the counter. Even Abigail leaned in.

"This kind of a haul deserves a special reward. And here's a Liberty head nickel to go with it. Three-cents bonus."

"Give it to Danny," Buddy said.

Mr. Halper held out the change, but Danny hesitated. Mr. Halper raised his eyebrows.

"Excuse me," Danny said. "Could I have regular money, please?"

"What on earth for?"

"We're just going to spend it. We don't need anything special."

"I get it," Mr. Halper replied. "Sure. Here's a dollar and two cents regular from the cash register. My compliments on getting so many."

Danny left the store quickly with Abigail right behind him.

"Danny Ryan!"

Oh no. Both names.

"How could you be so mean?"

"Who says I was mean?"

"You insulted Mr. Halper. He tried to give you those special coins, and you didn't appreciate it."

"I wasn't trying to be mean. All I wanted was regular spending money, not a prize."

"He was being nice."

"Nobody asked him to."

"You don't ask people to be nice. They just are."

"How would you know?"

Abigail was about to tell him how when Alfred rushed up to Danny.

"Are you crazy?" he asked. "Those are rare coins. You should have used them to start a collection."

"I need money right now! I'm telling both of you to get off my back."

This did not have the stonewalling effect that Danny had hoped. Instead, it brought on a new rush of accusations from Abigail and Alfred. Danny was on the verge of fleeing when Buddy came up.

"Danny didn't want to take rare coins because he knew we were just going to the Springs to buy airplane dope. He was being thoughtful. Give him some credit."

"What dope?" Alfred asked.

"For our project. And then we're going over to Al's Swap Shop to show him the model."

"Al's Swap Shop!" said Alfred. "I'm coming."

"What is this mysterious project?" Abigail asked.

"None of your business," Danny said, throwing a leg over his bike.

"I think I'll ride along with you," Abigail said, looking at Buddy.

"Fine by me," Buddy replied, taking the model out of Alfred's hands. "Let's hit the road."

Buddy, Alfred, and Abigail forged ahead. Danny rode along in the rear, replaying the morning's events: the mansion, the sliver, the pliers, the piles of garbage, the NuGrape, the dirty man and lady, the battleship. It seemed enough for a month's contemplation, but here he was riding along like none of it had happened, glancing up from time to time to see Abigail's little fanny bobbing up and down on her bike seat. And that, too, was strange. When had she ever been seen in the Springs? It was not a tidy place. Then there was Alfred, heading toward the swap shop as if his boundaries didn't exist.

Danny started to wonder if everybody's life seemed as weird to them as his did to him, but he never knew because they clammed up about it. This was a new and scary thought. At this point, Danny had to give up thinking. They had reached Sulphur Springs. Buddy stopped his bike and the others circled around.

"Which first? Hardware store or swap shop?"

"Swap shop!" Alfred shouted.

"I'll go to the hardware store," Danny said. "What do I get?"

"Let's start with two quarts of airplane dope," Buddy said. "Any color you like."

"Are you making an airplane?" Alfred asked.

"Couldn't say," Buddy replied, as Danny took off for the arcade.

Danny was afraid somebody might try to follow him, but Alfred and Abigail rode off with Buddy. This was luck. Danny glided into the cool shade of the arcade and pedaled down toward the rear entrance of the drugstore. Kids weren't supposed to ride their bikes in the central concourse but there was hardly ever anybody there. If there were any customers around, they went in from the Nebraska Avenue side. In the interior were dusty offices. Danny passed one with a sign saying "Bail Bondsman" and reminded himself yet again to ask someone what that meant. Inside the drugstore, he went to the counter and asked for two King Edward cigars. The clerk looked dubious.

"For my dad," Danny said.

"You sure?"

"I don't smoke."

"I hope not," the lady said, handing over the cigars.

To Danny's relief, the clerk at the hardware store knew about airplane dope. All he had was red, so Danny bought red and rode his bike over to the swap shop. Buddy was inside talking to Al. Danny walked toward them.

"Have a good time at the pool yesterday after I left?" Al asked.

"It was all right," Danny said.

"According to Frank, you almost wound up at the morgue."

"I was just coughing."

"He said you were trying to kill yourself."

"What!"

"Why did he think you were trying to kill yourself?" asked Abigail from behind a stack of galoshes.

"He got it all wrong," Danny said.

"I'm not surprised," Al commented. "Frank is prone to overexcitement."

"But why did he think that?" Abigail insisted.

Danny looked around helplessly, and Al Gallagher came to his rescue.

"Let's unwrap that mysterious bundle," he said loudly. "Where's little Al?"

Upon hearing this, Alfred put down a tin duck he was trying to make quack and hurried over, excited at the prospect of seeing his idol assess a new piece of salvage.

"I saw it a half an hour ago," Alfred announced.

"Well, you are one up on me," Al replied.

Alfred wiggled ecstatically and reached up to tug gently at the corner of the towel covering the model.

"All right then," said Al. "Here we go."

He whipped off the towel and stood contemplating the model, turning it left and right, sighting down its length and nodding in a knowing way that sent shivers through Alfred. He walked to an old desk in one corner of the shop, swept off the clutter, and placed the model on it, switching on a hanging lamp for better light. He opened a desk drawer, extracted a magnifying glass, and used it to pore over the model's every detail. Finally, he stood up.

"This guy was a craftsman, and he knew his subject. I was on this ship and remember it well."

"You never said you served on the *Missouri*," Buddy said.

"No, just was on board one time in Pearl. God, it was big. I wonder where this missing turret went?"

Alfred fished in his shirt pocket and carefully removed the turret, wrapped in tissue. Al took it, put it in place, and pronounced the model 99 percent complete.

"How much is it worth?" Alfred asked.

"Not a lot of money. Sailing ships are most prized, but this is still a thing of beauty," said Al, and then, noticing Abigail's bored expression, he added, "for those who like battleships."

"My dad was in the Quartermaster Corps," she said smugly.

"Men can't go into battle without underwear," Al said.

"There was a great deal more to it than underwear, I can assure you," Abigail said.

Al laughed.

"I know that, darling. God bless the Quartermaster Corps. I couldn't have gone in the water without them."

At this point, Al noticed Alfred making a strange face, and pretty soon everyone was staring at the boy, whose head was canted toward the back of the store, his eyebrows moving up and down torturously.

"Are you having a spasm?" Abigail asked.

"He's trying to call attention to something," Danny said. "He can never do it right."

"Could it be," Al asked, "that you think this model belongs in the back?" Alfred nodded vigorously.

"You're supposed to shut up about that," Danny said.

"What's in the back?" Abigail inquired.

"Now you've done it," Danny said.

"Oh, I guess one more won't make much difference," Al said, reaching for his keys.

Alfred raced to the back and stood next to the door like a dog on point. Abigail stayed at Al's hip, suddenly interested. Danny hung back, reluctant to look again at the spots of iodine he had left on Al's precious items. Buddy walked forward to look in as Al opened the door, but he had the air of a person who was revisiting familiar ground. Danny followed him and was pleased to discover that all traces of his mad iodine dance had been removed. The dummy looked as elegant as when Danny had first seen him. Either he had been dry-cleaned or dressed in a new tuxedo. Abigail was wandering about with a stunned expression. She stopped in front of a dressmaker's form on which was displayed an antique wedding dress. She reached out to finger the silk but drew her hand back.

"You can touch it," Al said.

Abigail rubbed her hand on her shorts and then studied her palm to make sure it was clean. She reached out again but could not bring herself to touch the garment.

"I better not," she said.

"Some other time, maybe," Al said. "So, little Al, where should we put the model? Do you see a good spot?"

Alfred looked this way and that. He put his thumbnail in his mouth and tried to look thoughtful. Danny felt he was overacting, but Al Gallagher didn't bat an eye, just turned to Buddy and Danny. He took out his wallet and extracted a hundred-dollar bill.

"This is what the model is worth to me," he said. "Do we have a deal?"

"Too much, Al," Buddy said.

"Who's the swap shop guy around here?" Al asked. "Don't insult my expertise."

"We won't take a hundred."

"Good Lord!" Al said. "Are you against free enterprise? What do you think we fought the war for?"

"That's too much. Make it fifty, and half goes to Danny," Buddy said.

"No way," Danny said. "You found it."

"You two are the sorriest businessmen I ever tried to make a deal with," Al said.

He took out a fifty-dollar bill, tore a third of it off, gave it to Danny and handed the remaining two-thirds to Buddy.

"Problem solved," he said. "I just bought myself a model at a discount rate."

With that, he ushered the kids out of the back room. Alfred was the last to go, looking backward and protesting that he had not yet decided where the model should rest. Al said that he would make that decision on his own, much to Alfred's obvious sorrow.

"Be quicker next time," Al said.

He herded them out the front door of the shop and told them to hit the road, but they hung around the door after Al had gone inside.

"I couldn't believe all those nice things were in the back of this store full of junk," Abigail said, waving dismissively at Al's display.

"I like it all," Alfred said.

"You would," Abigail commented, licking the end of her candy lipstick and applying a fresh coat of scarlet.

As if to demonstrate his point, Alfred walked to the diving suit at the shop entrance, put his arms around the waist, and gave it a vigorous hug.

"Alfred!"

At the sound of Mr. Bagley's clipped, evangelical voice, Alfred froze, his arms still around the diving suit. Danny turned and saw Alfred's father standing stiffly at the curb. His eyes were hidden behind his horn-rimmed sunglasses, but Danny could imagine how hard they must be, having discovered a disobedient son, not only outside his legal boundaries but making a display of himself on the streets of Sulphur Springs. Mr. Bagley opened the trunk of his car.

"Bring your bike."

Mr. Bagley swung Alfred's bike into the trunk and started tying the lid down with a piece of twine. He worked in a dreadful silence, fairly vibrating with wounded righteousness. Buddy stepped forward.

"Can I give you a hand, sir?"

"No, thank you. Get in, Alfred."

Alfred, who had so far been frozen like a pillar of salt, climbed in the car and Mr. Bagley joined him a moment later. Alfred did not venture a look backward, just sat staring ahead. Mr. Bagley started the car, but before he could move, Abigail ran to the driver's side and put her hand on the window frame.

"Can Alfred play this evening?"

Mr. Bagley looked at her for a long moment, pointedly taking in her scarlet lips.

"Alfred will not be playing for a while," he said, and drove away.

"That was an icy blast," Al Gallagher observed from the door of the swap shop.

"Alfred has boundaries," Danny explained.

"I see what you mean."

The four of them stood looking after Mr. Bagley's car, now passing over the Nebraska Street bridge. In a moment it was out of sight, but nobody seemed inclined to move on with the day. The little group just looked aimlessly around. Danny was trying to cope with the knot in his stomach. Then all of them spotted something across the street. Moving like an angel against the dreary backdrop of the Sulphur Springs arcade was the beautiful Donna. She looked neither left nor right, but Danny felt she knew their eyes were on her. He wondered what made her look as if she were floating.

"Danny," Buddy said, "will you see Abigail home?"

"What?"

"Will you make sure she gets home safe?"

"What for? She can take care of herself."

"I'm asking for a favor."

"All right, I guess."

With that, Buddy strode across the street toward the girl. Abigail looked on intently.

"Who's that?" she asked pointedly.

Al Gallagher laughed.

"Darling," he said, "that's a dream walking."

"I mean does she have a name?" Abigail said impatiently.

"Not that I know of," he replied, watching Buddy and the girl disappear into the arcade.

"It's Donna," Danny said.

"How do *you* know?" Abigail asked suspiciously.

"I met her."

"Where?"

"Never mind."

"You two get out of here, now," said Al. "You've had enough swap shop for today."

He went inside, and Danny moved very slowly to his bike, hoping that Buddy would reappear, but he didn't. Abigail stood expectantly next to her bike with her lips pursed. Apparently, she was set on Danny's going through with the ridiculous charade of escorting her home. Why was this necessary? Had a pack of wolves suddenly materialized in Nowhere? Even if it had, he would like to see a wolf with the grit to take on Abigail Arnold. But he had promised, so he got on his bike and glided down the street with Abigail close behind; however, they had just crossed the old bridge when she pulled abreast of Danny.

"Stop," she said.

Danny thought maybe her chain had come off, so he did as she asked, but when Abigail came to a halt, he saw that everything about her bike was in order. He looked at her inquisitively.

"What's wrong with you?" she asked.

The knot in his stomach came back. What kind of question was this? Who would even ask such a question? It could not be answered.

"I don't know what you mean."

He tried to pull away, but Abigail grabbed his handlebars.

"Why are you acting crazy?"

"I'm not acting crazy."

Abigail got off her bike, lowered the kickstand, and sat down at the side of the road. Danny wanted to ride off in righteous disdain, but he could not. Abigail knew it, too. That was the most infuriating aspect of the situation. He wanted to throw himself down and beat the ground with his fists, but he put on a cool expression.

"I don't ask *you* a lot of stupid questions," he commented.

"You don't have to. I'm normal."

"Okay, I'm crazy. Why do you have to butt in?"

"I want to know."

There was no reply for this. Danny sat down a few feet away from her.

"Then we'll wait," he said.

Abigail got a book out of her saddlebag and began to read. After ten minutes, Danny started to perspire. He got up and walked to the bank of the Hillsborough to have a look at the gator. As usual, he was sitting in the storm drain looking content and as usual did not move a muscle. Danny looked over at Abigail. She looked rooted to the ground, prepared to sit there all day. All right, then. If Abigail wanted an answer, he would give her one. He turned around.

"You win," he said.

"So start talking."

"Not here. You have to come somewhere with me."

"Is this a trick?"

"No."

"Are you lying?"

Danny got on his bike without further comment and pedaled away. In a few seconds, Abigail had caught up, and they rode in silence for ten minutes. A block from Hanna's Whirl, Danny braked and began walking his bike. He kept his head down.

"You look like you're going to a funeral," Abigail said.

"I don't know what I'm going to," Danny replied.

15

The short walk to Hanna's Whirl seemed very long with Abigail's eyes searching Danny's face for any clue to his concerns. It was tiresome to be under such scrutiny, but she was the only person he could think of who would give him a blunt, unsympathetic opinion, and he needed one because he was beginning to feel as if he was on the verge of being overwhelmed from the inside and the outside at the same time.

"Why do you keep looking at the ground?"

"Deposit bottles."

"Don't be ridiculous. What are you afraid of seeing?"

By this time they were within sight of Hanna's Whirl.

"That," he said, pointing ahead without looking.

"The river?"

"On the other side."

"Don't be silly. Look up and show me."

Danny slowly raised his head, and there it was, the moss-covered mansion, bigger than it had been that morning, leaning more heavily toward him, seemingly about to topple. Danny looked down again.

"You're actually afraid," Abigail said in disbelief.

Danny merely stared across the river, wishing the mansion would disappear but afraid of what might replace it.

"This is an interesting case," Abigail said. "Tell me what's bothering you."

Danny glanced up at the mansion again, but this time he did not look away immediately. The door was still ajar, but there was movement in the dark opening. As Danny watched, a young girl emerged. She was lithe and dressed in a 1940s style. Her blonde shoulder-length hair was rippling gently in the breeze. She was carrying a magnifying glass. Danny's eyes grew wide.

"What?" Abigail said, keeping her eyes on Danny's face.

"Is that Nancy Drew?"

"You mean my book?"

"Across the river."

"Nancy Drew is only a person in a book. She's not real."

"Will you just look?"

"No. I don't have to look to know that Nancy Drew is not over there."

Danny turned away and began to walk his bike toward home. Abigail followed him out to the road.

"You're in our neighborhood now," Danny said. "You can get home by yourself."

"I think you need a doctor or something," Abigail observed.

"Probably," Danny replied flatly.

It was out now. Soon everyone would know he was seeing things. He stood pondering the consequences but was shocked out of his reverie when Abigail planted a kiss on his lips and rode away, leaving him with a smear of cherry candy on his mouth.

Danny had never been kissed by anybody other than a family member. Under other circumstances, he would have been thrown into a state of disorientation, but since he was already disoriented, he simply stared after Abigail until she turned a corner, and though it was the last thing he wanted to do, he headed back to Hanna's Whirl to look once again across the river.

This time he kept his head up, staring doggedly at the mansion. He walked to the water's edge and sat down, never taking his gaze off it. He imagined his eyes were cosmic rays and tried to burn a hole into the mansion. He looked away and then back very fast. He held his breath until he nearly blacked out. He threw objects across the river, but they fell short. He yelled out, "What's happening? What's happening?" Nothing changed the mansion's aspect. At length he threw himself down, determined to stay by the river until he had figured out the mystery.

The mansion seemed to grow more threatening by the second. Danny was getting queasy, but then the young girl with the magnifying glass returned to the porch. Danny felt a little better. He jumped up and shouted, "Hello, Miss Drew! Could I have a word with you?" The girl did not acknowledge him. She simply moved around the mansion's veranda, examining things with her glass. She was on her knees, peering at the floor, when a bearded man came around the corner of the building and crept toward her. The girl was so intent on her investigation that she did not notice the intruder.

"Watch out for that man!" Danny screamed. Neither the girl nor the man seemed to hear him. The man came closer, full of menace. It was too maddening to bear. Danny threw off his shirt and dived into the Hillsborough. When he broke the surface, the mansion was gone.

Back on shore, Danny scanned the opposite bank for any trace of the mansion. He could see nothing and wondered if he had made it disappear by jumping into the river. He had followed Buddy's principle of doing something when you thought it was needed, but he didn't feel good afterward. In fact, he was more scared than ever. Danny struggled ashore. He sat down, picked up a water hyacinth, and sat popping its flotation bulbs, staring all the while across the water. No further scenes appeared. After a while, he rode away without looking back.

In a few minutes he was home. He stowed his bike and hung his soaking jeans on the line in back of the house. When he walked through the kitchen in his underpants, his mother looked up from her work.

"Going nudist?" she asked.

"Fell in the creek," Danny replied.

"Have you had lunch?"

"No."

"Well, better make yourself a sandwich. How did you do with the flea problem?"

Danny froze with one foot in the air.

"Don't try to joke yourself out of this! You get some clothes on, march across the street, and tell the Bagleys we never had fleas. I mean it!"

"Now might not be the best time. Mr. Bagley . . ."

"Not another word!"

"But Mom, look at my eyes. I'm not lying."

"I do not care about your eyes one way or another. This has to be done and the sooner the better. Do you want me to take you over there?"

"No."

"Get on your horse then! And come back with a report."

Danny went to the closet and found fresh underwear and jeans. The jeans were the only clean ones left, but they were the ones he had torn a couple of days before. As he had expected, his mother had repaired them with an iron-on patch. Ruth heard him sighing and called him into the bedroom. She seemed done in.

"Is something wrong?" she asked.

"Flea duty," Danny replied, holding his pant leg out for inspection.

"Mom did a neat job," Ruth replied.

"Yeah," Danny answered.

There was no point in complaining to Ruth. A bad jeans patch was nothing compared to her problems. He considered telling her about having seen Loretta that morning, but there were too many things about it that he couldn't tell. The safe topics of conversation in the Ryan house were diminishing fast, so he went back to the one that always seemed to work.

"Maybe we can draw later," he said, but Ruth didn't look like she had the strength to hold a pencil.

"That would be nice."

"Danny!" their mother called from the kitchen.

"I'm going!"

Danny rolled his eyes at Ruth and left, pausing in the living room to call to his mom.

"Here I go! Do you want to watch me go out the door?"

"Don't be funny. Just make sure you do it the way we agreed."

Danny went on his way, but his pace grew slower as he covered the distance to the Bagley house. Though it was only an unassuming cement-block home, it had taken on the foreboding feeling of the moss-covered mansion. Danny approached cautiously, relieved that he did not see Mr. Bagley's car on the premises. He peeked through the jalousies and spotted Mrs. Bagley sitting at the Formica dining table. Her shoulders were shaking. Danny was not quite certain, but it looked like she was crying, which meant this was not the time to discuss an absence of fleas.

He glanced over at his own house. If he returned there, his mother would just send him back. Couldn't anything be simple anymore? To make matters worse, his thumb was beginning to throb where the splinter had gone in.

He took a deep breath and knocked lightly on the door. Mrs. Bagley raised her head inquiringly. Danny knocked again even more faintly. She took a napkin and dabbed at her eyes.

"Please. Just a moment," she called.

"It's only me, Mrs. Bagley."

Danny observed her pulling up her socks and straightening her house dress. He was embarrassed and stepped back from the door. In a moment Mrs. Bagley opened it.

"Alfred can't come out, Danny," she said softly. "I think you know why."

"Yes, ma'am."

"You shouldn't encourage Alfred."

"Did he say I did?"

"No, but he wouldn't."

"No, ma'am. Did Mr. Bagley . . ."

Here Danny stopped and made a slight whipping motion with his right hand. Mrs. Bagley looked stricken. She put her hand to her throat.

"Mr. Bagley was on his way up to Land o' Lakes to look at some property when he saw Alfred. He was very unhappy about being put behind schedule. Alfred's punishment will have to wait until he gets back. That will be tomorrow at the soonest."

Danny nodded, and Mrs. Bagley burst into tears. She took a handkerchief out of her apron pocket and blew her nose. Danny shifted from one foot to the other.

"I'm sorry, Danny. This is no way for a grownup to act. I'm just tired. Now please go on. Maybe in a few days Alfred can come out. I don't know what will happen."

"Yes, ma'am."

Mrs. Bagley closed the door. Danny walked halfway back to his house before he remembered the fleas. Heaving a great sigh, he trudged back to the Bagleys' and knocked again. Mrs. Bagley only cracked the door this time.

"Danny, please."

"I'm sorry. I forgot that my mother sent me over to tell you something."

"Is it your sister?" Mrs. Bagley asked quickly.

"No."

"Thank the Lord for that."

"Yes, ma'am. Um. She wants me to tell you we don't have fleas. We never had fleas."

"Well, I never felt you did. What a strange message."

"I thought Mr. Bagley might have mentioned something about fleas to you."

"Why, no. Why would he if you don't have them?"

"I think I said something that gave him the idea we did."

"What on earth did you say?" asked Mrs. Bagley, opening the door wider.

The conversation was getting far too complicated for Danny's taste. He desperately tried to think of something that would stop the endless stream of questions. He could not confess that he had sent up a fog of talk about fleas to distract Mr. Bagley's attention from Alfred. That would only bring on more questions that would engender more lies. He needed a lie that would stop the process cold.

"I guess I said we had fleas, but I was making a joke. I think he took me seriously because he brought tobacco stems to our house to help with the fleas."

"Oh."

"Mr. Bagley didn't mention that?"

"There are many things Mr. Bagley doesn't feel he has to tell me," Mrs. Bagley replied.

"Anyway, my mom is afraid that everybody will think we have fleas because of what I said. But we don't."

"That's not a very funny joke, to say you have fleas."

"No, ma'am. My mom agrees with you."

"All the boys seem to be in trouble these days," Mrs. Bagley said. "Would you like a glass of tea, Danny?"

Danny found this possibility unsettling. He couldn't remember ever being alone with either of Alfred's parents. If it had to happen, Mrs. Bagley was certainly preferable, but she was acting strangely. The possibilities seemed ominous. However, he did not want to be rude, and perhaps he could do something to help poor Alfred, who was undoubtedly imprisoned in his room. Just the sound of Danny's voice might cheer him up.

"Sure," Danny responded. "I mean, yes, ma'am."

"Is that how you answer your mother, 'Sure'?"

Oh Lord, it was going bad already. Danny had forgotten to filter himself, and now he was in the soup. He looked up at Mrs. Bagley regretfully.

"She doesn't mind. We all talk that way in my family. It doesn't mean anything bad."

"I realize people are different," she said, ushering Danny into the house. "It just sounds undisciplined."

"I'm sorry."

"I don't know that you should be. The world is changing so fast these days. It's hard to sort out the good from the bad."

Danny was shocked to hear that Mrs. Bagley was having trouble of this sort. Prior to that moment, the most philosophical thing he had ever heard her say was "Cleanliness is next to godliness," a sentiment with which Danny heartily disagreed, though he did not say that to Mrs. Bagley, of course. Like so many of his maverick opinions, Danny kept that one to himself. No point in giving the adults more leverage. They had enough as it was. Mrs. Bagley set a large glass of sweet tea in front of Danny.

"Would you like a sandwich? I'm making one for Alfred."

"Could he eat with us?"

"No. He's to stay in his room, but I'll eat with you."

What could be more attractive? A one-on-one lunch with a Bible fanatic. The embarrassing silences would be exquisite. For a moment he hated her, but he instantly felt guilty about these uncharitable thoughts. He would have to remember to mention them to the priest at his next confession.

"That would be great," he said.

Mrs. Bagley made the sandwiches while Danny stared out the window, occasionally sipping his tea. Mrs. Bagley was good with the tea, plenty of sugar. When she was finished with the sandwiches, she took a plate and a glass of tea to the door of Alfred's room. It was around the corner, so Danny could not see what was happening, but he heard mumbling. A moment later, Alfred stuck his head out. He kept his arms and shoulders back, like a guy at the guillotine.

"Hey, Danny," he said.

"Hey, Alfred. Can you come out?"

"Nope. I can go to the bathroom."

"That's good."

"I was wondering if I could read that book while I'm in here."

"Nancy Drew?"

"Yep."

"Are you allowed?"

Alfred's head disappeared behind the corner for a moment. There was more mumbling. Then the head reappeared.

"Yes."

"I'll bring it over later."

"Thank you."

Alfred's head disappeared. There was more mumbling, and then it came back.

"Thank you, *Danny*."

"That's okay, Alfred."

Mrs. Bagley returned and set two sandwiches on the table. Danny reminded himself not to put his elbows on the table, a rule the Ryan family was aware of but did not enforce. In fact, the Ryan children found it advisable to read at the table, thus avoiding eye contact with their father, who might misinterpret a glance in his direction. Other families, Danny knew, absolutely forbade reading at meals. As he sat across the table from Mrs. Bagley, he wished he had a book to read.

"Danny, what is Alfred like?"

"Huh? I mean, pardon me?"

"Is he a good boy?"

"I guess so. He's a lot better than me, and I'm not so bad."

"Why doesn't he stay in his boundaries?"

"He does most of the time. Every now and then he gets excited and crosses over, but that's nothing. I mean, it doesn't mean he's bad. At least I don't think so."

"Don't you have some boundaries?"

"Not like certain streets. My mother just says stay out of trouble. She leaves the rest to me."

"That's awfully vague. I don't know if Alfred would do well with that kind of rule."

"You might be right."

Danny was immediately sorry he had said this, even though it was true.

Alfred was excitable, and his concrete rules did help keep him in check. Still, agreeing with an adult on such a thing was traitorous.

"That's an honest answer," Mrs. Bagley said.

This was too cozy. The next thing Danny knew she'd be inviting him to church.

"But I think he'd do okay if he could go a little farther on his own, like to the swap shop," Danny said. "He loves that place."

"I don't know. There are so many temptations. How do you resist them?"

Danny felt himself sinking deeper and deeper. He thought maybe he should fake a pain in his stomach and run home before he really fouled things up. In a minute he would be telling her about the picture of the "Barrelly Covered" lady and how he tried to keep his eyes off it, but that was sheer madness. He had better walk a more conventional line.

"I ask myself what my guardian angel would think."

"Oh dear," said Mrs. Bagley.

"I'm sorry. That's Catholic stuff. I shouldn't say it here."

"Do you talk with Alfred about your guardian angel?"

"No! I know Baptists don't like it. I'm sorry I brought it up."

"Angels are all right. It's just that we don't worship them."

"I don't worship mine either."

"That's good to hear."

Danny had to do something to get off the topic of angels. He didn't understand it very well himself. If he answered any questions about angels, he would certainly get something wrong and further destroy the reputation of the Catholic Church. There could be a serious sin in that, maybe even mortal.

"This is good tea," he said, holding up the glass.

"My goodness, there's blood under your thumb!"

"Just from a sliver. It's nothing."

"You haven't had good luck lately."

"No, ma'am," Danny said. "It's been a tough week."

Danny had the impulse to say just how tough, but he didn't. Mrs. Bagley could not help him. Not even an angel could. Everything in his life was so delicately balanced that it would take God himself to unstack it without causing the pieces to fall into a calamitous heap that Danny might never be able to crawl out from under. He took a bite of his sandwich and chewed silently. Mrs. Bagley watched him, and her eyes filled again with tears, but Danny was too consumed by his thoughts to notice.

A few minutes later Danny was on his way back to his own house. He was hurrying because he wanted to read the rest of *The Mystery at the Moss-Covered Mansion* before he turned it over to Alfred. Nancy Drew had appeared across the Hillsborough River in a perilous situation. Perhaps her book would help him understand why, and finishing it might even eradicate the mansion from his mind. That was to be desired. The other houses he had imagined had cheered him up, but the moss-covered mansion was sinister. Good riddance. Danny strode into his house and right into his mother's arms.

"How'd it go?" she asked.

"Okay. I had lunch over there."

"And about the fleas?"

"Taken care of."

"What did you say exactly?"

"We don't have fleas. We never did. The fleas were a joke. It didn't go over."

Danny's mother thought for several seconds before she released her hold on his shoulder.

"I suppose that's good enough, though I don't know if we'll ever fully recover. Well, since you've had your lunch, you can go right down to see the Arnolds. Let's get the whole thing taken care of."

"Can't I have a minute's rest?"

"No rest for the wicked, and the righteous don't need it," she replied.

"Okay, I'll take Abigail's book back," Danny said, heaving a pointedly beleaguered sigh.

"Oh, my poor baby! He can hardly take a single step. How can I be so cruel as to send him out in this condition?"

"Yeah, yeah."

"And do not fail to let me know how it goes."

Danny retrieved *The Mystery at the Moss-Covered Mansion* and headed down the street, planning to postpone the flea explanation until after he had read the rest of the story. He would do his reading in the weeds near the Arnold house. With a little luck, he might observe Abigail leaving, whereupon he could rush over, make his flea explanation, and get away without seeing her. He settled himself on the ground and opened the book.

Forty-five minutes later he arrived at the last page. The book had been a Pandora's box of gypsies, escaped monkeys, plane crashes, car chases, heart attacks, disguised heiresses, and tin cans full of money, with a mean-tempered leopard thrown in. Danny had to admit that a great deal happened in the book, and an important point was that the man at the mansion who seemed so menacing turned out to be an artist with a gruff manner but good intentions. All along, he was suspected of horrid acts, but in the end, he was okay.

This was Danny's favorite part of the book, that and the fact that everything turned out well, which come to think of it was what he liked about the movies he saw at the Springs Theater. Of course, there were a few in which nice people ultimately were defeated or died, but Danny left the theater if he thought they were going in that direction. He couldn't understand why anybody bothered to make such stuff.

Danny looked again toward the Arnold house. He had glanced at it many times during his reading and had seen no one come or go. If Abigail was there, he would just have to bear it. He placed *The Mystery at the Moss-Covered Mansion* in the crotch of a tree and headed for the front door of the Arnold house. He knocked and was surprised when Mr. Arnold answered the door in white shirt and a tie. Danny was not sure exactly what Mr. Arnold did for a living, but he was unusual in Nowhere because he dressed up to go to work.

"You're Danny, aren't you?" he said pleasantly.

"Yes, sir."

"Come on in. I'll get Abigail."

"Oh, no sir!" Danny said. "I want to talk to you."

"Is that so? Well, let's sit on the porch here. Would you like a soft drink?"

"No, thanks."

"Okay, shoot. What's on your mind?"

"My mom sent me down. Uh . . . she says thanks for the banana stalks."

"Oh, she's very welcome. We have a lot of them. I really don't know if they'll work with fleas, but I've heard so much about it, I was glad to have a chance to see if they'd have an effect. We never had fleas ourselves."

"Yeah, well, that's the thing. We don't either."

"No?"

"It's a misunderstanding."

Mr. Arnold stared at Danny for a moment and then a look of realization flooded over his face.

"Oh, I see. Of course not. Tell your mother it's forgotten."

There was something in Mr. Arnold's manner that was a little unnerving, but Danny couldn't put his finger on exactly what. He was not threatening or mean. Quite the contrary. Danny carried on.

"I made a stupid joke about fleas and everybody took it the wrong way."

"That's so common," Mr. Arnold said. "I can't count the times I've had the same thing happen to me."

Danny shifted in his seat. Things seemed to be going well. Why did he feel so uneasy?

"Are you sure I can't get you that soda?" Mr. Arnold asked.

"No, sir. Just to be clear. We don't have fleas and we never did, okay?"

"Absolutely!"

"I'm not just saying that we don't have fleas. I'm telling you we actually don't have fleas."

"And I'm saying that I understand and am happy for you."

"I'll be going then."

"Danny, you are welcome here anytime. I've enjoyed talking to you. Give my best to your mother."

Mr. Arnold opened the door, and Danny walked out, pausing a few steps down the path to turn around. Mr. Arnold was still standing in the doorway. He gave Danny a hearty wave. Danny waggled his fingers back and headed home, thinking the Arnolds were the most exasperating family on earth.

16

Danny retrieved *The Mystery at the Moss-Covered Mansion* and headed over to Alfred's house. He decided to bypass Mrs. Bagley and slip around to Alfred's bedroom in the back. The casement window was cranked open, and from ten feet away he could hear Alfred humming to himself. By the time Danny had crept to the window, Alfred had stopped humming. Danny arrived just in time to hear Alfred mutter something that sounded like "Abigail," but he couldn't be sure. It was probably his imagination.

"Alfred!" Danny hissed.

Alfred jumped off his bed and dropped to the floor out of sight. A moment later he rose, hugging his pillow.

"You scared me," he whispered.

"What am I supposed to do?"

"You shouldn't hiss."

"I don't want your mom to hear."

"Why not?"

"She's asking too many questions about stuff."

"What?" Alfred asked, suddenly fearful.

"About why I made up the flea story and whether you're a good boy or not."

"What did you say?"

"I said you were a lot better than me."

This did not seem of much comfort to Alfred, who cast his eyes downward. Behind him, Danny saw the door to Alfred's room start to open. He ducked out of sight, leaving Alfred looking bewilderedly out the window.

"Alfred," Mrs. Bagley said.

For the second time inside a minute, Alfred jumped a foot in the air.

"I didn't mean to scare you, son," she said. "I just came in to see if you needed anything."

"No, ma'am," Alfred said stiffly.

"Don't be so cold. You know your mama loves her little boy."

From beneath the window, Danny could hardly believe his ears. Mrs. Bagley was a diligent housekeeper and cook, but this expression of motherly affection was unprecedented. Danny was so intrigued that he risked a look in the corner of the window. Mrs. Bagley was crushing Alfred against her portly frame. The top of his head was pushing up into her breasts. This was shocking, and Danny dropped down, too embarrassed to look any longer. He heard Mrs. Bagley ask, "Would you like a biscuit with apple jelly?" Alfred declined.

Danny could have killed him for acting so suspiciously. Alfred never turned down food. He had a heightened system or some such thing that caused him to burn calories almost instantaneously. Mrs. Bagley was always pushing food down his throat just to keep him from wasting away. Danny could hear the note of concern in her voice when she said "No? Are you sure?" Alfred said he was. When she left, Danny rose angrily and rammed his head into the casement window. He stifled a cry of pain and clapped his hand to his scalp. Alfred came back to the window and looked on sympathetically. Every kid in the neighborhood had run into a casement window and was familiar with the ensuing pain and feeling of helplessness.

"Open the screen and take this book," Danny said through clenched teeth.

"How will I say I got it?" Alfred asked, not moving to unfasten the screen.

"Don't say anything. Just take it and hide it."

"I can't. She'll find it."

"Does she search your room every day?" Danny asked.

Alfred made a face that suggested his mother did exactly that. Then his expression turned to one of horror. At the same moment, Danny felt something trickle down the side of his nose. It was crimson. His run-in with the window had been more damaging than he had realized.

"Go to the bathroom and get me some toilet paper," Danny said, "and don't forget to flush the toilet."

"I don't have to pee," Alfred replied.

"So your mother won't suspect, stupid."

"Okay."

Danny waited expectantly, his fingers pressed with all the force he could muster against his scalp. The minutes passed. He heard Alfred's mother call, "Are you all right?" Alfred answered that he was. Shortly afterward, Danny heard the toilet flush, and Alfred came back with a wad of toilet paper.

"Why were you gone so long?" Danny whispered as Alfred passed him the tissue.

"It took me a while to go."

Danny had learned that there was no use trying to explain to Alfred about subjects such as flushing toilets for effect alone. He never learned, and Danny doubted he even understood the principles involved.

"Glad you were able to squeeze some out," Danny commented dryly.

"Yeah," Alfred said.

Danny wiped his head with half the toilet paper and showed the result to Alfred, who reluctantly shifted his eyes to the area.

"It's cut."

"I know that! How bad?"

"It's like a half-inch long, up in your hair where the corner punched in. Blood keeps coming out."

The first half of the tissue was a mess, so Danny dropped it and pressed the other half to his scalp, making sure to put his finger right over the wound.

"That's stopped it," Alfred said, beginning to look a little woozy.

Danny continued to apply pressure while Alfred stared into the corner of the room. After several minutes, Danny raised the tissue.

"Looks better," Alfred said, "but it's still oozing."

Having made this diagnosis, he sat down heavily on the edge of his bed.

"Okay," Danny said, continuing to hold the tissue on his scalp. "I will go around to the front door. Give me time to get there. Then call your mom in and say you want that biscuit after all. While she is in here, I will ring the bell and leave the book on the step. That way, I don't have to see her, and you get your book. Okay?"

Alfred looked thoughtful.

"You want the book?" Danny asked peevishly.

"Yeah."

"Then you better say 'Okay,' or I might throw it in the creek. I'm tired of messing with it."

Alfred nodded his head, and Danny crept around to the front. He looked in the window, saw Mrs. Bagley heading for Alfred's room, placed the book on the steps, rang the front doorbell, and dived into the bushes. In a moment, Mrs. Bagley opened the door and found *The Mystery at the Moss-Covered Mansion*. She picked it up and looked from left to right.

"Danny?" she called, and receiving no response, closed the door.

Danny poked his head up out of the bushes and looked inside the Bagley house. Mrs. Bagley did not head toward Alfred's room. Instead she sat down at the dining room table, opened the book, and started to read. Danny watched Mrs. Bagley's lips move for several minutes before he left.

The afternoon was waning. His father would be home soon. That thought brought on a nauseous moment, but he fought it back. The important thing right now was to get the cut on his head under control. He did not feel like explaining another wound to his mother or sister. They had enough to worry about. If it would stop bleeding, he could cover it with some ingenious hair combing. He was glad there had been no haircut money for several weeks. His mother had trimmed around his ears and shaved the back of his neck, but the rest was luxuriant.

He took a look at his tissue wad and shuddered. It was a mess. This was the first time he had ever had occasion to wish he carried a hanky. His mother had suggested it many times, but he had always refused. Eventually she had given up, except on Sunday when he went to mass. She insisted he take one then. But now he was developing an appreciation for what a hanky could mean in an emergency.

At the door to his house, Danny heard his mother talking to Ruth in the bedroom. He darted to the bathroom and closed the door. On the washbasin, he found his father's styptic pencil. He had seen him use it to stop the bleeding when he nicked himself shaving; however, if he had time, Mr. Ryan preferred putting a little piece of toilet paper on the cut and letting it dry. This method was unsightly, and Danny considered the pencil much preferable. However, he needed to get cleaned up before he could use it.

He took off his clothes and stepped into the concrete shower stall. There was no time to fire up the water heater, so he would have to take a cold one. He braced himself and stiffened for several seconds as he endured the first blast of cold water, then quickly soaped all over with a special emphasis on his scalp. In the Ryan house, they used Ivory soap. It was cheap, and Danny had liked that it was advertised as being "ninety-nine and forty-four one-hundredths percent pure" until he had asked his father, "Pure what?" His father had answered, "Animal tallow, probably." Danny had inquired as to what "animal tallow" was and had been dismayed to find out that it was animal fat. "We used to make our own soap on the farm out of the leftovers," his dad had said. "Most soap is basically animal fat with lye and a couple of other things." This took the shine off the purity claim, but as long as he had to use soap, Danny was satisfied with Ivory.

After a good wash, he stepped to the mirror and parted his hair. He could see the cut in his scalp. It was clean but beginning to bleed again. He took the styptic pencil, applied it to the wound, and immediately discovered why his father preferred the toilet paper method. An intense, highly focused stinging sensation sent him hopping around the bathroom, vowing to wear a beard when he grew up.

It was awful but did not last long. When he examined the results in the mirror, he was satisfied. No blood. Unfortunately, the cut lay in the natural part in his hair, so to obscure it, he would have to make his part on the opposite side. This proved easier in concept than in practice, but Danny discovered he could accomplish it if he created a large wave on his forehead. This was a style some boys affected, but Danny had never found it compelling. Yet he made do and eventually created something that looked intentional. He put on his clothes and strolled into the kitchen. His mother was just coming into the room.

"Good Lord!"

He looked up at her innocently.

"What made you decide to do that?" she asked.

"Just something new," he answered casually.

"It certainly creates an effect. Let's show Ruth."

They walked to the bedroom door. Danny's mother told him to wait outside for a minute.

"Ruth, I want to show you something," he heard his mother say.

"I'm awfully tired, Mom."

"Oh, you'll want to see it. I doubt it will last long. May I present the new Danny Ryan!"

Danny walked into the room, and Ruth burst out laughing. He turned to the side, and she laughed harder.

"He looks like he has a bun on his forehead! Oh, turn all the way around. You can even see it sticking up from the back!"

Ruth was gasping with laughter.

"I don't think it's that funny," Danny commented.

"Au contraire," Ruth said weakly. "You mustn't step out of the house like that, really. I'll fix it for you."

"I think I'll keep it this way for a while," Danny said.

"You didn't go down to the Arnolds' like that, did you?" Danny's mother asked.

"No, I did it afterward."

"Why didn't you heat some water?"

"I was in a hurry."

"Mom," said Ruth, falling back on her pillows, "the inspiration for this hairstyle hit him, and he had to try it as fast as possible! You should understand that."

Danny ran his hand preeningly along the side of his head and peered into the dresser mirror.

"How did it go with the Arnolds?" his mother asked

"Smooth as silk," he replied.

"Who did you speak to? Not Abigail?"

"Mr. Arnold. He said he understood perfectly. Call him up. He'll tell you."

"There's something suspicious about this," she observed.

Mr. Ryan appeared suddenly in the doorway.

"What are you doing in here?" he asked gruffly.

"Just talking, Dad," Ruth said in a very small voice.

"Just talking," he replied, giving the words such a nasty turn that Ruth gulped.

"Harold, let's go in the kitchen," Danny's mother said.

Mr. Ryan's lip curled, and he raised his hand. His wife did not cringe. She just stared quietly at his face. Danny thought she might be imagining what he looked like in times past, maybe in his Lincoln costume, but she did not have time to do much imagining. Mr. Ryan slapped her face and then looked at each of the children. His expression did not soften as he stared at his ailing daughter and then at his son standing like a statue in the corner of the room. Danny wondered what his father was seeing. It could not be his family as they really were. He must be imagining something threatening and horrible.

"Mom!" Ruth whispered and tried to rise from the bed.

Mr. Ryan snorted and walked out of the room.

Mrs. Ryan rushed to Ruth's side and gently pressed her back into the pillows.

"It didn't hurt," she said. "He didn't mean to hurt me. He's just on edge. I'll take care of it."

She tried to leave the room, but Danny blocked her path.

"Leave him alone," he begged. "You'll just make it worse."

She leaned down, kissed his cheek, and moved him gently to one side.

"You have to trust me," she said. "He's sick. We have to make allowances."

Danny watched helplessly as his mother left the room. He climbed in bed with Ruth, and they sat together silently. In a few minutes, Ruth fell asleep, leaving Danny to watch the doorway, expecting some form of disaster to come through it any minute. He felt the slightest slip on his part could spell doom. He went over all the things he had touched or influenced during the last few hours, right down to carefully washing and replacing his father's styptic pencil in exactly the position on the sink in which he had found it. He felt that in that instance, at least, he was all right. Even his father's keen perception could not possibly detect the minute amount of material that had come off the pencil. Or could he? The man had a supernatural radar, and you never knew when it would flick on or where he would aim it.

The light at the window faded. Danny sat in the dark, listening to Ruth's unsteady breathing. Then his father began to cough. The spell went on and on, sometimes nearer to the bedroom and sometimes farther away. Just as Danny was about to run screaming from the house, it stopped. He rubbed his arm nervously and discovered he was covered in perspiration. That was no good, sweating in Ruth's bed. He rose quietly and sat down on the floor. Eventually, he drifted off to sleep.

He woke in the middle of the night and made an effort to get up to go the couch, but he could not find the energy. It was much nicer in the bedroom, even on the hard floor. He could hear Ruth breathing more easily now, and he could take in the faint scent of perfume and lotion that made the bedroom so different from the rest of the house. All things soft and feminine were concentrated at the bedroom end. He turned over and went back to sleep, not waking again until morning. The sky was brightening when he got up and made the short walk into the kitchen. His mother was sitting at the table with a cup of coffee. His father had already left. Danny went to the fridge to get some milk for cereal.

"Good morning," his mother said. "You didn't make up the couch."

"I slept on the floor."

"That won't hurt you. The Japanese do it all the time."

"I didn't say I was hurt."

"I thought you might think you were."

"Nope."

"Why don't you go to the pool again today. It will be a little treat."

"I think I'll just mess around. Thanks, though."

"Well, light the water heater before you go. I want to give Ruth a bath."

Danny ate some cereal and then went into the heater closet. He was the preferred heater lighter in the Ryan family. The closet was tiny and you had to get down on your knees and peer into the firebox to see when the kerosene started flowing in. At that point, a twist of flaming paper had to be thrust into the firebox, and then the result observed until it was certain that the flames were at their proper height. If you put in the twist too soon, it might burn down and be put out by the incoming kerosene. If you waited too long, the fire might be extinguished by too large a puddle of kerosene.

It was amazing to Danny that a flammable liquid could actually put a fire out; however, sometimes, for reasons inexplicable, the big puddle of kerosene would ignite and that was bad because then the fire would blaze too high, making a roaring sound in the stovepipe and scaring everybody to death. However, if all went well, the usual procedure was to let the heater run for fifteen minutes and then turn it off and use up the resulting hot water.

Danny watched the fire until it was burning properly and then went back into the kitchen. His mother had gone in to check on Ruth, so he took the opportunity to slip out the back door and into the trees beyond. He couldn't bear to sit around pretending things weren't out of whack, but his mother would have it no other way. She would discuss almost anything else freely, but not her husband. Danny had observed the same reluctance in Mrs. Bagley and wondered if it was a rule of married life.

Whatever the reason, it made communication difficult when the main problems seemed to be caused by husbands. Danny dreaded the prospect of being a husband someday. He would hate being so troublesome. The only really happy couples Danny had observed were in the movies, though the Arnolds seemed happy. However, he would have to see more of them to make an informed judgment. You could never tell what was going on in a house from the outside.

Having nowhere else to go, he headed for Buddy's place. Some canoe therapy might cheer him up if he could avoid the splinters. As he approached, he heard hammering and found Buddy at work. He had done a great deal since yesterday, having applied the orange crate slats to one side of the canoe and part of the other. With the slats on, the project was beginning to look like a tidy craft. Danny's mood improved at the thought of one day getting into the canoe and going down the river. There was a sense of freedom in that kind of traveling, different from riding a bike. On the river, you were driven by a big never-ceasing force. It held out the prospect of going far away.

He and Buddy worked together, finishing the slats and smoothing down the edges in preparation for laying on the canvas skin. Buddy was a good instructor, and Danny felt like an asset to the operation. He noted to himself that the world looked better when you were making progress toward something worthwhile. Around noon, Buddy's dad emerged from the Airstream. He came wordlessly into the shop, nodded to the boys, and walked over to the workbench. He picked up a big wooden clamp and twisted it open. Then he threw up and fell down clutching his stomach. Buddy got him to his feet and walked him toward the trailer, but halfway there, he shrugged Buddy off and turned to Danny, who was following at a respectful distance. Danny thought he was going to catch some more biting commentary and braced himself.

"I apologize," the man said with great formality. "I am sorry you had to see that, but I suppose you may have seen worse. If you haven't, I know you eventually will. May God spare you as much as possible."

"That's fine, Dad," Buddy said. "Let's go in now."

The two disappeared into the trailer, leaving Danny wondering whether to stay or go. He didn't feel he could just disappear without a word, so he went back to the canoe and continued working. To his surprise, Buddy joined him shortly and took up his tools as if nothing had happened. Danny stared at him in wonder until Buddy noticed the look on his face.

"Dad hasn't been right since the war," Buddy said. "He took it a lot harder than most. Al's coming over. We might have to move Dad back to the V.A. hospital."

Buddy gave this speech in a matter-of-fact way, without any note of complaint or judgment.

"Maybe he'll get better," Danny said.

"Maybe," Buddy answered, turning back to the canoe.

Before too long, Al drove up and went into the trailer. A few minutes later, they heard laughter and Al emerged.

"You give him some Pepto?" he asked Buddy.

"Yep."

"Where'd he get the grog?"

"You tell me. I clean the trailer."

"You think Danny's bringing it to him?"

Danny was surprised to be brought into the conversation, but he did his best.

"Somebody else must bring the booze. I could bring him cigars, though."

This was the first time he could remember having the occasion to use the term "booze," and he was pleased at the effect.

"If we could limit him to cigars, we'd be in good shape," Al said, laughing.

He shook his head and walked over to the canoe. Danny and Buddy showed him their progress, and he helped them stretch the canvas, which was secured above the waterline with brass tacks. The work went fast with Al's assistance. Once the canvas was on, Buddy brought out Cokes, and they sat under the roof where they could appreciate their work.

"How's Alfred doing?" Buddy asked.

"Locked in his room," Danny replied.

"How long?"

"Don't know. His dad's out of town." Danny was not sure how much he should say, but he took a chance and added, "I'm afraid he might get the belt."

"The belt! For hugging a diving suit!" Al exploded.

"He was outside his boundaries. Mr. Bagley takes Alfred's boundaries pretty seriously."

"That poor little innocent," Al said. "Well, pretty soon the swap shop won't be there to tempt him."

"What!" Danny said.

"I'm moving it out of the Springs. There's too much salvage to be contained in my present quarters. Got to have room for expansion."

Danny was stricken, and he showed it. No swap shop at the Springs. That was inconceivable.

"Things change, son," Al said. "You can't let it get to you. You might want the swap shop to stay, but if my dad was alive he would be delighted to see it go."

"Why?"

"He was around when Sulphur Springs was something else. It was beautiful. Everything looked good."

"What happened?"

"First there was the Great Depression. Everything in the whole country was on shaky ground. Even so, the Springs was keeping up. Then a hurricane hit. It rained so much that the dam broke, which flooded everything and caused a lot of damage. Along with the depression, it was too much. The area couldn't come back and it went pretty far downhill. Dad lost our house at the Springs, but we stayed around. He actually had an apartment in the hotel where he could look out and see my sign. He gave me hell about it."

Danny had heard many references to the mysterious Great Depression. Maybe he would look it up in the encyclopedia; no, the encyclopedia was too old for that, but he would find out some way what forces had destroyed the Springs. It might clarify a great deal.

"It's best to stay light on your feet," Al concluded. "You avoid a lot of useless misery that way."

Danny nodded as if he understood.

17

~~~~~~~~~

Al sat with Danny and Buddy a while longer, and then went into the trailer to check on Buddy's dad. When he came out, he was chuckling.

"Bart's got the metabolism of a rhinoceros," he said, "but even a rhinoceros can drink himself to death if he's dedicated. Nothing's worked for the last nine years; I don't see what will work now. If you want to pen him up again, we can try. I wouldn't blame you."

"We'll make out," Buddy answered.

Al punched Buddy on the shoulder and headed toward his truck, but he stopped and turned to Danny.

"Be careful with the booze, Danny," he said. "You can see that Bart will never build his boats, and a lot of people are moving to Florida who would buy a nice boat at a good price."

"Don't you mind when he says things like that?" Danny asked after Al had driven away.

"Why? He's just telling the truth. We both know Dad's near the end of his rope."

"Can't something be done?"

"We can work on our canoe. It might cheer him up if we finish it."

The boys spent the next couple of hours putting on coats of dope. After a while, Danny got a little woozy from the fumes, and Buddy took him behind the trailer to show him an ingenious device he had made for transporting a canoe. It was simple, just some bicycle wheels and a few other parts that slipped under the canoe and were secured with stretchy bands.

"You can even pull it behind your bike," Buddy said, "as long as you don't try to turn any sharp corners."

"Buddy!" Bart yelled from the Airstream. "Is Danny still here?"

"No, Dad."

Buddy put his finger to his lips and waved Danny down the road.

"That damn Al has tied me down."

This was the last thing Danny heard as he left. When he came to the main road, he considered his options. There was no use going to the Bagley house with Alfred in quarantine, no use going to his own house with the memory of last night hanging in the air, no use going to Halper's store with its inquisitive proprietor, and no use going to Hanna's Whirl with its confusing apparitions. Somehow he was drawn toward the fish hatchery. Very little bad could happen at the fish hatchery if he stayed away from the pools, and he might see the girl again. He followed the path along the creek and came to the spot where he and Alfred had met the beautiful Donna, so long ago it seemed. He was flabbergasted to find her there again, just as before.

"What are you doing here?" Danny asked bluntly.

"The same as you," she answered.

"I'm not doing anything."

"You are a very unusual boy then," she answered. "Most people are always doing something. Perhaps you are watching me as you did at the Springs two days ago."

So, she had seen him and must think him pretty low. He wanted to say it had not been his idea, but why should she believe him? He took a step back down the path.

"Don't be contrite. Why don't we wait together for a while?"

The girl's tone was soft and inviting. He sat down several feet away. She seemed to find this funny, and she flashed her white teeth. Once again, Danny was struck by how out of place she looked in this little corner of the woods. She belonged more properly on a movie screen, but even on this unglamorous trail, she had chosen the perfect spot to sit amidst the foliage with her flowered dress pooling out picturesquely around her. Danny hadn't the slightest doubt that when she rose, she would have no speck of debris on her. She would be perfect in the rising and perfect in the completion of the rising.

"There's a big snapping turtle in this creek," Danny said suddenly.

"Is this to be our subject? Snapping turtles?"

She was right. He had commenced with a flaky Alfred Bagley–style comment, but when he tried to come out with a Danny Ryan comment, he did even worse.

"I imagined I saw you across the river a couple of days ago. You were at a little house having coffee on the porch with a dog. You looked across the river. I thought you were looking at me."

"Did you think I was beautiful?"

Now that was definitely an improper question. It suggested a shallowness of character. She knew she was beautiful. Danny sat silently.

"You did not find me beautiful?"

"Okay. You were beautiful," Danny admitted, trying to shame her with his frankness, "if it's so important to you."

"How did my beauty make you feel?"

She was impossible. Danny shook his head.

"It is a difficult topic?"

She asked this kindly. Danny had no idea what she was driving at, but he nodded.

"What other things do you find beautiful?"

"Excuse me?"

"Where is the beauty in your life?"

Why did she keep asking about beauty? Did she have it on the brain? Danny wondered if she was speaking in code. But why would she, sitting on a little trail by a creek in the middle of Nowhere? It made no sense.

"Pobrecito," she said.

"What does that mean?"

"Poor little one."

This was insulting in numerous ways. Danny felt a flash of irritation.

"Don't call me that!"

"I must, because you cannot answer a question about the most important thing in the world."

"What!"

"What is the world without beauty?"

"Could you be a little clearer?"

"What in this life warms you?"

"Uh . . ."

"You must learn to accept the warmth."

Okay, she was touched. If she were not so good-looking, she would be in an institution. Obviously, she had to be handled with kid gloves. He would distract her with something more commonplace.

"How do you know Buddy?"

"In the same way I know you."

She was making less and less sense, but why did Danny feel stupid? She seemed so at ease throwing out perplexing questions and comments. Was she just tired of ordinary conversation? Could it be as simple as that?

"You're from Ybor City, right?"

The girl rose. Danny had been right. Nothing smudged. Nothing out of place.

"May I ask you something?" she said.

"Sure."

"Will you think about what we have said today, sitting here in the forest together?"

There was nothing to think about, but Danny nodded. Her eyes flashed.

"Make use of your chances, Pobrecito. Don't live a life of regret."

She moved off, leaving Danny to ponder beauty and warmth. What was the point of it? He was too busy trying to manage an uncertain world to focus on beauty, and the warmth thing didn't make any sense at all. But now that Donna was gone, Danny felt bereft, and he wandered back up the creek, eventually entering the thicket where he had run into Abigail a couple of days before. It felt cozy. He threw himself down and tried to think about beauty.

The most beautiful things were in the movies. That was evident. Most everything else seemed drab by comparison. Danny had once seen a movie that was set in Florida. It was about fighting the Seminoles. He had been shocked at how beautiful Florida had looked on the Technicolor screen. Where was that Florida? They must have done something to it. Still, there were things in Florida he recognized as beautiful. The waving grasses in the clear water of a spring run. In a diving mask, it was almost like watching a movie.

Danny was elated at having thought of something real that struck him as beautiful. He wished he could have effortlessly tossed it off to the girl as if he had a hundred such examples. But she would probably have directed another impossible question at him and spoiled his triumph. He wondered where their talk would have wound up if he had given all the right answers.

Probably in circles. Danny tired of thinking about beauty and fell asleep. He didn't wake up until Alfred Bagley shook his shoulder.

"Isn't this where Abigail comes?" Alfred asked.

"Yeah, I guess. What are you doing out of your room?"

"I was looking out the window, and I saw that bloody tissue you dropped. I wanted to get it before somebody found it, so I opened the screen and climbed out, but I couldn't go back in."

"Why not?"

"I don't know. I felt sick to my stomach."

"What about your mom?"

"She's working in the garden."

"How long have you been gone?"

"Fifteen minutes maybe."

"We've got to get you back! Your dad will kill you."

Alfred looked around the thicket as if he would like to set up housekeeping and live there for the rest of his life. Danny thought there was little chance that the diligent Mrs. Bagley would not have discovered that Alfred was out of his room. However, they might get him back soon enough to prevent her from calling the police or, perhaps worse, Mr. Bagley. She had been acting strangely of late, and she might be maneuvered into ignoring the incident.

Maybe they could confess that Danny had gone to the window and then say Alfred got so worried about Danny's head wound that he went out to check on him. The timeline didn't quite match up, but that could be blurred, and the evidence on Danny's scalp would be persuasive. It was a harebrained story, but that was the beautiful thing with Alfred. People expected improbable behavior out of him. Danny pushed Alfred to get him going. He moved with exasperating slowness, and then stopped cold, refusing to jump over the creek.

"Let's get going!" Danny shouted.

"Look at that big turtle!"

Danny saw that the alligator turtle was back in his old spot. This was all they needed, an enticing distraction to increase Alfred's reluctance.

"We'll look at him later! He's always there."

"How do you know?"

"I've seen him before."

"With Abigail?"

"Yes, get a move on, for Pete's sake."

Alfred did as commanded, but he required constant prodding. Danny took them through the woods to a point where they would emerge in the position least likely to be seen from the garden, where Mrs. Bagley might still be working. They would be crossing open ground, and a length of street, but they might make it without being detected. If this worked out, it would be the greatest stealth operation the two had ever pulled off. If only Alfred were not acting like a bag of sand! Danny pushed him into the open and dragged him along toward the Bagley house. They reached the back without incident, and Danny began to hope things might turn out well.

At Alfred's window, they found the situation just as he had left it, with no sign that Mrs. Bagley had been in his room. The screen was off, lying on Alfred's bed. Even the bloody tissue was sitting on the window ledge where Alfred had placed it before he was seized by the compulsion to run away. Danny stood for a moment observing the scene, trying to think of any factor that needed attention before he put Alfred safely back inside. He could think of nothing, but when he turned around to give Alfred instructions, he was gone. Danny glanced about and spotted him rounding the corner of the house nearest the garden, heading straight for his mother.

Danny sprinted after Alfred and took him down with his hand over his mouth, a technique he had learned from a war movie. Luckily, there was a cover of weeds between the house and the garden, so Mrs. Bagley, whom Danny had glimpsed briefly, could not see them. Danny could feel Alfred's lips moving.

"Be quiet. Do you want to get caught?" Danny said, removing his hand.

"I don't care."

"Well, I do. Just do me a favor and go back in your room. I'm going to try to get you out of this thing."

"What will you do?"

"I don't know yet, but it won't work if you keep piling crime on crime!"

Alfred bit his lip. Danny had come up with some amazing escapes. He might do it again.

"Okay," he said.

"Wait here just a minute," Danny said.

He slithered forward through the weeds to a point where he could see Mrs. Bagley. As he had hoped, she was engrossed and had not seen anything of the boys. She had on her straw sun hat and canvas gloves, but her hoe was leaning against the garden shed. Instead of gardening, Mrs. Bagley was sitting on a stool in the doorway of the shed reading *The Mystery at the Moss-Covered Mansion*. Danny recognized the dust jacket.

"She's reading that book!" Alfred hissed, having crawled up behind Danny.

"Pipe down. This is a break for us. Let's get back."

"She never gave it to me," Alfred muttered.

The boys crabbed backward and then crawled around to Alfred's window. Danny was in a fever to get Alfred back into his cage before the situation blew up. As exasperating as Alfred was, he was essential. Where would Danny be if Alfred were forbidden to see him or were shipped off to some Bible reform camp? The days would be empty. He grabbed the bloody tissue, put it temporarily between his teeth, and gave Alfred a leg up to the window ledge.

"Alfred!"

Mr. Bagley had come around the corner and found them like that. His searing gaze took in the open window, Alfred's precarious stance, Danny's intertwined fingers under his foot, the bloody tissue in Danny's mouth. This was as bad as it could get. Danny spat out the tissue.

"Mr. Bagley . . ."

"Silence!"

Mr. Bagley moved forward and yanked Alfred down from the window ledge where he had been struck as motionless as a pillar of salt. Danny stepped out of the way.

"I hurt my head," he began.

"Go to your own house," Mr. Bagley said flatly, dragging Alfred toward the garden. This was where Mr. Bagley meted out punishment: in the shed.

Danny looked at the black leather belt around Mr. Bagley's ample waist. How could little Alfred bear up under even one lick from that awful thing with its bright silver buckle? Danny could not go home. He had to do something. He ran around in front of Mr. Bagley, who was dangling Alfred by one wrist, the boy's shoe tips barely touching the ground.

"Don't punish Alfred. He's a good boy."

"Go home."

"It's all my fault!"

Mr. Bagley brushed past Danny, who followed a few paces behind, desperately trying to think of some action that would not make conditions worse. Nothing workable came to mind. Mr. Bagley drew Alfred relentlessly on, but stopped at the edge of the garden. Here he was confounded by the sight of his wife, not working but reading a book of unknown origin with such attention that she did not even note her husband's appearance on the scene. He stood for a moment trying to make sense of what he was seeing. Finally, he spoke.

"Woman, walk this way!"

Mrs. Bagley looked up in confusion. She spotted her husband, tried to struggle up too quickly from the stool, and fell on her backside. Danny cringed. Alfred laughed. Danny wondered how he could do that. He was in dire circumstances, yet he could not help himself. Mr. Bagley let out an exasperated breath and crossed the garden to his wife.

"Go in the house."

Mrs. Bagley got up off her knees. She looked at her husband and then at her son, hanging like a mop.

"What is the trouble, Mr. Bagley?" she asked.

"This is between a son and his father. Go in the house like you were told."

"I will go, but Alfred should come with me."

"Alfred will stay here."

"Mr. Bagley, you are in temper. Remember Proverbs 29:11."

"Is that your Bible in the dirt?" asked Mr. Bagley, glancing down at *The Mystery at the Moss-Covered Mansion.*

"No. That is something else."

"Then go inside and find your Bible."

Mr. Bagley made a move as if to enter the shed, but Mrs. Bagley grabbed up her hoe and stood in the doorway with the handle across her stomach.

"You won't bring our son in here," she said. "In all else I will obey, but this will stop."

Mr. Bagley dropped his arm, but Alfred was so limp that he just puddled at his father's feet. The sun beat down as the seconds passed. Mr. Bagley took out a handkerchief and mopped his brow.

"It's hot out here," Mrs. Bagley observed, getting Alfred to his feet. "There's a pitcher of tea in the refrigerator. Alfred and I have been wondering about that property in Land o' Lakes. Why don't you tell us about it?"

Danny backed away into the weeds. He thought it would be much better if he pretended not to have seen any of what had just happened. Once the Bagleys had moved off, he sneaked over and retrieved Nancy Drew. Then he darted back over to Alfred's window and picked up the bloody tissue, which he put in his pocket, rebuking himself for having forgotten it in the first place. The whole mess might have been avoided if only he had been more thorough.

He was still not sure what the ultimate outcome of the day would be. Mr. Bagley might be in the house this very moment beating the daylights out of Alfred and Mrs. Bagley. He crept around to the front window and peered in. The three of them were sitting stiffly at the table drinking tea. Mrs. Bagley had the big family Bible out, and she was thumbing through it.

"What are you doing?"

Danny whipped his head around so quickly that he scraped his cheek against the concrete wall. Abigail Arnold was standing a few feet away with her arms crossed.

"You love to peep, don't you?"

"Will you shut up!" Danny hissed. "You don't know anything about what I'm doing."

The door to the Bagley house opened. Mrs. Bagley looked at Abigail and then at Danny, up to his waist in the azaleas.

"Go play somewhere else, children," she said. "We're trying to pray."

"In the middle of the afternoon?" Abigail asked.

"Shut up!" Danny said, climbing out of the bushes.

"That's not nice, Danny," Mrs. Bagley observed, turning to Abigail. "Prayer is good at any hour, dear."

"I suppose if you need it," Abigail said.

"Well, we do, so please go on and give us our quiet time."

"Yes, ma'am," Danny said quickly, before Abigail could offer any more caustic remarks.

He took Abigail's hand and led her away. She resisted but he clamped down and jerked her along.

"You're hurting me!"

"Not very much."

"Any hurting is too much!"

But Danny did not stop until they came to the edge of the Arnold property. Then he turned her loose.

"Here's your book. It is now officially off my hands. I think Mrs. Bagley and Alfred would like to read it, so you could offer it to them if you want, but not until tomorrow! Something happened, and they shouldn't be bothered today."

"What happened?"

"It's private."

"If it's private, how come you know?"

"Do I have to tell you the story of my life? Can't you just clam up for once?"

"You're bleeding, you know."

Danny felt his face and, sure enough, there was blood oozing from the place he had scraped against the block wall of the Bagley house. He reached into his pocket and got out the toilet tissue he had stuffed there.

"What on earth is that?" Abigail asked, stopping Danny's hand before he could apply it to his face. "It's covered with dried blood!"

"From yesterday," Danny said, suddenly tired.

"You're getting chewed up," she said. "You need to be more careful."

"I'll make an effort," Danny commented, lying down on the ground and closing his eyes.

"Well, you are not putting that awful thing on your face. Let me fix it."

Abigail drew a crisp hanky out of her pocket and dabbed at the blood. Danny opened his eyes and saw her face close to his, officiously going about her work. At this range, it was easy to see how pretty she was. When she was farther away, she was usually doing something so irritating that you didn't notice. He closed his eyes again.

"So, how did you like Nancy Drew?" she asked.

"I'm glad the man didn't hurt her," Danny replied.

"The gypsy?"

"No, the guy with the beard. He was sneaking up on her, and I couldn't get her attention."

"Not that again!"

"I must have had a dream," said Danny, coming out of a half-sleep.

"What am I to do about you?" Abigail asked.

"You don't have to do anything," Danny said.

"Well, somebody needs to. I can't be the only one who notices you are in a sorry state."

"Other people keep their mouths shut about me," Danny said, but he was thinking of the beautiful Donna, who did not shut up about him at all.

"Those people don't have the right attitude," Abigail said. "If someone is going off course, they need to know it. You can't get better doing the same old thing."

"There's nothing else to do."

"Why won't you just tell me what's wrong?"

There was something new in her voice. Danny looked up at her. Could she be crying? Ridiculous! He sat up.

"I wouldn't know where to start," he said, looking past her.

"You never talk to me, not really," Abigail said, dabbing at her eyes.

"Can you believe my dad runs the machine when they wrap those little Christmas loaves of Holsum Bread?" Danny said. "He's the best wrapper they have."

Abigail sighed, stood up, and started to walk toward her house.

"But he won't be doing it anymore," Danny continued, "because he's got flour in his lungs."

Abigail turned around.

"Say again?"

"When you get it in there you can't get it out."

"Flour in the lungs?" Abigail repeated, touching her chest.

"He's sick."

Danny wondered what would happen now. He felt like crying himself, but he knew it wouldn't help. Abigail walked back and put her arms around him. He felt his strength leaving. That was no good. If he were any weaker, he might make a fatal mistake. Then he heard a cry from down the street.

"Danny! Danny!"

Alfred came running up but stopped a few yards away when he saw Abigail's arms around Danny. He stood gaping and shifting from one foot to the other.

"Shouldn't you be praying?" Danny asked Alfred, pushing Abigail's arms downward.

Alfred recovered himself and began jumping up and down.

"Yeah, but your house is on fire!"

18

~~~~~~

The three children ran down the street together. When Danny's house came into sight they could see the front door standing open and a wisp of smoke ascending from the far end. As they approached, Danny's mom and Mrs. Bagley came through the door supporting Ruth.

"Go help Mr. Bagley," Mrs. Ryan said to Danny.

"You two stay out here," Mrs. Bagley added, speaking to Alfred and Abigail. "Don't get in the way."

Abigail made a face that suggested she could not imagine herself being in the way, but she obeyed, turning her attention to Ruth. Alfred ran down to the end of the house where he could better take in the disaster. Inside, Danny found Mr. Bagley wedged into the heater room, propping open the flue with the end of a broom handle. The stovepipe was cherry red. Mr. Bagley turned his head when Danny came to the door, and the flue cover slipped off the end of the broom, causing a mighty roar of flame in the pipe. Mr. Bagley quickly reinserted the smoldering broom tip and the roaring subsided.

"Can you get up on the roof?" he asked.

"Yes, sir."

"Go up and see what it's like around the pipe. We can probably do without the fire department. The kerosene will burn off in a few more minutes."

Danny streaked to the mulberry tree at the end of the house and clambered up onto the roof, followed closely by Alfred. It took them only a couple of seconds to reach the heater chimney. The smoke they had seen was coming from heated tar. No flames were visible on the roof. Alfred went to the edge, lay down, and hung his head over the eave to shout to his father through the back room window.

"It's not burning!"

"Speak louder," Mr. Bagley yelled.

"It's not burning!" Alfred screamed.

Danny winced. When Alfred really raised his voice, it went through your head like an ice pick.

"That's fine, Alfred. You and Danny keep watch and make sure it cools off. Stay away from the edge of the roof."

Danny left Alfred staring with fascination at the chimney, clambered down the tree, and went back to the heater closet. Mr. Bagley's face was dripping with sweat, his curly brown hair matted on his forehead. The heat from the pipe had turned his face rosy.

"I could spell you on that, sir," Danny said.

Mr. Bagley looked down at Danny. He smiled.

"I'm sure you could, but I will stick to my post, just to say I saw it all the way through."

Danny knew it was getting late. His father would be home soon, and he should not find a pack of strange people around his house, even in an emergency. Danny felt he was the only one of his family with focus enough to appreciate the danger. Ruth would be contending with the effects of leaving her bed, and his mother would probably want to serve everyone cake. But how to handle it?

"Mr. Bagley," he said, "I have to tell you something."

"Yes?"

"But it will have to be between us. You can't tell anyone else."

Mr. Bagley looked over and saw the concern on Danny's face. He thought for a moment and looked at the stovepipe, which had faded to a less violent shade of red.

"I can't make that promise without knowing what you're going to tell me. My conscience might not let me uphold it."

"Well, if you think it's okay, will you keep it secret?"

"I think I can do that."

"It's not good for my father to find all these people at our house. He's been nervous."

Mr. Bagley gave Danny a quizzical look.

"He might get mad."

Mr. Bagley looked again at the stovepipe. Danny dreaded the questions he knew would follow, just like the priest in the confessional, always scouring for details. Mr. Bagley didn't speak for a moment. Then he turned back to Danny and pointed to the flue.

"Do you see what I'm doing?"

Danny nodded.

"Keep doing it until the pipe is a normal color. Don't put any more kerosene in the heater until your father comes home."

"Yes, sir."

Mr. Bagley tried to hand over the broom handle to Danny without letting the flue drop, but he was too big for such an exchange. The flue closed while Danny was taking his position, but the roar was less than before.

"Thank you, sir," Danny said as Mr. Bagley left.

Outside, Danny could hear Mr. Bagley quickly explaining that the emergency was over. When Alfred called to him from the roof, Mr. Bagley said, "Come down, Alfred." When Mrs. Bagley said she would stay and help with Ruth, Mr. Bagley said, "Her mother is the one to do that. We will be on our way." After a moment's silence, he said, "Abigail, go home to your parents. They will be worrying."

"No, they won't."

"They may have heard of the fire. Go home."

Even Abigail could not budge him. He accepted Danny's mother's thanks but did not permit a prolonged scene. In a couple of minutes he had cleared everyone out of the area. Danny sagged against the wall with relief. The stovepipe had turned grey again, but he stood for another ten minutes to make sure. When he dropped the flue there was no reaction at all. He knelt on the floor and made sure the fire had burned out. Then he set aside the broom handle and went to the bedroom. Ruth was back in bed with her eyes closed. Mrs. Ryan took her son by the shoulder and led him out of the room.

"Let her rest," she said.

"Mom," Danny said, "is there some way we can keep from mentioning this to Dad?"

"I don't see how."

"Could we say as little as possible? Keep the Bagleys out of it. Make it seem like no big deal?"

"Don't you think he's liable to find out about it and feel we're hiding things from him?"

"He never talks to anyone."

"That's not true."

"Around here, I mean."

"Let me handle it. I was the one who made the mistake with the heater."

"No! The heater is my job. Let me say it was my fault."

"That would be lying."

"Who cares! We have to keep him calm!"

His mother looked down at Danny, who was wringing his hands in frustration. She patted his head.

"You're taking too much on yourself. Why don't you try to rest? Lie down on the couch."

It was the same old story. Adults said they would handle it and then everything went to pot. Danny put on his best face. He stopped wringing his hands.

"You're right," he said. "I'll go outside for a while."

"Good. Go play until dinner."

Danny left the house but not to play. He headed down Florinda Street to wait for his father. If he could not stonewall the heater fire, he should be the one to reveal it. Nobody else could do it right. Halfway to Sligh, he sat down on the far side of the drainage ditch with a knot in his stomach.

Everything would depend on his father's state of mind. That could not be predicted, but Danny would be able to tell at a distance. If his father walked in a certain style, sort of sideways, it was certainly bad. If he came straight ahead, it was probably okay. Danny lay back, closed his eyes, and tried to remember when this fact of life had become clear to him. Just in the past couple of years, he guessed.

A thousand images of his father walking, sitting, standing, kneeling, and lying down passed through his mind. In each instance, he knew immediately the man's frame of mind, just from his configuration, but the signals were usually too subtle to describe. He opened his eyes and glanced down toward

Sligh. Nothing yet. He closed his eyes again, thinking back to that era long ago before they moved to Nowhere, when things had been mostly right.

"Hi."

Danny opened his eyes and saw Abigail standing there.

"Everything okay?" she asked.

"Yeah. Goodbye."

"What?"

"Go on. I'm waiting for my father."

"Can't I wait also? I want to tell him I'm sorry about the flour."

"No way. He doesn't like to talk about it."

"I don't believe that. He might pretend he doesn't want to talk, but you have to keep trying. People don't always say what they mean."

"You don't know anything about my father! Do you think he's like your dad, sitting around offering people sodas? My dad is dangerous!"

Danny immediately regretted this outburst. He had never spoken of this to anyone outside the family. What was happening to him? He couldn't control his imagination or his mouth these days. Every time he turned around, he seemed to be making things worse.

"Did the fire upset you?" Abigail asked.

"Leave me alone!"

She sniffed and walked away. Danny felt bad, but he could not permit her to remain, and there was no time for the lengthy grilling he would have to undergo if he showed the slightest bit of friendliness. It was a funny world when you had to be mean to be nice. He was beginning to like Abigail, but he could not let his feelings rule him right now.

He saw his father turn the corner and come walking toward him. The sun was dropping beneath the trees, so it was hard to make out his gait, but as he got nearer it appeared he was more straight than sideways. Danny allowed himself to hope. He hopped up.

"Hi, Dad."

"Hello, Danny-boy. What are you doing down here?"

Things were looking good. His father had called him "Danny-boy."

"I have a confession to make."

"Oh?"

"The water heater got out of control today."

"Was it your fault?"

"I wasn't around to do it. Mom was busy with Ruth. I should have stayed to help her."

"You can't stay all the time."

"But I should have been there," Danny said, preparing for the most delicate part of the procedure. "She had to call Mr. Bagley to help."

"Bagley came over?"

"For a few minutes until I got there."

"He's gone now?"

"Yeah. He was just there until the fire died down."

"What did he do?"

"Held the flue open with a broom handle."

"That's quite a picture," Mr. Ryan laughed. "How'd he fit in there?"

"Almost didn't."

"Well, let's see what the situation is."

Danny took a deep breath and walked with his father toward the house. A few feet down the road, he saw Abigail crouching in the brush. She really was a most provoking person. Thank God his father didn't see her. That was all he would need to set him off, someone in the bushes spying on him. Danny could not understand why people couldn't just get out of the way and let him operate. Everything would go better that way. At the house, Harold kissed his wife on the cheek.

"I hear there was some excitement today," he said.

Danny looked pleadingly at his mother. She looked back impassively over her husband's shoulder.

"Nothing much," she replied. "The heater went wild."

"Well, let's see if there's any permanent damage."

He walked back to the heater closet and looked upward.

"Come here, Danny," he said.

Danny stuck his head into the closet.

"See up there?" Harold said, pointing to the boards around the stovepipe.

"They're scorched," Danny said.

"A little longer and they'd have gone up. It was lucky Bagley was around."

With that, his father closed the subject and went in to see Ruth. This was a familiar pattern. He did not seem to remember when he had been bad, and if he did, he apparently expected his family to put it out of their minds and act as if nothing had happened. Danny heard mumbling talk coming from the bedroom. Ruth would be sweet, not out of fear like Danny, but because that was her way. She could forgive; Loretta could not. For his part, Danny could only grow wary and false.

Mr. Ryan stepped into the doorway and beckoned to his wife. She walked toward him. Danny started to follow, but his father said, "Not now, Danny." He was not angry. This was something else. The knot returned to Danny's stomach. More mumbling from the other room. It had that ominous sound. Danny started to tremble. What now? You just got one thing fixed and another thing started. Was there no end? His mother emerged from the bedroom, serious-faced.

"Ruth is not well. Probably just upset by the fire, but we can't take a chance. You'll have to go over to the Bagleys'."

"Can't I just stay here?"

"Not alone."

"I'll be okay."

"No."

"But they might not want me over there."

"Don't be ridiculous. They are a strange bunch, but they're human beings."

With that, she put some underwear, a pair of pajamas, and a few toiletries into a paper bag. She dialed the phone and spoke briefly with Mrs. Bagley, giving her the number of Tampa General Hospital and describing the situation as an "emergency." This word had a profound effect on Danny's stomach knot. He sat on the couch.

"Get up and tell Ruth goodbye. You can come and see her tomorrow if she has to stay over at the hospital."

"What's wrong with her?"

"She feels very weak. They'll give her something to perk her up."

Danny walked toward the bedroom. He wracked his brain for something to say or do to affect the flow of events. There was nothing. The best he could do was to put on a cavalier front. He walked jauntily into the bedroom. Ruth was being lifted by their father, blanket and all. This drained him of all jauntiness. He stood staring.

"Don't look so shocked," Ruth said. "I just need one of those delicious IVs. I'll be dancing on the roof before long."

"Yeah," was all Danny could manage.

"Ta ta!" Ruth said as they swept past Danny, and she brushed her hand against the top of his head.

Ruth was stowed in the back seat of the car and Mrs. Ryan climbed in with her.

"Take a bath and put on clean clothes before you go to the Bagleys'," she said, patting Danny's cheek as she closed the car door.

With that they sped off, leaving Danny in the front yard staring after them. Across the street, he saw the Bagleys standing on their porch. He waved and pointed to his house.

"I'll be over in a few minutes," he shouted. "I need to take a bath and get some things."

"There'll be lots of hot water!" Alfred yelled.

"Shush," Mrs. Bagley said. "Don't be too long, Danny. Would you like me to come there?"

"No, ma'am. I'll hurry."

Danny went in the house. For a moment he felt an overwhelming sense of relief. The house had been emptied of every person or circumstance that could be the source of friction. He threw himself down on the couch and relaxed. It was an exquisite feeling, but he was soon overtaken by guilt. How could he indulge himself so? He went to the closet and found the slip of paper containing Loretta's number. She should know about Ruth. He dialed and listened to the ringing for a couple of minutes. Not there. He would call her again later. Right now he had to get a move on, or Mrs. Bagley would be knocking on the door.

He showered and got into clean clothes. He picked up the bag his mother had packed and removed the pajamas. They were no good at the Bagley house, where they slept in their clothes. He would do the same. With a heavy heart, he opened the couch and withdrew his rubber sheet. Soon the Bagleys would know his awful secret. The only thing worse would be to wake up in their spare room having soaked their mattress with his urine. He stuck the sheet in his bag. Maybe he could make a joke about it.

When he arrived at the Bagley house, he was ushered inside and made to feel welcome, too welcome. It felt unnatural and added to the general sense of strangeness. Alfred was the only one operating within normal limits, but he was sky high. Danny could only guess at what this day must have meant to him, with all its bizarre twists. Mrs. Bagley took Danny's bag and walked toward the spare room.

"Excuse me," Danny said.

She needed to be warned that there was something disgusting inside.

"I'll lay your things out," she said firmly.

"Sit down, Danny," said Mr. Bagley. "Tonight we're going to have our Bible reading before dinner."

What had he done to deserve this? He sat in a living room chair while Mr. Bagley thumbed through the New Testament. At any moment, he expected to hear a cry of revulsion from the bedroom as the sheet was discovered, but in a few minutes, Mrs. Bagley emerged from around the corner and sat down.

"There," she said, "that's all taken care of."

"Did you . . ." Danny began.

"*All* taken care of," Mrs. Bagley said, giving Danny a significant look. Mr. Bagley looked up quizzically.

"What will we hear tonight, Mr. Bagley?" she asked.

"From Luke," he said, and began to read:

And he came down with them, and stood in the plain, and the company of his disciples, and a great multitude of people out of all Judaea and Jerusalem, and from the sea coast of Tyre and Sidon, which came to hear him, and to be healed of their diseases; and they that were vexed with unclean spirits: and they were healed. And the whole multitude sought to touch him: for there went virtue out of him, and healed them all.

Mr. Bagley stopped there, much to Danny's relief, although his suggestive silence was unnerving. Like a good Catholic, he had ignored this Protestant Bible reading. But some reaction was clearly in order, so he tried the one that usually worked with Mr. Bagley.

"Yes, sir," he said, using his most heartfelt tone of voice.

Mr. Bagley nodded sagely and turned to Mrs. Bagley and Alfred in turn, and each of them said, "Blesséd be the name of the Lord." Last of all, he turned to Danny. This was a sticky situation. Danny didn't want to be the one to suggest that the name of the Lord was not blesséd, but fooling around with Protestants in religious matters was perilous. He nodded affirmatively, and after a moment, Mr. Bagley bowed his head and intoned a heartfelt rendition of the Lord's Prayer, known to Danny as the Our Father, another one of those disputes that looked inconsequential on the surface but seemingly could be the difference between an eternity in heaven and an eternity in hell.

Danny suffered through the tag that Protestants added, "for thine is the kingdom, and the power, and the glory forever," quite sure that the very hearing of it put at least a venial sin on his soul. He would be working it off in purgatory. He hoped his guardian angel would understand, and he fervently hoped the praying was over for the evening, but he had to endure the blessing at dinner and to his amazement, there was another brief prayer session before bed. The Bagleys went early to bed, and Danny remarked to himself that if anything was blesséd about the evening, it was this fact.

At long last, he could climb into the bed in the spare room. Upon doing so, he recognized the familiar rattling sound of his sheet. He was sure Mrs. Bagley intended to keep his bladder problem a secret, for which he was very grateful. She was showing a heretofore hidden depth of character; however, the very thought of her handling his soiled sheets was too humiliating to consider. He would avoid that if he had to stay awake all night. With that promise in his head, he promptly fell into an exhausted sleep and woke in a huge sopping puddle.

He peeked out the window. There was no hint of light in the sky. His jeans were wet, everything befouled. There was only one thing to do. He would take the sheets to his house, get new ones, bring them back and remake the bed. With luck, all this could be done before the Bagleys woke. He would have some explaining to do when Mrs. Bagley discovered alien sheets on the bed, but that was the lesser of two evils. He quietly stripped the bed and crept to the breezeway door, the farthest from the bedrooms. With great care, he opened it and slipped out. The night air was cold on his urine-soaked body, and he hurried to his house, where he dumped the wet sheets in the laundry tubs. He went into the water heater closet and lit the heater. There might be some warm water left from earlier in the day, but Danny wanted it scalding.

While he was waiting, he went into the kitchen, closing the door behind him, just as he would have done if his father were in the back room, and headed toward the closet to get fresh sheets. Halfway there he remembered that he had not called Loretta. It was four in the morning, but he had to get the word to her. He retrieved the scrap of paper from his jeans. It was soaked with urine. A fresh wave of self-loathing swept over him, but he dialed the number and waited. It rang many times before a sleepy male voice answered the phone.

"What! What!"

"Is Loretta there?"

"Who in hell is this?"

"Her brother, Danny."

"God damn! What time is it?"

"It's an emergency."

"Jesus Christ. Wait. She's on the couch."

Danny prepared for what he knew could be a long wait. Loretta was hard to wake up. He occupied himself by transferring her number to a clean piece of paper. This made him feel better. He even scuttled to the closet to get some clean clothes. When he got back he could hear voices at the other end of the line, very small in the background, like cartoons. He made out the words "emergency" and "leave me alone." A minute later, Loretta came on the line.

"This better be good, Danny."

"They took Ruth to the hospital."

"Oh no! When?"

"Yesterday afternoon."

"And you're just calling me?"

"I tried. You weren't home. They've got me over at the Bagleys."

"And the Bagleys don't have a phone? Never mind. It's my own fault. What happened?"

"I'm not sure. There was a fire."

"What!"

"Not much of one. The water heater flared up, but they had to take Ruth out for safety, and she was low afterward. The next thing I knew, they were taking her to the hospital."

"How's he reacting?"

"He's okay so far."

"St. Joseph's?"

"Tampa General."

"I'm going now."

"Okay."

"I'm sorry for how I spoke earlier. You know what I'm like in the middle of the night."

"Sure."

"I love you."

"Me too."

Danny hung up the phone and sat down on the couch. He didn't like the way he felt, as if he were in a tiny space. He knew that there was a wider world, that he could walk out the door, that he could go through the woods, but he felt as if all he would see wherever he went would be nothing more than ugly patterns on a blanket that was smothering him. He began to breathe hard. Perhaps the shower would calm him down. The water must be hot by now. He walked through the kitchen wringing his hands.

When he opened the door to the back room, he found it in flames, and there was nothing to be done about it. Kerosene had run out of the water heater and spread the fire all over the floor. The unpainted wood was going up like kindling. He gazed spellbound as his father's bed started to smolder. Danny's own sheets were already afire in the laundry tubs. For a moment, the heat felt good, but then Danny went cold. He closed the door and walked to the phone. The fire department's number was on a little red sticker fastened to the back of the cradle. He dialed and when the lady answered, he gave the address and said the house was on fire.

"You don't sound very concerned," the lady said suspiciously.

Danny put the receiver down and got into his clothes. He could hear the lady squawking away. He put a few comforting things in his pockets and picked up the receiver again.

"I'm leaving the house now," he said.

The lady squawked again, but Danny hung up and walked out the front door. He got on his bike and rode over to the Bagleys', reentering through the breezeway door. In a moment he was at Mr. and Mrs. Bagley's bedroom door.

"Excuse me," he said. "Our house is on fire again. I already called the fire department."

Having said that much, Danny turned and walked back toward the breezeway door. He could hear Mr. Bagley saying, "Did someone just speak,

Mrs. Bagley?" And Mrs. Bagley replying, "I believe Danny said the Ryan house is on fire. I'll get up. He may be dreaming about this afternoon."

That was the last Danny heard before going out the door. He climbed on his bike and pedaled into the night. He looked across at his house but could see no sign of flames. He knew he should stay and explain everything, but he could not face the prospect. Besides, it was increasingly clear to him that he was doing more harm than good. Every time he made a move, things got worse. It was better if he was not around.

As he rode along, he asked his guardian angel to help him breathe. It was getting harder and harder to do so. Danny uttered the plea without much hope. He wasn't sure he deserved any easy breaths. He went to the only place he could think of. In twenty minutes, he reached the Connolly property. There was a note on the door of the Airstream:

"Gone to the emergency room. Dad sawed off his thumb."

19

Danny read the note several times, growing more and more agitated, his head filling with images of his friend's father at the table saw. When he could stand no more, he threw himself on the ground in frustration but immediately jumped up with the frightening conviction that he must keep moving or die of a crushing, indefinable malady. He had to escape, but where should he go? Every possibility seemed equally dreadful. His heart was racing.

Then he thought of the river. He could get onto the river and let it take him away. If he eventually drowned in the Gulf of Mexico, what was so bad about that? His guardian angel would lead him to purgatory where he could begin burning the sins off his soul. He would be out of this life where it seemed he could do nothing but add more sins and more suffering. Succumbing to one big wave on the sea was a cheerful thought compared to the prospect of being slowly gnawed to nothing by life on earth. He walked to Buddy's and worried the unfinished canoe down off its mounts. Forget the final touches. It would float, which was all that mattered.

Buddy's canoe carrier was behind the Airstream, and in a few minutes Danny had secured the canoe to it and hooked the assembly to his bike. He knew he was on the right track. His breathing was more regular, and he no longer heard his pulse pounding in his ears. He battled his way down the sandy access road, but after he hit the pavement, he began to make good time.

In a few minutes, he was pulling into his accustomed spot near Hanna's Whirl, keeping his eyes averted from the opposite bank. Buddy's carrier had worked to perfection. Danny was in a fever to untie the craft and get it into the water. He felt as if he were on the verge of exploding, but when he risked a glimpse across the river, the scene stopped him short.

The house across the river had changed. It was no longer the looming Nancy Drew mansion but something smaller, something he could hardly believe. Stranger still, it was clearly visible in the gloom of early morning, shining like an image on a movie screen. He shook his head to clear his imagination. Still the scene remained. He turned back to the canoe. The morning dew was good lubrication, and the craft slid easily over the grass and into the water. Danny climbed in from the stern and sat, holding the canoe in place by grasping a knot of grass on the bank beside him. He feared that water would leak in due to some mistake he had made during construction, but as the minutes passed, he felt nothing but the bobbing of the current beneath him.

Several times, he nearly committed the canoe to the current, but he could not tear his eyes from the image on the opposite bank. If it had been anything else—castle, ranch house, skyscraper, cathedral—he would have ignored it, but it was the one thing he could not ignore: his own house. He wanted to run away, but he was drawn across the river.

Once he had made up his mind, the transit was easy. His canoe cut easily through the water and in a few strokes, he was to the opposite bank. Danny put his hand in the river and splashed some water on his face. He cleared his eyes, half-expecting the chilly shock to make the house disappear, but it remained. He clambered out of the canoe, pushed it safely up onto the shore, and stood before the house, the river flowing around his calves, tugging at his pant legs.

In all respects it seemed to be the Ryan house, though with a slightly grainy quality and giving off a radiation that was warm on Danny's cheeks. Danny stepped out of the river and stamped his feet. There was a tingling in his hands and legs, but it was not painful. He was on the verge of striding forward when a shadow fell across the door. For a moment, he thought it might be his father, and he stepped back, but it was Ruth. She swung open the screen door.

"Hi, sweetie. Come in."

This was cruel. His sister was in a hospital somewhere with a needle in her arm. Danny turned away.

"Danny. It's okay. I promise."

"Who are you?" he asked, turning back.

"I'm Ruth."

"Why are you here?"

"The usual reason, I guess."

"What's that?"

"What do you think?"

"Is there anyone else in the house?"

"No. Just me. The others are in the backyard."

"What others?"

"Come in and see for yourself."

Ruth came out on the steps where Danny could see her more clearly. Her neck wasn't swollen. She looked in the pink.

"Aren't you sick?"

"Not right now."

Danny wondered why he was not sick himself, sick to his stomach. This house and all that went with it was outlandish. He was now in his father's world, where nothing could be trusted. Who could tell what awful visions were in store? But he had passed over to the other side of the river. There was nothing to be done about it, nowhere to run, no way to hide.

"Are you coming in?" Ruth asked.

"Why not?" Danny answered.

He climbed the steps and walked into the house. It was a little brighter than he expected. Usually the blinds at the Ryan house were pulled down and closed. Mr. Ryan felt this kept the house cool, even on a hot summer day. Loretta would walk in and yank them up, saying, "My God, can't we at least have some light in here?" But the open shades could not fully explain the softly glowing quality of the house. The furnishings and arrangement of the room were just as Danny had experienced for years, but the light altered everything. It may have been coming from the back room. Ruth slid onto the couch and put her feet up.

"Do I seem different?" she asked.

"Yes, ma'am."

"Oh, please! 'Yes, ma'am'?"

Danny averted his eyes. Ruth shrugged her shoulders, reached under a pillow, and withdrew a tablet. She handed it to Danny and sat back expectantly.

"Open it," she said.

Danny sat down at the end of the couch and thumbed through the tablet. He stopped at the drawing he had worked on with Ruth a couple of days before. His contribution was still there, a bank note sticking out of a bulging bank. It looked as he remembered it: pretty good, but with the unmistakable shadow of his first grotesque effort clearly visible underneath it. Ruth handed him a pencil.

"Try again," she said.

"You should start over. I fouled this one up."

"Try anyway."

Danny looked first at the drawing and then at the pencil, which he noted had a fresh eraser. He glanced at Ruth. She was wearing her usual sweet expression but without the tightness in her face. She looked beautiful. Danny wished he could tell her, but he didn't want to seem a sissy. He went back to the drawing. With little hope, he applied the eraser to the haunted bill.

"This is a great eraser," he said excitedly.

"Isn't it?" Ruth replied.

Danny brushed away the eraser dust, but he could see no trace of what he had erased. He brought the sheet close to his face, and still he saw nothing of his mistake. Something fell onto the page. Danny realized it was a tear, and he thrust the tablet aside and wiped his eyes. He was too ashamed to look at Ruth.

"Look out the window, sweetie," Ruth said.

Danny wiped his eyes again and looked into the backyard. It was not what he expected. Instead of the jungle that was behind the real house, here he saw an endless sweep of prairie grassland bathed in sunlight.

"Where is this?" he asked.

"Nebraska."

So this was Nebraska, not in a yellowed photograph but in Technicolor. He was seeing it as if in life, only better. It looked nice, but there was something odd about the people near the house.

"Is that Abraham Lincoln?" Danny asked.

"No, sweetie. That's Daddy."

"Who's that little girl holding on to his leg?"

"That's Loretta."

"She likes him?"

"She adores him."

"Is that Mommy in the chair?"

"Yes, dear."

"Is she happy?"

"Yes, dear."

Danny hung his head. All happy. That was something anyway. He was glad he had seen it. Now he could go. He started to rise.

"You haven't finished the drawing."

"I cried on it."

"That just makes it so much the better," Ruth said, showing him the page.

He saw that his tear had caused no damage, neither spot or blotch, and Ruth was holding the tablet out with such a look of expectation that he could not refuse.

"You asked for it," Danny said.

He took the pencil and with three bold strokes drew a bill that fit in perfectly with the others. He showed Ruth.

"Not bad, huh?"

"It's a thing of beauty, sweetie."

Danny thought this was the finest compliment he had ever received, but he was tired. It seemed those three strokes of the pencil had taken all his energy. He wilted and fell forward into Ruth's arms. For a moment he reproached himself but then he remembered she wasn't sick and could bear his weight, which was lucky because he couldn't stay with her anymore. Everything went black.

Danny woke on the bank of the Hillsborough. The house was gone and the sun was well up. He blinked, looked around, and made for the canoe. It was where he had left it, still pulled up out of the water. He pushed it into the river, climbed aboard, and headed downstream, still under the influence of his vision. Perhaps his angel had arranged it. Everything seemed subtly altered, even the darkly flowing Hillsborough.

The houses beyond Hanna's Whirl soon appeared on the riverbank. He paddled quietly by them, noting all the features he could not see from the road: the docks, the patios on the water. People waved at him as he passed. One man shouted, "That's a nice canoe. Did you make it?" Danny shouted back, "Some of it."

Soon he was approaching the Sulphur Springs bridge. He veered to check out the alligator in the drain. As he came close, the gator slithered into the Hillsborough. At last Danny had seen him do something other than wait. He paddled to the spring run flowing from the Sulphur Springs Pool. The complex had a different aspect when seen from the Hillsborough, if anything more interesting. The bathers looked at him with envy, Danny thought. Buddy had been right. An orange crate canoe could make a big difference in a lot of things.

Danny continued down the river, moving slowly like the hyacinths, drifting as much as paddling. The time for lunch came and went. He didn't feel hungry. The shoreline was a parade of green parkland, oily industrial sites, and grand estates. There was no telling what would pop up next. The bank was alternately beautiful and ugly. He accepted each scene for what it was, but he was grateful for the beautiful things and for the sun on his face.

At some point he knew he would come to the Lafayette Street bridge where he would be able to see the Moorish spires at the University of Tampa. And beyond that the Hillsborough would lose itself in Tampa Bay. What would he do when he arrived at river's end? He might just keep paddling until he reached the Gulf of Mexico and beyond that the Atlantic. One way or another he would see it through. The bridge and its spires came and went.

The current carried Danny onward. Ahead was an island where the river forked, one side leading to a series of docks and the other to open water. On the point of the island was a complex of buildings. Its dingy brown bricks and big smokestack looked familiar. Then he realized that he was approaching Tampa General Hospital. It looked different from the river.

The buildings loomed before him, blotting out all possibility of escape. He had been wrong to think he could paddle away from his problems or sink gratefully beneath the indifferent waves. This grim edifice on the bank of the river was no work of his imagination. Tampa General was implacably rooted in reality. So the decision was made for him. He would not be setting out on his own for the wide Atlantic. He would land at Tampa General Hospital and see what shape his family was in. There was no escaping it, not really. Danny paddled to the seawall and found a dock. A curious groundskeeper came over and helped him haul the canoe up on the lawn.

"Couldn't wait to finish her, huh?" the man asked.

"Emergency," said Danny. "My sister had to come here last night."

"Came to see your sister," he replied, nodding. "Well, don't you worry about your canoe. I'll keep an eye on her for you."

Danny thanked the man and started to walk toward the hospital, but out of the corner of his eye, he saw an outline that caused him to stop. Sitting on a bench facing the river was his father in a strangely upright posture with his hands on his knees and his eyes staring toward the opposite bank. Danny watched him for a couple of minutes, but Mr. Ryan did not move.

It was as if someone had switched off the electricity. Danny was well aware that his father could sit very still. In fact, it was one of the many warning signals that he kept a sharp eye out for, but today his father was not just still, he looked more like a thing of stone. Danny's first impulse was to creep onward to the hospital, but he found himself more curious than fearful. What was his father looking at, or what did he *think* he was looking at?

Danny approached indirectly and stood ten feet behind the bench, leaning with one hand against a tree. He squinted his eyes at the opposite bank, but no floating vision appeared to him. If only his father could see what Danny had seen that morning, a family healthy and at peace, what a difference that might make to him. However, the stiffness of Mr. Ryan's body did not suggest he had any such thing in view. As Danny stood there, a disturbing sensation began to grow within him: a feeling of being watched. He looked around and saw nothing unusual, yet the trees, the grass, the pavement, even the water in the river channel was suffused with a growing sense of malice. He felt as if he were a target. Danny struggled to understand what had brought this about. Had he tapped into his father's mind? Was this the terrifying hell his father occasionally inhabited?

That was a new thought. Danny had been so frightened of his father that he had never considered the possibility that his father might himself be frightened. But what could Danny do? At this moment, the whole world seemed full of paralyzing bad intentions. He tried to remember his vision of Ruth and the shining plains of Nebraska. This gave him strength, and he resolved to go to his father and have it out. He would discover once and for all what the matter was.

It was a scary thought, so he made a silent plea to his guardian angel for help, but when he opened his eyes he saw a familiar figure ambling toward his father. Buddy. Danny wanted to cry out a warning: "My father is not in his right mind. Stay away!" But all he could do was shrink behind the tree trunk and hope Buddy would pass without incident. That did not happen. Buddy paused in front of Mr. Ryan. As always, he seemed composed. Danny noticed that the sense of threat in the air had diminished. He wondered if his father felt that.

"Hello, Mr. Ryan," Buddy said. "Do you remember me? I came to your house a couple of nights ago."

Harold Ryan continued staring silently ahead. Buddy waited for a moment and then sat down on the bench.

"I wanted to tell you something about Danny. We've been spending a little time together. Usually, I don't bring people home because my father is a drinker, and he gets out of hand sometimes. But Danny took Dad in stride. He has a lot of understanding for a ten-year-old. You must be proud of him."

Buddy looked over at Harold Ryan, who did not look back.

"I'm here now because of my dad," Buddy continued. "He accidentally cut his thumb off."

Mr. Ryan remained silent.

"I forgot to unplug the table saw," Buddy said, after a moment.

At this, Mr. Ryan took his hands off his knees, rose, and without a glance left or right, walked away. Buddy studied him as he strode stiffly along the path bordering the river. Then he stretched out his legs, crossed them at the ankles, and gazed out at the Hillsborough. Danny watched him for a few seconds but could not bring himself to go forward; however, the atmosphere of malice had dissipated. Whether because of Buddy's arrival or his father's departure, Danny could not say.

At length, he turned and, without making himself known to Buddy, walked through the grounds toward the hospital entrance. Several passersby gave him a second look. He was scruffy and barefoot. His mother would not be happy about that. He made his way through the big doors and walked to the reception desk. The lady at the desk eyed him dubiously.

"I'd like a room number, please."

"Are your parents around here?"

"They're with Ruth Ryan. I'm her brother."

"You're the little boy everybody's looking for!"

"I don't know anything about that."

"My God, the whole county is on the watch! You come back here immediately."

The lady put him in a little room with a bed and a sink. As usual the adults were making a fuss over nothing, but Danny seized the opportunity to hop up on the sink and start washing his feet. Clean feet might blunt his mother's disappointment in his appearance. He ran the water between his toes and applied some funny-smelling soap to them. At this moment, his mother burst into the room. She yanked him off the sink and smothered him with kisses. Danny hardly knew how to react. A moment later, Loretta burst into the room and took her turn. When she finally let him go, Danny started to say something, but he slipped and fell on his rear end. He looked up sheepishly.

"I was washing my feet," he explained. "I guess I look pretty bad."

"Danny, where on earth have you been? Mrs. Bagley is beside herself. She and Alfred have been praying nonstop for the last five hours."

"I wasn't thinking about that."

"What on earth were you thinking?"

"I felt funny."

"What do you mean?"

This was a moment that called for the utmost delicacy, but Danny had no delicacy left. There was no explaining what had happened, and no subtle blend of truth and fiction occurred to him.

"I don't remember anything," he said.

"Nothing about where you've been?"

"Nope."

"Wait a minute!" Loretta put in. "We can work backward. You remember coming in the hospital."

"No."

"You don't remember the receptionist?"

"No."

"What do you remember?" Mrs. Ryan asked.

"Was I washing my feet?"

"This is too much!" Loretta said. "He's lying."

Danny's mother looked deeply into his eyes. Danny looked back unblinking.

"I don't know, Loretta. He doesn't have that guilty expression."

"So he finally learned how to beat the eye test. It had to happen some-day," Loretta said.

"I guess we'll have to have you examined," Mrs. Ryan said.

"No," Danny replied firmly. "I'm okay. Let's go see Ruth."

With that, he headed for the door, looking backward impatiently. Mrs. Ryan and Loretta were in a head-to-head conference. Danny cleared his throat loudly.

"All right," Loretta said. "But you haven't heard the end of this."

The three of them walked to a hospital elevator. Danny's mother kept her hand on his head. As they waited for the car, her fingers found the cut under his hair.

"What's this?"

"That's old. Ran into a window."

"Danny, you have to be more careful," she said, kneeling down and taking him in her arms. Danny looked up at Loretta. She shook her head. Something was up. The elevator car arrived, and they stepped in along with several other people. When the doors opened again, they revealed a waiting room containing a dozen people, seemingly frozen in place. Mr. Ryan was standing with his hands at his sides, glaring at Loretta's boyfriend. The young man had taken a boxing stance.

"Don't go shoving me!" the boy shouted.

Mr. Ryan said nothing, just moved menacingly toward him. The boy took a step backward. A nurse standing nearby said, "Sir! The security man is on his way. Please, no more trouble." Loretta bolted into the room and placed herself between her father and the boy.

"Leave him alone!"

She stepped toward her father. He drew his right arm back.

"Go on!" Loretta shouted. "I'm tired of waiting!"

"Who is he?" the boy said, pulling Loretta backward. "What's his prob-lem?"

"He's my father! He thinks everybody's out to get him, and he's right about me!"

She tried to fly at her father, but the boy held her back.

"Let me go," she screamed. "I'll tear his eyes out!"

At these words, Mr. Ryan shuddered and glanced about, seemingly see-ing for the first time the circle of people surrounding him, their eyes wide. They were a pathetic lot—an elderly lady with a walker, a handful of haggard relatives waiting for word of their loved ones, three children in pajamas, a wispy nurse reaching toward him. He ran his hand over his head and looked at a stain on the front of his white baker's shirt. Ruth must have thrown up as he carried her. Across the room, Danny saw two substantial security guards enter. They stopped and looked over the scene.

"What's the trouble?" one of them called to the nurse, who pointed at Harold Ryan.

"Please, Harold," Mrs. Ryan said softly, holding out her hand. "Think of Ruth."

Harold Ryan turned and looked at his wife. He assumed her exact posture, complete with his hand held out in a pleading fashion. Then he screwed his face into a mask of sarcasm. It was ghastly. The crowd shrank back.

"You're insane," Loretta said, looking her father in the eye.

Upon hearing those words, Mr. Ryan strode to the stairs and exited the room.

"What's he done?" asked one of the security guards.

"He shoved that man," said the lady with the walker.

"Anything else?"

"Just what you saw," said the nurse.

"You want us to go after him?"

"Please, no," said Mrs. Ryan. "He's been under a strain."

"What about you, pal?" asked the security guard. "You're the one he shoved."

"Let it go," the boy said.

"You can have him arrested for all I care," Loretta declared.

Then, as if remembering something crucial, the nurse crossed the room to speak to Danny's mother. Danny knew what it was about. Everything was clear to him. That was the last thing Danny saw as he stealthily followed in his father's path out the exit door.

Once he was on the stairs, he raced down six flights and burst into the lobby. His father was not there, but Danny caught sight of him striding across the hospital grounds toward the river. When Danny caught up, Mr. Ryan was standing with the toes of his shoes over the edge of the seawall. He was holding his right fist in front of his face, slowly rubbing his thumb against his first finger.

"Dad," Danny said loudly.

Mr. Ryan turned around. He began to make the terrible face.

"Don't do that, Dad. I know you feel bad, but here's something that will make you feel better."

Danny thrust an emergency King Edward into his father's hand. Mr. Ryan stared at it for a long moment.

"Did I ask for a cigar?" he asked vaguely.

"I just brought it in case you wanted one."

Mr. Ryan looked up from the cigar. Some of the tension left him.

"I do think I'll have a smoke," he said.

Without further comment, he walked off. When he was fifty feet away, he stopped, lit his cigar, and continued walking.

Danny was not sure what he had accomplished, but at least he had done something. He felt good about that. Not far away, he could see a splash of red, his canoe. The groundskeeper had turned it bottom up. There was a bit of hyacinth stuck near the prow, still green and sporting a fresh purple flower.

"She brought you downstream with no problem, am I right?"

It was Buddy.

"Yeah," Danny said.

The two looked out at the Hillsborough for several seconds. Then Danny remembered himself.

"How's your dad?"

"He'll survive."

"Danny!" someone called from the hospital entrance.

It was his mother with Loretta alongside. They were coming toward him, trying to look natural. His heart went out to them. He knew they had come to tell him Ruth was gone.

20

Danny sat on the bank of the Hillsborough staring out at Hanna's Whirl. All around him were the sounds of heavy equipment. The land by the river was being cleared. Big piles of brush would later be set afire as part of the cleanup. It was neat to play in the revamped landscape, but it was a temporary pleasure. Soon the property would be divided into lots and covered with tract homes.

According to Al Gallagher, the houses on the river would cost the most. If you could only glimpse the river, you would pay less, and still less the farther away you got. Al had handled the sale of Bart Connolly's property and knew what he was talking about. Bart's land and shop had fetched a modest price, but it was enough to offset the expenses his sister in North Dakota would incur for minding him until he either rallied or drank himself to death. "Maybe he will do better far away from the water," Al had said.

Across the river, Danny saw nothing strange, just an unremarkable riverbank, but pretty. His days of desperate imagining were over, and it was plain that Nowhere was becoming Somewhere. The signs were all about. Many of the streets were being dug up to accommodate the city sewer extensions. The neighborhood was full of intriguing, cannonball-shaped torches burning at the top of enormous piles of dirt, warning people to skirt the excavations.

Mr. Bagley was in a state of high excitement and was building a new house nearby for his family, this time on a larger corner lot. He had purchased several other parcels of land in the vicinity and was putting up homes at a sparkling pace. God had been good to the Bagleys, and Mr. Bagley had in turn been good to the Ryans. He had rebuilt the back room at cost, this time with a proper bathroom.

To Danny's mind, this new construction just pointed up the general shabbiness of the Ryan house, which was more clearly than ever a relic of the past, but at least it was not as crowded as it once had been. Ruth had gone to a better world, everyone agreed. Danny wished that the send-off had not included the requirement that he kneel at the coffin and gaze upon her waxen face before they closed the lid and lowered her into a grave at the Garden of Memories cemetery. He would have preferred to remember only the glowing beauty he had seen across the Hillsborough on the morning of her death. He had pondered that experience until he could ponder it no more. He might have been delirious, but what of it? He remembered it more clearly than most supposedly real experiences. He was grateful for the memory.

And his father was gone. He had returned to the mysterious Nebraska and the legendary Armour and Company packinghouse where he had worked twenty years before. He was too old, but the union shop steward remembered him singing in a quartet at union meetings and told the company, "You will hire this man." His father must have been something back in the Abraham Lincoln days. Before he left, he had told Danny, "The one thing they can't take away from you is your work record," and he showed Danny his union card from long ago as if it was an Academy Award. It had been in his wallet all along.

When he got on the Greyhound bus, he turned to the family and said, "I always know what direction I'm going in Omaha. In Tampa, I could never keep north, south, east, and west straight." He appeared to be looking forward to knowing the directions again. Danny had handed him a box of King Edwards at the last moment. Harold took it and said, "Thanks, son."

The remaining Ryans were staying in Tampa. One of Marjorie Ryan's wealthy employers had gotten her a nine-to-five job in a health food store, and she was making good. There was talk of setting her up in a store of her own over in St. Petersburg. She was bringing home all sorts of weird stuff to eat, but Danny didn't mind. It eased the budget, and there were many debts to be paid. Whole grain bread was not as tender and squishy as the Holsum loaves his father used to get, but you couldn't have everything. He salted his organic peanut butter sandwich when his mother wasn't looking. She had started taking health foods very seriously.

Loretta had come home as soon as their father was gone. She would stay at the Ryan house through her high school graduation. The couch was empty now. Danny was sleeping in the new back room on a real bed. He had apparently outgrown the need for his rubber sheet, though it was kept at the ready just in case. Loretta and his mother slept in the other bedroom, where Ruth had spent her last days. So, the setup was more conventional, but to Danny's mind the house would never be normal. Even so, there was talk of reupholstering the living room furniture. Danny thought this a futile gesture and would have been happier if the whole place had burned down on that hectic night so many weeks ago. He never said this out loud, of course.

"Danny!"

This cry came from Alfred, who raced up on his bike, full of nervous energy.

"Buddy's at Halper's. He sent me to find you."

"Is that Buddy's wagon?" Danny asked.

"Yeah! He gave it to me. Now I can haul stuff around!"

Buddy had tended Al's Swap Shop while Al Gallagher had taken Bart Connolly to North Dakota and had been staying with Al since his return. This was the way Bart had wanted it. "You gave me your childhood," he had told Buddy. "Now I'm giving you your manhood. Drop in and see me in a couple of years." Bart had also given some advice to Danny before leaving for North Dakota.

"Don't saw your thumb off."

"Got it," Danny replied.

"Good," Bart said, "because you're one of those guys who's hard to teach a lesson."

Bart had patted Danny's shoulder with his thumbless hand. There was a lot of fondness in the gesture. Danny often thought about it in the years to come.

On the way to Halper's store, Alfred nearly ran off the road a couple of times, proudly looking back at Buddy's wagon rattling behind. When they got to Halper's, they saw Abigail's bike parked in front next to Al Gallagher's truck, and they walked in just as Abigail was saying, "You're too young to go in the Navy." She was speaking to Buddy, who was leaning against the front counter. Danny thought he looked the perfect midshipman in his jumper and bell-bottom trousers. Buddy laughed.

"That's a matter of opinion."

"No, it's not. It's a rule."

"Not a very strict rule if you know how to handle it," Buddy replied.

"You don't handle rules. You obey them."

"Spoken like a true quartermaster's daughter," said Al Gallagher, who was lounging in the shadows.

"Let's have a drink on the house in honor of our new swabbie," said Mr. Halper, throwing open the big cold-drink case full of sodas of every kind. Danny liked to fish around in the case when it was nearly empty. Your hand came out numb from the cold. Al Gallagher and Buddy had Cokes, Alfred had a peach NeHi, explaining that he had never had peach and since this one was to be free, he would make the experiment. Abigail got a Yoohoo for herself and one for Danny. Danny did not properly consider Yoohoo a soft drink—after all, there was milk in there somewhere—but he didn't want to insult Abigail. She had been sweet to Danny in the days after Ruth's death. Mr. Halper preferred a cup of tea, which he always had ready behind the counter.

When everyone had a drink, Mr. Halper raised his cup and said, "To Buddy. Hanna's Whirl is proud to send such a young man into the Navy. He will make a fine engineer. Keep 'em afloat, Buddy!"

Buddy looked from one face to another as everyone joined in a little cheer. Danny tipped up his Yoohoo and drank deep of chocolaty goodness. Abigail had made an excellent choice after all, but maybe any drink would have tasted right after such a cheer.

"Yes, sir," Mr. Halper said, but his voice faltered, and he dropped his eyes.

Buddy straightened up and pulled down the front of his jumper.

"Are you going?" Abigail asked.

"Just after I talk to Danny for a minute. I'll say goodbye to everybody before I leave."

Buddy put his arm around Danny and ushered him out of the store. They walked around to the back and sat down on one of Mr. Halper's benches.

"Al and I left the canoe and the carrier at your house."

"Thanks."

"You'll get some use out of it," Buddy said, fishing in his wallet and extracting part of a torn $50 bill. "Al says we can tape our pieces together and the bank will take it."

"I'd rather keep my part," Danny said.

"Me, too," Buddy replied.

The boys sat quietly for several minutes.

"Let's go back," Buddy said finally.

Danny nodded.

"Oh, I have a message for you," Buddy said.

"Who from?"

"She said you would know. She told me to say, 'Beauty is waiting for you.'"

"Does she say that kind of thing to you?"

Buddy smiled.

"Welcome to the party, brother. Let's go around front."

They found everyone congregated in the parking lot. Al was already sitting in his truck, but he had the door open with his legs swung out. Alfred was in the seat next to him, going through the glove compartment. Abigail was standing on the end of one of the benches with her arm around Mr. Halper.

Buddy went over and shook hands with Mr. Halper.

"Always a free soda at my store for our boys in uniform," Mr. Halper said.

"That's a good offer, Oscar," Buddy said easily, turning his attention to Abigail, who had leaned forward with a pucker. "You want a kiss goodbye?" he asked.

"Of course. Isn't it customary?"

"Can't ignore custom."

Buddy grabbed Abigail and laid a lingering movie kiss on her lips. It must have lasted ten seconds. Alfred fell out of the truck laughing. Danny held his breath. When Buddy let Abigail go, she plopped down on the bench with her eyes glazed.

"Young lady. You'll never get another one like that," Mr. Halper said, smiling.

"Come on before somebody calls the cops," Al yelled from the truck.

Buddy walked to the rider's side, but before he got in, Abigail recovered herself, ran to him, and threw her arms around his waist.

"I'd rather not go," Buddy said, patting her cheek, "but things change. They can't stay the same."

With that, he got into the truck, and Al drove him down the street and out of sight. The kids hung around the store for a while. Mr. Halper treated them to another round of drinks, but they didn't taste the same. After a while, Alfred and Abigail rode away toward home. Danny sat on a bench in front of the store for quite a while. The sun dropped lower in the sky. Every now and again, Mr. Halper came out and asked Danny if he was all right.

"Just relaxing," Danny would say.

"That's what you should do," Mr. Halper would reply.

Late in the day, after the construction sounds had stopped, Danny mounted his bike, rode to a spot near the fish hatchery, and from there made his way to the place where he had twice seen Donna. She was no longer working at the fish hatchery. Maybe she had gone away to Hollywood to be a movie star. That was where she belonged, but maybe she would be in her old spot on the trail.

When he arrived at the scene, she was not present, only the memory of her. He considered sitting in the place where she had sat, or hovered, or whatever she did, but he would have felt like a fool. Then he decided to do it anyway. Nothing special happened, but he didn't feel as foolish as he had thought he would. After a few minutes, he left. The light was going, and he wanted to see Hanna's Whirl once more before the close of day.

He pulled in and got off his bike. Across the river, only a few stray sunbeams cut through the grey dark and shone on some purple hyacinths clustered along the bank, still blooming. To his right, he could see nothing but shadows, nothing of the changes. For a moment, all seemed as it had been, but then Danny thought about the big alligator turtle who had been plying the creeks and had seemed so fearsome. Weeks ago, Danny had mentioned the turtle to Al Gallagher, who had said immediately, "Let's go get him."

"What for?" Danny had asked, hoping that Al did not have turtle soup in mind.

"Let's take him up to Green Swamp. He'll do better there."

So Danny, Buddy, and Al had found him, wrestled him into the back of Al's truck, and set him free in Green Swamp, the source of the Hillsborough. Now, on the night of Buddy's leaving, Danny was watching the river and thinking that some of the water flowing in front of him might have passed over that very turtle's back. It made him shiver.

The patches of light across the river were darkening. Danny had hoped that the mysterious Donna would step into one of them and make a dramatic gesture that would clarify everything. She didn't. But she had sent him a message. That was something to think about.

The sky was red now. Everything on the Hillsborough was reduced to beautiful black silhouettes. Danny cast one last gaze across the river and then rode away.

John Ames has a master's degree in English from the University of Florida, where he was a Ford Fellow. After graduation, he built a rustic house and lived for several years on the edge of a spiritual community located near Gainesville, Florida. John's search for enlightenment ended when he decided that he was living too far from a movie theater. He moved inside the Gainesville city limits and taught English and film for thirty years at Santa Fe College.

He has produced and acted in numerous short films and videos, including the cable TV series "The Tub Interviews," wherein all the interviewees were required to be in a bathtub. For ten years he reviewed movies for Gainesville's National Public Radio affiliate WUFT. He has appeared as a standup comedian and has designed and marketed Florida-themed lamps. He coauthored *Second Serve: The Renée Richards Story* (Stein and Day, 1983) and its sequel *No Way Renée: The Second Half of My Notorious Life* (Simon and Schuster, 2007), and *Speaking of Florida* (University Presses of Florida, 1993).